I0461125

LEAVING IT ALL BEHIND

by Peter Holdroyd

NVP Publications

Published by NVP Publications
Norwich
www.nvppublications.uk

This printed edition published 2015
Copyright © 2015 Peter Holdroyd
All rights reserved.

ISBN-13: 978-0-9933409-3-2

Peter Holdroyd lives in a village near Norwich in eastern England, with his wife of more than 40 years. He has written short stories since the age of 12, when he was given a second-hand portable typewriter and taught himself to touch-type.

It was not until the early years of the 21st century that he decided he should learn more about the art and skill of writing, and began attending Creative Writing courses at the local university, which – happily – enjoys a world-wide reputation in this field. In the years since then, he has written several novels in various genres, from crime to sci-fi to romance, but through them all runs a streak of humour.

Peter and his wife have a son and daughter, and two grand-daughters.

CHAPTER ONE

Seymour Whittle closed the door of the Consultant's office behind him and turned round slowly, looking blankly at the people still waiting their turn. Everything suddenly went black and he slid inelegantly to the floor.

He woke to find someone shining a bright light in his eyes.

"How are you feeling now, Dr Whittle?"

He gazed up into the eyes of a nurse. "Bloody awful. How d'you think?"

"I think you should remember you're diabetic. You need to eat."

He was laid on a trolley, he realised.

"I was kept waiting. Besides, I didn't feel hungry."

She looked at him with polite scepticism, he thought. He had no real excuses: he knew better than to skip meals. He'd been diabetic – late onset Type 2 – for three years, so there was no valid reason for his failure to take lunch. His low blood sugar was perhaps not enough by itself to cause a blackout, but the bad news from the Consultant had probably made things worse. He'd received confirmation of his diagnosis, first put forward as a possibility a month earlier, that he was suffering from amyotrophic lateral sclerosis, ALS, a degenerative failure of the brain which commanded the muscles of his body. It was, as Seymour well knew, a life sentence, and a short one at that.

Since being warned, he'd come to accept that his time was up. He'd already experienced a certain loss of control of his feet, and he'd begun dropping crockery, something he'd rarely done in the past. He occasionally had a little fit

1

of the shakes. The disease would progress until he became completely immobile, and it would finally interfere with the autonomic functions of heart and lungs and he would die.

"I'll park you just up the corridor from A&E. Then I'll get a doctor to see you and we'll have to consider discharging you."

He nodded as the nurse left, reflecting that the NHS was all about throughput these days, in and out in a flash.

"Wham, bam, thank you ma'am," he muttered.

"I beg your pardon?" A woman on the next trolley was staring at him with raised eyebrows. She was perhaps in her fifties, he thought, but still good looking, her skin smooth and scarcely lined.

"Well?" she prompted.

"Sorry," he said, "I was thinking about something."

"I think I'd come to that conclusion unaided," she said, "I wondered whether you were talking to me, and if so, whether I'd missed something allegedly exciting."

"No. It was a stray thought about the NHS today. I'm afraid I live alone and am at that stage in my life when I very often give voice to my thoughts if only to break the silence."

"What happened to your wife?" she asked.

He tilted his head, frowning.

She pointed. "You wear a wedding ring."

"Ah. She died three years ago."

"Sorry to hear that," she said. "By the way, my name's Harriet Blythe."

"Seymour Whittle."

"The nurse called you Dr Whittle. Do you work here?"

"No. I was a GP. Gave up a couple of years ago. After my wife died, work suddenly seemed less important. I had the means to retire, so I did."

"Must be nice, being able to retire young."

"Yes, but I wish she'd been around to share it with."

She was silent for a moment.

"I have a daughter," she said. She glanced up at him. "Do you have any children?"

"A married daughter, Kay, and a son who's still looking, called David. What's your girl called? Any grandchildren?"

Harriet looked slightly affronted. "Her name's Charley, short for Chalcedony, and she's single. Do I look old enough to be a grandmother?"

Seymour grinned at her. "Grandmothers are getting younger every year."

She sucked her cheeks in and considered him a moment. "Good answer," she said. "Any grandchildren yourself?"

"No. Kay's been married five years, but she's still only twenty-eight, so I suppose there's time yet." He looked down. "At least, *she* has time."

Harriet peered at him from under her eyebrows. "What does that mean?"

"It means I may die in the next few months, and almost certainly within five years."

"Oh."

He wondered how much to tell her, but on the basis that she was a total stranger and he couldn't imagine their paths crossing again, he thought it might be an idea to air the matter.

"I have something called ALS. Most people know it as motor neurone disease."

Harriet chewed her bottom lip. "Oh, dear," she said, "that's very serious."

"I know," he said, drily.

"But you might live for years?"

"Yes, but most of the time I'll be immobile and totally dependent on others. It's not how I'd choose to die, believe me."

"We don't all have the privilege of dying the way we want to," she said. "I've been told I probably have multiple sclerosis. It is also – as *you* probably know – ultimately fatal."

"An unpleasant condition," said Seymour.

"Not to worry," she said, "there are some very good drugs about can deal with the pain."

He could find nothing to say. They were silent for a moment, then Harriet smiled determinedly.

"I'm working out what I want to do in the time that's left," she said.

"Very laudable," replied Seymour, "but after you've gone, will anybody care?"

She shook her head slightly. "You misunderstand. I'm not talking about the things that need doing in order to benefit my daughter – she'll be my sole beneficiary – I'm talking about the things I've always put off doing, but have always wanted to."

Seymour nodded. "I see. I suppose that's a good idea. Yes. Perhaps I ought to try it myself."

"Could be fun," Harriet said with a gleam in her eyes.

"Do you have something in mind?"

"I've always wanted a big red sports car," she replied. "Never could afford one – can't now, either, but the credit card company won't know I shan't be making my usual payment."

He grinned. "Throwing caution to the winds, aren't you? What if you're still around when the payment is due?"

She shrugged. "Either I'll simply not pay, if I can't afford the minimum amount, or – " She hesitated.

"Or?"

"I'll drive it into the sea or something. Kill myself."

Seymour twisted to face her fully. "You can't do that!"

"Why not?" she asked levelly.

"While there's life..."

"Huh! And remind me, what is my life expectancy with MS – more to the point, what's my quality of life going to be like?"

He stopped while he considered her words.

"I suppose you can take that line, if you want," he said grudgingly.

"I want to die when I decide," Harriet said, "not just because some awful bug has eaten away at some vital organ. I mean, how undignified that could be: suppose I was out with Charley, at the theatre? Or worse still, driving my sports car? Could be disastrous."

"If you were dead, I suppose you'd be relieved of the embarrassment."

"I might not be. I might find myself standing in front of St Peter at the Pearly Gates, blushing and naked. Naked would be bad enough."

"Oh, I can quite see how blushing would make it so much worse." He found himself grinning despite himself. "You wouldn't be blushing just *because* you were naked?"

"Being naked doesn't usually make me blush, Dr Whittle. I've been around too long."

He was silent for a moment. "Anything else on your list?"

"There might be, but it's your turn. What would you very much like to do before turning up your toes?"

He stroked his chin with long fingers. "I've always wanted to fly a helicopter," he said. "Years ago, I had a PPL – that's a private pilot's licence – but only for fixed-wing aircraft. Always wanted to learn to fly a helicopter, but never seemed to have the time."

"Will you have time before your condition makes it impossible?"

Seymour held his hands out in front of him, the fingers spread and straight, looking for signs of tremor. Almost imperceptible, but he knew that the symptoms of ALS came and went, each time coming back a little worse than before, and never quite receding as far as the last time. It was like a tide coming in: wavelets would advance up the beach, then retire a little way, before advancing further the next time, and retiring not quite as far as before.

"Maybe," he said.

"Isn't there something somewhere that says, "Physician, heal thyself"?"

"St Luke's Gospel, chapter four, verse twenty-three," he supplied promptly.

Harriet studied him for a moment. "Ever tried LSD?" she asked.

Seymour lifted an eyebrow in surprise. "No. Now you mention it, I have no idea what any of the drugs they go on about are like."

She shook her head in amazement. "You mean, when you were a medical student, with all the others, you never had a tab of acid or a quick spliff?"

He looked at her askance. "I see you know the street names. Do acid and spliffs form part of your recreational pleasures?"

She grinned mischievously. "Not so far."

Seymour looked at her properly and confirmed his earlier impression that she was very attractive. He shook his head.

"I was from a so-called respectable family," he said, "We didn't do drugs – unless you count alcohol and tobacco. My father drank himself to death, and used to smoke like a chimney – big fat cigars, Cuban if he could get them, otherwise from anywhere he could be persuaded to believe they'd been rolled on the sweaty naked thigh of some Latina sexpot."

A chuckle escaped Harriet. "And were there a lot of those?"

"Apparently. Judging by the number of cigars he got through. He reckoned he occasionally found a pubic hair trapped between the leaves of tobacco. They were the ones he enjoyed most."

She turned her head to scan the corridor. Between their two trolleys and the next there was a gap of several yards. She looked back at him.

"Encourages me to believe I did the right thing in never smoking cigars," she said. "I wonder if they ever bring you a mug of tea in here or whether they just expect us to live on our reserves of fat until we peg out."

"Don't know, but I think there's a service bell here somewhere..." He peered at the tubes and cables emerging from the wall behind him until he found one with a red button sticking out of the pad on the end.

Harriet had turned to look at him, and guessed what he was about to do.

"Seymour..." she said.

He pressed the button. "Yes?" he replied, looking up as a red light started flashing over his bed, while a high-pitched ululation made conversation difficult. "Yes?"

"I think that button is the one they use to send for the crash cart or the undertaker."

"Ah. Not, actually, room service, then?"

The nurse who'd spoken to him earlier appeared in the corridor pulling a trolley loaded with aids to resuscitation and skidded to a halt beside Seymour. He watched her with an expression of wide-eyed innocence. She glared at him, pressing the reset button to silence the alarm.

"Dr Whittle! Did you press the emergency call?"

Seymour looked suitably chastened. "I'm sorry, nurse, but my friend here was beginning to suffer."

The nurse looked across at Harriet.

"Is that true, Mrs Blythe? Are you suffering? If so, from what?"

Seymour rested his fingers lightly on her wrist, indicating with a shake of his head that he wanted to whisper in her ear. She pursed her lips while she bent to listen.

"She was beginning to suffer from the sort of dehydration you get when there hasn't been sight of a mug of tea in hours," he said, holding on as she tried to straighten up and pulling her back down. "I might add, I am beginning to suffer from that self-same form of dehydration myself. So, do you think you could manage two cups? White without for me, I don't know Mrs Blythe's preference."

He released her. She glared at him through eyes which were almost closed.

"If you use the emergency call again when it isn't an emergency, I shall report you to Matron."

"You know, nurse, that I am as putty in your hands, just that I'm running a little low on tea." He smiled winningly at her.

"I suppose you think I have nothing better to do than bring you mugs of tea any time you feel a bit thirsty?" she said.

"But think how much better it makes me feel. And that's your job isn't it? Make the patients feel so well they'll go home?"

"It might be your definition, but it isn't mine. My job description is laid down by the management, and says nothing about making mugs of tea for patients."

"How about," Seymour began, in his most reasonable tone, "you show me where the kettle and the makings are kept and I can help myself – and of course, Mrs Blythe?"

"There's a machine in the waiting area."

"Those things make terrible tea. Haven't you got some of the real McCoy in your rest-room?"

"Yes, but it belongs to the staff. I can't give you free rein to help yourself, or Mrs Blythe."

"Oh," said Seymour, bowing his head.

"Oh, all right," she said capitulating to the soulful gaze he lifted to her face, "I will, on this occasion, advance you two teabags and some milk from my personal supply, provided you replace them."

Seymour looked up and beamed at her. "Nurse, you are truly an angel."

Her lips twitched. "I want full restitution of the teabags," she said.

"I am at your command, nurse," said Seymour, smiling humbly.

He watched as she pushed the trolley back down the corridor. A smile played across his lips. He dropped his gaze to Harriet.

"I haven't enjoyed myself so much for a long time," he said.

Harriet grinned at him. "You're very brave," she said. "Think how many ways she can get back at you if you really annoy her."

Seymour buffed the nails of his right hand against his shirt and examined them. "Nurses were always a push-over for us doctors," he said.

Harriet laughed.

*

Harriet's daughter put down the telephone and stared at it like a viper lining itself up to strike. Her partner in their architectural design business, Colin Milner, looked at her across the cluttered top of her workstation.

"Mothers!" she exclaimed.

Colin waited. He'd seen the signs before: she'd tell him if she wanted him to know what was bugging her – and she usually did. True to form, she looked up and glared at him.

"My mother is obviously going mad," she announced vitriolically.

"What's she done this time?" he asked.

"She has been visiting the hospital over pain in her limbs – without telling me! – and they've told her she's got multiple sclerosis that will kill her quite quickly. She sounds so calm about it on the phone – says she's had a while to let it sink in – and today she's met an old man who is also dying and they've made a list of things to do together before they go."

She bit off her words. Her mouth worked for a moment, then her face crumpled and fat tears welled up in her eyes and rolled down her cheeks. She grabbed a tissue from a box beside her monitor.

Colin stared at her: she'd had many run-ins with her mother, but he'd never seen her weep before. Her usual response was fury. The sight of his feisty partner weeping was unnerving. He stood up.

"Uhm, would you like some water?" he asked, fidgeting on the balls of his feet.

Charley gave a gusty sob into her tissue. Colin took it as a yes and went into the office's small kitchen to fetch one. He returned and put it on her desk. She seemed to have stopped crying and was mopping up.

"Thank you," she muttered into the sodden paper handkerchief. He passed her a fresh one. She dabbed her eyes again.

"That's terrible, Charley," he said, "And she never said anything to you? Surely she can't be dying?"

She drew in a great shuddering breath, mopped her eyes again and nodded.

"That's what's so awful," she said, adding in a small voice, "She didn't tell me she was ill."

"Do you want to go and see her? I can manage without you for a couple of days."

She smiled damply. "Thanks, Col, but she specifically told me she didn't want me hanging around." She sobbed again, noisily.

"I can understand that," he said, unwisely.

Charley flared up immediately. "What do you mean, you can understand that, huh?"

Colin had regretted saying the words as soon as they were out of his mouth. "I only meant that – well, every time you see your mother, you bully her."

"I do not!"

"You do."

"Do not!"

He clamped his lips shut.

After a moment, she said contritely, "Well, I don't mean to."

"The truth is, you and Harriet live in peace – but only when you're miles apart."

"You make me sound as if I'm a real bitch."

Colin cracked a brief smile, wiping it off his face as quickly as it appeared.

Charley pursed her lips mulishly. "I know that look! It says, 'if the cap fits'. I am not really a bitch."

"I've worked with you long enough to know that underneath your crusty image beats the soft and tender heart of a true romantic heroine."

She stared at him for a moment before a smile dimpled her cheeks.

"You bastard," she said without heat, "I'm not like that either."

He grinned at her. "I know you'd like the world to think so. Don't worry, your secret's safe with me."

She grabbed an elastic band from her desk tidy, stretched it over a finger-end and let it fly at him.

"You're still a bastard."

He held up his hands. "I'm a man. All men are bastards; isn't that your view."

"All the ones I know," she said. "You're maybe not so much of one. You have your good points."

He rolled his eyes. "Any more compliments like that and I shall insist you write them down so I can show my wife. She won't believe me otherwise."

She drank some of the water.

"Anyway," he continued, "just what are you going to do about your mum?"

Charley scowled. "I don't know. One of the problems of living so far away is that I can't easily keep an eye on her."

"Just what is she thinking of doing? What's on this list?"

"She wants to buy a big red sports car." Charley stared at him accusingly. "I mean, with one breath she tells me she's only got weeks to live, and in the next, she says she

11

wants to buy a big red sports car. Says she's always wanted one."

Colin's eyebrows rose. "So what's wrong with her buying a big red sports car before she dies, if that's what she wants to do? It's her money, isn't it?"

"That's just it: I don't think she has that sort of money."

He grinned at her mischievously.

"You're worried you might have to pick up the tab."

"You make it sound as though that's the only thing I care about," she complained.

"So it's not true, then?"

She dropped her gaze for a moment before looking up at him again.

"It's all right for someone like yourself: middle-class family, public school and wanting for nothing. Mum and I had nothing. She brought me up single-handed – "

"Yes, I know," he said, "and she made a good job of it. What about your father? Why didn't he help out?"

"Nobody knows where he is. Well, my mother says she doesn't. Says she can't remember his name sometimes. Apparently I was the result of a knee-trembler at the back of a dance-hall. You'd think they'd never heard of condoms back then," she added disgustedly.

Colin looked at her askance. "Are you trying to say you wish you'd never been born?"

"Yes." She hesitated. "No. I mean no. I'm glad to be alive. But it would have been better for her if she'd had a termination."

Colin shook his head. "You're a strange woman, sometimes, Charley."

She stiffened.

"Does it ever occur to you," he continued, "that she could have had a termination and chose not to? Because she wanted you?"

Another frown crossed Charley's striking features.

"Why on earth would she want to be burdened with a brat when she didn't have to be?"

"Why does any woman want a child?" asked Colin.

"Having me kept us both poor. It wasn't my fault."

"Of course not. Did she ever blame you?"

"Colin! Stop behaving like a psychoanalyst. I'm okay with my mother. It's just that I don't want her hurting herself. She's never driven a fast car before, and..." Her voice tailed off as she stared blankly at her desk. "Oh sod it!"

She reached for the telephone.

"Police," announced a female voice a few moments later.

"Can I speak to Mike English, please."

"One moment please. I'll see if he's in."

There was a brief ringing tone before the call was picked up.

"English. Can I help?" said a deep and mellifluous, chocolate-brown male voice. Charley's insides gave their usual little lurch of interest as she heard it.

"Mike, it's Charley."

There was the slightest hesitation before he spoke again. When he did, his voice lacked enthusiasm.

"Oh."

She rolled her eyes. "Hi," she said in her sunniest voice, "how're things with you?"

"Just wonderful. Peaceful, uninterrupted sleep periods. And you?"

"Would you mind if I interrupt this afternoon's sleep period and ask you something?"

"I thought we'd said all we needed to."

She bit her lip. "Please don't make this harder than it is."

Something in her voice must have survived its journey along the telephone lines.

"What's the matter?" he asked, with a hint of concern she'd been listening for.

"I need your help."

In the pause which followed, she could almost imagine him staring at the phone incredulously. She waited.

"I'm sorry, Charley. I just had to sit down. Shock, you know – then I realised I must have misheard you. Thought for a moment you said you needed my help."

She sighed gustily. "Please don't mess around, Mike. I'm worried about my mother."

"What about her?"

"I think she's going to kill herself."

"Oh yes? When?"

"Please take this seriously. She's going to buy herself a big red sports car and she's only got a few weeks to live and she's never driven a fast car before."

There was silence on the end of the telephone. It seemed to drag on. Eventually, he spoke.

"And how is she going to do it?"

"How should I know? I didn't even know she could afford one."

Charley felt the tears rising again and grabbed a fresh tissue.

"No, I meant, how will she kill herself? And if she's going to die anyway – that is what you said, isn't it? – why would she commit suicide in the interim?"

"I don't mean she'll kill herself deliberately: her last car was a Fiat Seicento – she's certain to have an accident in anything with a big engine."

"Ah," said the disembodied baritone, "so it's only a… let's say, a risk that your mother might kill herself if she buys a big red sports car?"

"Yes. Well! It seems like a big risk to me."

"Okay. I don't know your mother as well as you do. You never got round to introducing us. Look, I'll do what I can, but if your mother hasn't broken the law, there's not a lot the police can do."

Charley sniffled. "Okay. I – I understand," she said.

There was an awkward pause before he said, "I *will* try. But don't expect much. I take it there's a reason why you can't go and see her, as you're so worried?"

"She's told me she doesn't want me to visit her." She bit her lip.

"I see," he said, "that does throw a spanner in the works. I take it, if she's planning to buy a new car she isn't *feeling* very ill?"

"It would seem not. I expect she's on drugs."

"Prescribed or recreational?" he asked, a spark of professional interest in his voice.

Charley took the phone away from her ear and looked at it as if it had crawled out from under a rock before putting it back.

"Prescribed! My mother's no angel, but she wouldn't use illicit drugs."

His voice was placatory. "All right, all right! Just remember, I don't know your mother as well as you do. Perhaps you could give me your mother's details."

Charley quickly provided the information asked for.

"Right, then. I'd better get moving."

Charley, listening to the even temper of his voice, was beginning to wonder if she might have been hasty when she dumped him. Every time he spoke his voice was causing little ripples deep inside, and it was disconcerting.

"What are you going to do about it?" she demanded.

"Well, I could ring her nearest police station and ask them to arrest her for being in possession of a big red sports car in a public place, or be thinking of attempting suicide."

"You're not taking this seriously, are you!" Charley said.

His calm, unflappable voice, sounded hurt.

"I am! Really. But there's a limit to my official interest. We have serious crimes – murders, rapes, arson – to deal with, and if I'm honest with you, they have to take priority over the possibility that your mother might – I stress the word, might – do herself some injury. I'm sorry, I guess this isn't what you want to hear, or the way you see it, but I have to try to be objective or, basically, I'm not doing my job."

The mulish expression had appeared again. "All right," Charley said, "I'd rather hoped you might make a bit of an effort, considering it's my mum we're talking about."

"I'll do the best I can."

She hung up.

Colin had been wrestling with a Bill of Quantities for a client who'd commissioned a six-bedroomed mansion based on one he'd seen on a television programme. Charley didn't envy him the task. She glanced at her watch and figured she could put in an hour's work on it herself.

CHAPTER TWO

"I still don't know why you want to blow thousands on a sports car," grumbled Seymour. He stirred his coffee.

He and Harriet had been discharged on condition that they took things easy and avoided stress. They'd been provided with powerful drugs to take. He felt fine.

Harriet blushed, he noticed. "I just do."

He harrumphed.

She looked up at him. "You probably wouldn't understand, being a man."

Seymour felt affronted. "I am a doctor. I have a history of listening to women and learning about what bothers them."

Harriet lifted a sceptical eyebrow. "I'm not 'bothered', as you put it. It's just something I want to do."

"Yes, but why?"

She picked up her mug and studied him over the rim. Outside the coffee shop, a taxi-driver was berating a cyclist for going the wrong way in a one-way street.

"If I tell you – doctor – you've to promise not to laugh."

"I promise. Get on with it."

"Let me ask you this: I bet you live in a big house, bought and paid for, investments in this and that? Probably your children went to public school and university. In short, you probably have no financial worries compared to a lot of people."

Seymour shrugged.

"Well, I had this silly dream," she continued, "I wasn't a bad-looking girl – more freckles than I'd have liked, but hey! – and we were poor. I went to see a movie: it was that James Bond film with George Lazenby and Diana Rigg.

There was this scene towards the end when they're married and driving away from the wedding in his open-topped sports car, to the strains of Louis Armstrong singing "All the Time in the World", and she looked so glamorous and sexy."

She broke off, lost in a memory.

"So, what happened then?" asked Seymour.

Harriet looked up. "Oh, someone shot her."

Seymour rolled his eyes. Then looked at her narrowly.

"Is that how you want to go out? You're driving along in the flash car and someone you don't see, with a rifle, puts a period to your existence?" He leaned closer. "Is that what you want me for? To be your assassin?"

She laughed, punching him lightly on the shoulder. "No! It was just the glamorous and sexy bit. I want to drive round in a red sports car wearing the shortest skirt I can still get into, showing as much cleavage as won't get me arrested, with my hair done up, and dark glasses. I want every male eye on me; I want them all wanting to get me to themselves, down and dirty."

He blinked. "Would that be all together or one at a time?" he asked dourly.

She laughed.

He watched her. It was a long time since he'd seen a woman laugh. His wife had once been like that, when he'd met her, but twenty-six years of living with him and bringing up their children had worn her down. The last two years, after the cancer, she'd rarely laughed, but neither had she complained. In the end, she'd slipped away from him, going gently into "that good night" against which Dylan Thomas urged rage, leaving him to cope alone. He'd given up his medical practice after she'd died, when he'd found it difficult to give it the same commitment as he had before.

He had never been good at coping. He'd put so much of himself into the practice of his profession, he'd had little room left in his life for either his family or other pastimes. Sally had always made things right; she organised him and the children, she channelled what spare energy she had into being a local magistrate, and he'd had no idea of the effort she routinely put in to make his life tick over smoothly. No idea at all until suddenly she was no longer there to look after him.

He found his vision suddenly blurred and dashed away the moisture which had crept into his eyes.

He looked up at Harriet.

"I've been thinking about what I said about learning to fly a helicopter."

Her expression was serious. She hadn't missed his moment of introspection and she wasn't about to make jokes about what he wanted.

"Why don't you?"

He looked up at her. "I don't think these days I'd pass the medical," he replied.

"They wouldn't necessarily know. I mean, you're only on a pain-killer, it isn't going to affect your ability to fly, is it?"

"But they're bound to ask."

"So? Lie."

Seymour stared at her. "I'd never get a licence."

"I thought your aim was to fly, not to get a licence?"

He thought about that. "Hmm. True."

"Let's go to a flying club that has a helicopter. You could go for a half-hour pleasure flight to begin with."

He looked at her with a glint of excitement in his eyes. "I could, couldn't I!"

"Just as soon as I've got my sports car, I'll drive you there."

He leaned closer to her. "I believe some credit cards carry insurance that writes off the outstanding balance on the death of the cardholder," he said softly, "Mine do."

"Why are you whispering?" she asked.

"Because incurring a balance in the knowledge that you're not going to be around to clear it is probably fraud."

"I'm going to be cremated, so they won't even be able to dig me up to arrest me."

Seymour sat back and focussed on her from a distance before leaning forward again so he didn't have to raise his voice.

"You're going to corrupt me, a man of impeccable background, with no points on my driving licence, and only one small peccadillo on my criminal record."

She was immediately curious. "How small?"

Seymour pursed his lips primly. "As a youth, I fell from grace when I was caught attempting to defile a fifteen-year-old Lolita who was, I thought, desperate to be defiled. I gather my real sin was in not using "something for the weekend", which I was far too shy to ask for. This was a Tuesday anyway. Her father found us, on the brink, so to speak."

"And for this you got a criminal record?"

"Her father was a policeman. I got off with a Caution. I also got a clip round the ear, which I never told anybody about."

"And what happened to Lolita?"

"Well, my street cred was shot, of course. I think she got someone else to defile her the following week."

Harriet sighed. "Ah, the hormones are difficult to re-sist."

"This coffee's getting cold. Let's go find a car show-room. Got your card with you?"

She shook her head, amused.

"Never mind, I've got mine," he said, standing up.

They settled their bill and stepped outside into the April afternoon.

*

Seymour climbed out of a taxi later and went into his house. As he went up the two steps to the front door, at the end of a long path through the garden, the quietness of the place struck him, as it had every day of the last two years since Sally had gone. It was cold, too, no longer the place of comfort and relaxation it had once been.

He flicked lights on in the hall and living room. There was news about to start on the television. He switched it on. Before sitting down, he took a glass and a bottle of malt whisky from a sideboard and poured himself a shot. He had been warned against mixing his medication with alcohol, but he thought it could hardly harm him more than the insidious disease eating its way through his brain.

By the time he'd emptied the glass, he was feeling sleepy, and settled down in his favourite armchair to have a nap. Minutes later, the doorbell rang and he heard his daughter come into the house.

"Dad?" she called from the hallway. She entered the living room, followed by her husband, as Seymour came fully awake.

"Hello, Kay." He remembered it was the night when Kay, son-in-law Mark, and sometimes David usually came for dinner. "Oh, damn," he muttered, "I'd forgotten it was Thursday."

Mark greeted him briefly before positioning himself at one end of the settee from where he could see the television, while Kay crouched next to Seymour.

"Where've you been, dad?" she asked, "I've been trying to ring you since Tuesday. Have you been away?"

"Sorry. Look, I haven't gotten around to cooking."

She arched her eyebrows. "Oh! Never mind, Mark can get us a Chinese take-away – will you, Mark?" she asked, raising her voice slightly to command her husband's attention.

"Huh? Oh, yes," he said, standing with his gaze still on the screen as if reluctant to tear himself away. He turned to Kay.

"What would you like?"

"Just get a set meal for three," she suggested. "She glanced at her father. "I take it David isn't coming?"

"He hasn't said so," said Seymour.

She redirected her attention to Mark. "Just for three, then. I'll put some plates to warm while you're out."

After Mark left, Kay sat in the easy chair next to Seymour and looked a question.

He scratched his head. He knew that he really should tell his daughter about his diagnosis, but he also knew that she would make an enormous fuss of him. He gritted his teeth and chose duty.

"I've been in hospital for a few tests," he said.

She stared at him, wide-eyed.

"Dad! What's wrong with you? I didn't know you were ill."

"Oh, it's nothing – ." He was going to say serious, but realised that was stupid. "They say I've got a degenerative illness."

Kay covered her mouth with her hands, horrified.

He watched her, realising that in some way, his condition might be harder for her to bear than it was for him.

"There's no easy way to put this," he said.

She stared at him, eyes wide with distress, hand still clamped over her mouth.

"It's called ALS. Amyotrophic lateral sclerosis. Motor neurone disease."

Her eyes, he saw, were beginning to fill with tears, but still she held herself steady.

"It means that I might not have many months to live. It could be weeks, but however long, I will be progressively losing control of my body."

Her tears began to roll down her cheeks, across her fingers, and she blinked rapidly to clear them. He reached out and put a hand on her arm. She moved forward to embrace him, cheek to cheek. He held her as she finally allowed her grief and anguish visible expression.

"Oh, dad! Surely not you?"

"Why not?" he asked her softly.

"But I can't lose you. You're still a young man."

"Young for my age, you mean," he said with a grin. He could feel his own eyes beginning to flood.

"You're only fifty-eight. That's nothing. You could have another thirty or forty years ahead of you."

He shook his head, but said nothing, while they simply held each other tightly.

He patted her back. "Look on the bright side," he said, "I'll be with your mother a lot sooner than I'd expected."

Kay sobbed quietly.

"You shouldn't distress yourself, Kay. We're all dying from the moment we're born." He thought of Harriet telling him something similar. "It's the natural order of things: we see our parents off."

She refused to be comforted. He held her firmly and held her away from him so he could look at her.

"Now you must stop this, Kay," he said. "When your mother died, you were strong. Be strong again. I really can't do with you weeping on me."

He smiled gently at her.

"Oh, dad," she said again. She bit her lip and looked round for something to mop her eyes with. Seymour passed her the box of tissues.

"Now, why don't you tell me how work is going?"

Kay snuffled again. "Dad, how can you talk about that when you're dying?"

"Because I know it means a lot to you."

"Not more than you do!" she said indignantly.

"I'm old enough to look after myself," he said, clasping his fingers.

"What do you mean?"

He smiled at her. "I have plans."

"What plans?"

"Well, I expect they'll include long walks and plenty of fresh air," he said at last.

Kay was unconvinced. Something in his tone of voice made her suspicious. She frowned.

"Just where will you be walking?"

He shrugged. "Round town? Perhaps out in the country. I'm not lacking in wind or limb – yet. Anyway, I have a companion for these, uh, excursions."

Kay stared at him. "Who?"

"She's called Harriet Blythe. Met her in hospital. She's in the same boat as myself, only weeks or months to go. So you see, she won't let me do anything that might harm me, in case it harms her."

It was Kay's turn to look at her father speculatively. "This Harriet, what's she like?"

Seymour shook his head, schoolmasterly. "Ah, your youth shows, my dear. When you get as old and decrepit as me, you're really pleased if anyone of the opposite gender speaks to you. To find one who wishes to be in my company is so unusual – and welcome. You don't worry too much about the fine detail."

"What "fine detail"?" asked his daughter, keen to mine him for facts about the mysterious Harriet.

"I mean I don't know her that well."

"What does she look like?"

"She's... average. For her age," he said eventually.

Kay studied his expression, which he was keeping as bland as possible. "Hmm!"

Seymour gazed at her suddenly, all blue-eyed innocence, before turning to stare at the television, while Kay gazed unhappily at him until it was time to walk through to the dining room and lay out the place settings before Mark returned with the food.

*

The lift in the tower block where Harriet lived was in its usual non-working condition. She adjusted her grip on the carrier bags she had in each hand, and turned towards the stairs. She was glad, on such occasions, that she only had to climb six flights to the third floor. She felt sorry for those living further up. Despite the ache in her leg, she took the first two flights without a break, pausing on each landing thereafter. At the half-way landing between second and third floors, a black youth trotted up the steps behind her. She recognised him as Eddy from the eighth floor. He glanced at her from under his hood as he arrived.

"Hello, missus," he said.

"Hello, Eddy," she replied. "No school?"

"Ah've finish wid dat, missus. I ain't hangin' aroun' there any longer."

"Blotted your escutcheon, did you?" Harriet asked.

He looked up at her sharply. "Ah ain't got one o' dem fings, missus."

She smiled to show she wasn't being offensive. "It just means, got into trouble."

He smiled back. "You clever lady. Fine wuds."

"I can teach you lots of fine words, if you wanted, Eddy. And please call me Harriet, not missus."

He looked at her askance. "Why I want to learn fine wuds? What I need 'em for?"

"Could help you with a career," she suggested.

He laughed, teeth gleaming white against his black skin.

"I got a career, missus – Harriet. An' all wid-out de fine wuds."

"So will you be moving away from this awful place into the countryside?"

He grinned. "Maybe."

Harriet leaned close to him, smelling his sweat and the sweet damp scent of cannabis.

"I have a good idea what your career is, Eddy, and if it doesn't lead to the fine house in the country, it could land you behind bars. Language skills are a surer start to a life of wealth and ambition."

Eddy turned his whole body so he could see past his hood that they were alone.

"What makes you t'ink you can teach me lang'age skills what my teachers couldna in ten years?"

"How much do you want to learn?"

"Jus' s'posin' I did, how long?"

"Let's do it in steps. On approval."

"What's dat?"

She raised an eyebrow, while an obvious analogy came to mind. "Suppose you were selling something, but instead of taking cash on delivery, you sold it on approval. That means you'd be paid if your customer liked what you'd sold and decided to keep it, after trying it. Otherwise, they return the goods to you. That's selling on approval. Sometimes known as Sale or Return."

"You don' say!" said Eddy. "You mean people sell gear wid-out getting dere han's on de money?"

"If seller and buyer trust each other, or the goods are low enough in value for the seller not to be too inconvenienced if he never sees them again. Certainly not every seller offers goods on approval."

She looked into his eyes under the hood.

"What I'm suggesting is that if you will undertake to come and see me for an hour every day for the next two weeks, and go along with what I try to teach you, then at the end of that time, you can decide whether you want to learn more, or if you think it's a total waste of time."

He pursed his lips. "An' what do you want for doin' this?" he asked sagely.

A thought appeared in her mind that was so alien to her that she daren't mention it. "C-can I take a rain-check on that, Eddy. I'll think about it."

Eddy frowned at her and walked to the other side of the landing and back.

"So, you teach me words, an' maybe you want something' or maybe not. Huh?"

"That's right," Harriet smiled.

"An' I can leave any time?"

"I don't see you as a quitter, Eddy, but yes, you can give up if you can't get along with it."

He thought for a moment. "Okay. We start now?" he said suddenly.

"Oh, okay," said Harriet. "You'll have to wait for me, because I'm not as nimble as I used to be, and it takes longer to get up these stairs."

Eddy grinned and took her arm supportively. "No problem, missus, uh, Harriet, we go up togevver."

Her flat, when they reached it, was cold. She turned the heating up, drew the curtains and switched on some lights. Eddy watched.

"Whocha drawing de cu't'ins for, Harriet? Dey ain't nobody can look in when you're dis far up de sky."

She directed him to a comfortable chair. "It makes the room seem warmer, and I'm not so aware of being this far up the sky," she said. "Would you like some tea? I'll see if my milk's survived in the fridge."

"Ah pre-furr vodka an' tonic, yes."

"Well, I'm afraid I don't have any vodka," she replied, "and anyway, if you're going to be learning things, you don't want your head swimming in alcohol. We can have a sherry at the end of the session, if you'd like, but tea's on offer now. I'm having some anyway."

Harriet went into the small kitchen and filled the kettle. She noticed Eddy standing in the doorway.

"Do you want a cup?" she asked.

"Okay," he said.

They waited until the tea was brewed and took their mugs back into the living room.

"I don' know," he said when they were seated opposite each other across a low table, "I's wonderin' why I really need to speak good." He glanced up at her cautiously. "I got a li'l business goin', an' if I speak like you, my customers gonna t'ink I gone over to de udder side."

Harriet sipped her tea before replying. " 'F I done gonna tok dis way when I wid you, you might t'ink I gone over to de udder side, too. But is just de way I choose to spik at dis time."

Eddy stared at her. "You takin' de piss?"

In her normal voice, she said, "No. I'm trying to make the point that you wouldn't have to speak like I do when you're conducting your, uh, business. Horses for courses, Eddy. But speak like I do and you might, God help us, widen your circle of acquaintances."

"Dat ain't what you really t'ink, is it? You wouldn't want me to 'stend my bizniss into a wider circle 'f 'quaintances."

"What you do with your business is up to you. I think you could change careers to one less likely to see you deprived of your liberty. But you need to get to grips with the language, and then maybe you could get yourself a few qualifications."

Eddy thought for a moment, frowning at her. "But why you doin' dis for me? I nothin' to you."

"I like you Eddy, and I don't want to see you getting into trouble. I just think you've had a bad start to life, and if we can put that right, you have the potential to do great things – good things. Don't waste your talents: one day it'll be too late to change."

He drained his cup. "Okay, where we start?"

*

Charley checked her makeup in the vanity mirror set into her car's sun visor before getting out and joining Colin on the pavement outside the Ten Bells Tavern.

"I don't know why I let you talk me into having a drink after work," she said to him. He held open the door for her.

"Because I hoped it might cheer you up a bit," said Colin.

"You think I need cheering up?"

They found a table.

"A bit," he said. "What do you want to drink?"

"A spritzer, please. Plan on having another drink after, 'cos I buy my round."

"As I well know," he said. "I wish you wouldn't be so insistent – I prefer a pint of beer in a pint glass, but I can't drink two pints, so when you want to buy a round as well,

I have to settle for two half-pints. Can't we arrange that I buy the drinks one time, and you buy them the next?"

She shrugged, grinning. "Oh, if you want to," she conceded.

"Good!" He turned away and insinuated himself through the crowd to the bar counter.

Charley took the opportunity to see if there was anyone she knew in the bar. She became aware that a voice she recognised was in discussion with someone. She saw Mike English and a young woman perched on bar stools either side of an elegant wrought-iron table with a red leather inlaid top.

He hadn't changed since she'd last seen him, two months ago, when they'd had a row over yet another date he'd missed and she'd decided to end their relationship. He was broad-shouldered and narrow waisted, and looked like a rugby-player. He had dark hair and eyes, and tanned, Italian looks. She watched his gestures as he spoke to the woman in the chocolate-brown voice she remembered so well. She could almost taste it: the voice alone was enough to make her feel comfortable and warm. She closed her eyes for a moment.

"Your spritzer," said Colin, putting both their drinks down on the table and bringing her thoughts back to earth. "You all right? You looked miles away."

She smiled at him. "I was just having a pleasant daydream. Mike's over there – " she nodded her head in the man's direction: Colin looked round.

"Nice girl he's got," he said.

Charley looked at him. "Does your wife mind you looking at other women?"

"Nah! I think she actively encourages it. Sometimes I think she'd like me to clear off for a bit, have a torrid affair to get it out of my system, and come back to her. Then I wake up. Not in this lifetime."

She grinned at him. "You poor hard-done-by married man," she said, "Anne looks after you and the children, adds considerably to the Milner family holiday and retirement funds, and you wouldn't trade her for all the tea in China – you know you wouldn't."

Colin shushed her. "Keep your voice down, I don't want these attractive young women around us to stop wanting my body."

"Why? What would they do with it? You're not twenty still. You've got some mileage on the clock, as my mother frequently tells me." She glanced over at the policeman. "You know, she's used that metaphor for years, it's only just struck me: I wonder how long she's had this dream of a big red sports car?"

The noise level in the bar had unaccountably dipped as she spoke, and her words carried to the two people sitting at the wrought-iron table. Suddenly, Mike turned and locked his eyes on hers. Charley gulped and her mouth dried. He smiled, spoke briefly to his companion, and slipped off the bar stool. A moment later, he was towering over Charley.

"Hello."

She felt heat rising up her throat and into her cheeks, and knew she was blushing.

"Hello, Mike," she said. She managed a small smile.

He turned to Colin. "Mike English," he said, holding out his hand.

"Colin Milner, Charley's business partner."

"I think she mentioned you, when we, uh, when we were–"

"A few months ago," she inserted.

The girl Mike had been speaking to came over and touched his shoulder.

"I'd better get home, Mike," she said. "See you tomorrow."

He glanced round at her. "Okay. G'night, Jane." He looked back at Charley, then Colin, who was watching Jane through the window as she strode away.

"Jane's my DC," Mike explained. "We just popped in for an after-work drink. As you probably recall," he added, looking at Charley, "the nick's almost next door."

"That's more or less what we're doing," said Colin.

"Ah. I see," said Mike. He smiled. "Can I get you one?"

"I'm okay," Charley replied, touching her glass.

"How about you, Colin?"

"I'm okay as well, thanks. In fact I'm just going to finish this off and leave you to it."

Charley tried to catch his eye, not at all sure she wanted to be left 'to it' with the man-mountain and his deliciously tasty voice. Colin avoided her gaze, drained his glass and relinquished his chair to Mike.

"See you tomorrow, Charley," he said. "Bye," he added to Mike, and went out into the street.

Mike took his place facing Charley and looked into her eyes.

"Tell me about your mother," he said, "and I mean, I'd like to know about her as a person, the way you know her. We're not in the nick, and I'm not on duty now, so let's just talk about her so I can see her through your eyes."

His voice was still sending ripples of pleasure through her. Below the table, out of his sight, she clamped her knees together. She was finding it difficult to concentrate. She lifted her glass jerkily to her lips, splashing wine on her blouse as she did so. She drained the glass, suddenly aware that one breast felt cold and damp. She glanced down and saw the splash had landed on her right nipple, and the wet fabric had become translucent. The nipple, responding at least partly to the coldness of the drink, had stiffened and was pressing against her blouse. Too late now to wish she was wearing a bra. She guessed before she looked up where Mike's gaze would be focussed, and she was not wrong. Another wave of heat and embarrassment swept across her face. He held out a clean folded handkerchief.

She took it, but excused herself. "I'll just go and dry off," she said, rising from her seat.

Mike stood up, too. "I'll replace your drink," he said, "what would you like?"

She had a fancy for something a bit stronger than the spritzer.

"A gin and tonic, please," she said.

He watched her cross the bar to the washrooms. She was very trim, he thought. He had other thoughts, too, but tried to push them out of his mind.

They'd met when she'd had her purse snatched in the shopping mall three months before. The purse had never been found, but Charley and Mike had found themselves attracted to each other, and it had been no surprise when they started going out together. He'd soon found she had very definite ideas which sometimes clashed with his own, but despite their occasional arguments, their relationship had lasted – until he'd had to break one more date and she'd told him she was fed up with his unreliability, and ended it.

He ordered the drinks, deciding to join Charley in a G and T.

She still looked as good as ever, he thought. She reappeared across the bar and he watched her weave past the other customers to their table. He felt a pang of regret that they no longer saw each other, but didn't want to try to resurrect their affair and risk her running away a second time. On the whole, he decided, it was probably better to stick to a professional relationship, in which he treated her like any other customer, as the management liked to call them these days. Rather like doctor-patient, he thought, he must try not to be seduced by his feelings for her.

Unfortunately.

He picked up the glasses and bottle and took them to their table.

"So tell me about your mother," he said when they were both seated comfortably.

Charley took her time pouring most of the tonic into the gin.

"She's fifty-five and she's dying."

His expression grew serious.

"That's very young. What is it? Cancer?"

"MS. All I remember is that she said she had only a short time to live."

He reached out spontaneously and touched her upper arm in sympathy. She felt something like electricity pass between them and was once again conscious of his nearness and masculinity. He exuded a very slight scent, spicy and clean, which she breathed in and savoured.

"That's really terrible," he said. "What about your father? I don't remember you ever mentioning him, or brothers or sisters."

"I don't know who my father is. There's just me and my mum, and she tells me she's forgotten his name." She sniffed and flipped open her bag to look for a tissue.

He waited while she dabbed her nose. She looked him in the eye.

"She told me I was the result of – and I quote – 'a knee-trembler at the back of a dance-hall'."

Mike grinned wryly. "I haven't heard that term used in years. She sounds like a very forthright lady, your mother."

"She is. She can be very stubborn, and I think she can be her own worst enemy."

"Hence your concern for her safety if she gets behind the wheel of a much more powerful car than she's used to."

"Yes. I'm convinced she could have an accident if she buys this big red sports car she's decided she must have."

He nodded. "I begin to understand, I think." He glanced at his watch. "It would be nice if I knew more about her – and you. I was wondering, if you're not busy, if you'd like to have dinner with me." As soon as the words were out of his mouth, he regretted them as being outside the policeman/client relationship he was intending to maintain.

Charley looked up. He expected her to bawl him out, but suddenly her face broke into a grin.

"Well, I admit to feeling hungry," she said, "which is a bit of a surprise: I didn't think I'd be able to eat a thing."

He saw the colour rise to her cheeks.

"Okay," she said, "where shall we go?"

"Do you like Italian food? There's this little place called Trattoria Italia, just along the street. It's very good."

"Do you think we'll get in without a booking?" she asked.

He glanced at her sideways. "We'll see."

He guided her ahead of him out of the Ten Bells into the street. Turning right, he walked on her left towards a pedestrianised side-street, halfway down which was the illuminated sign of the Trattoria Italia.

As they approached, Charley saw through the window that the place was packed.

She shrugged. "Oh well, we'll have to try somewhere else," she said.

"Don't give up just yet," said Mike, pushing open the door.

A middle-aged man in a blue-checked apron, balding head and cultivated moustache was by the till at the rear of the premises. He looked up as the door opened and his face broke into a beaming smile. He surged forward.

"Ah, Mr English, I have your table," he said beckoning Mike and Charley into the restaurant. Sure enough, tucked in a discreet corner, away from the windows and the eye line of most other diners, was a small table laid for one. The proprietor produced a cigarette lighter and lit the table's candle while Mike eased Charley into a chair. A waitress brought a second chair and laid a second cover.

When they were both seated, he glanced up at her, smiling.

"Guess that was lucky, huh?" he said.

Charley pursed her lips and studied him askance. "Very," she said accusingly, "I could almost believe you had it all planned."

"The truth is I eat here most nights I get off at a reasonable time, and old Guglielmo keeps the table free for me."

For some reason, she liked that he was on name terms with the proprietor.

"Guglielmo? That's Italian for William, isn't it?" she asked.

Mike smiled. She had the thought that his bulk dwarfed the table.

"We have this joke: he calls me Old Bill and I call him Young Bill, which is quite a compliment, considering he's about twenty years older than me."

Oh, God, she thought, what am I doing here? Mike's voice was still weaving its spell. She eased her thighs apart below the table and made a huge effort to concentrate her thoughts on her mother.

The waitress placed menus on the table.

CHAPTER THREE

"I daresay we can let you handle the controls for a few minutes during the flight," the Chief Instructor of the helicopter flying school said to Seymour. His smile was patronising.

While the two men negotiated the details of a pleasure flight the following week, Harriet was gazing at the posters and photographs on the office walls. They were mostly what she expected – aerial photographs of Breydon and the county beyond, oil and gas production platforms in the southern North Sea, the helicopters themselves in their working modes as camera platforms and power line checkers. Then one poster caught her eye.

"Seymour," she called. He was busy paying for his flight and didn't answer.

"Seymour!"

He turned, putting his credit card away. "Yes?"

"I'm going to put this on my list," she said, tapping the image on the poster.

He gazed at it. "Well just as long as you don't drag me up there," he said.

She smiled and went to him, tucking her hand in his arm and gazing up into his face.

"Seymour! Is it possible that you are afraid?" she asked.

He pursed his lips and looked away. "I'm just a bit old for that sort of thing."

"Oh," she said, "so you're not afraid of heights."

"I think that at my time of life it's stupid to take risks. I don't mind being high up if there's a railing or a wall preventing me seeing the ground."

"So you are?"

He pursed his lips again and dropped his gaze. "No... just worried I'll lose my balance and fall. Prefer to keep my feet on the ground."

She regarded him quizzically for a moment before turning to the Chief Flying Instructor.

"Just how do we go about arranging to do a parachute jump?" she asked sweetly.

*

It wasn't a particularly warm day. Seymour was wearing a long woollen overcoat, gloves, a scarf and a cap. Next to him, behind the wheel of her new bright red Mazda sports car, Harriet adjusted the driving position again. She was still experimenting to find the best and most comfortable one having only that morning picked the vehicle up from the dealer's, where she'd paid for it with her credit card. She was wearing a red dress which rode above her knees and her hair was held back in a scrunchie. Her one concession to the temperature was a stylish jumper.

"I don't know why you won't close the roof," Seymour complained, "then we could get some heat going."

"You can have the heater on, dear, " she said, patting his knee, "but I want the roof down. I can't wait for the summer before doing it."

He muttered something she didn't hear as the engine fired into throbbing life.

"Pardon? Didn't catch that," she said, glancing at him.

He looked at her. "I said I can't believe you didn't get all this out of your system when you were a girl."

She stared through the windscreen as the car pulled away from the heliport.

"Didn't have the wherewithal – and none of my boyfriends did either," she said.

"Surely you don't need a car, especially one like this, to attract men's glances – I take it that's why you're freezing to death rather than wearing warm clothing?"

She shot a quick glance at him, a smile curling her lips. "A compliment: thank you, Seymour."

He grunted. "You could die from hypothermia before the other thing gets you," he said.

"If you're going to rain on my parade, I shall take you home and then cruise round the red light district, or something."

He pursed his lips. "With what in mind? I don't believe there are any male prostitutes down there, if that's what you were thinking of."

"Seymour!" she scowled. "A compliment in one breath and an insult in the next! Perhaps I should take you home."

She angled her head to see his face in the driving mirror. She was pleased to see a flush of embarrassment colour his normally pallid cheeks. She drove into the centre of Breydon and grabbed a parking bay in the High Street. Seymour had remained quiet after her rebuke, but she hadn't time to leave the punishment in place for long. She looked at the large imposing building on their left.

"I suppose respectability runs all the way through you," she said to Seymour, "like the words in a stick of Yarmouth Rock."

"I thought it did," he said quietly. "I can see I owe you an apology."

"I knew you were a nice man, deep down," Harriet said as she leaned over and kissed his cheek.

"Are we friends again, woman?"

"As much as we shall ever be."

He lifted his eyebrows. "Are you thinking there's a limit to our friendship?" he asked.

She gripped her fingers and looked down at her hands.

"I think it would be silly of us to think there's any future for our relationship," she said. She turned towards him and for a moment their eyes met before she looked down again. "It will only make it harder for the survivor when one of us goes if we – well, I know it's unlikely, but we can't rule it out – if we were to fall in love. Won't it?"

Seymour regarded her thoughtfully. After a moment, he nodded.

"I suppose you're right." If he was disappointed, it wasn't evident from his expression.

"Harriet is always right, Seymour. Just repeat that to yourself every now and then and we'll get along just fine."

"We don't need to complicate things by falling in love, however unlikely," he said.

"Agreed. Ever felt like trying to rob a bank?" She looked again at the building they were parked outside. Its pillared and porticoed exterior was the epitome of the grandiose and respectable establishment banks had always professed to be. Seymour studied it briefly before turning to look at Harriet, a strange gleam in his eyes.

"Curiously enough," he said, "I've never given it a thought."

"It would be very dangerous," she said.

Seymour pursed his lips. "But quite exhilarating."

Harriet smiled. "Do you reckon we'd be up to it? Capable?"

Seymour rubbed his chin. "You mean, walk in, demand a bag-full of money and get away before we're arrested?"

She nodded. "Hmm."

He shook his head. "I think they have very good security devices to prevent people taking cash out over the counter."

"You mean security guards, CCTV?"

"And the rest: I think they have shutters built into the counters that close off the cashiers' area."

Harriet looked down, discouraged. "Sounds as if it's a non-runner of an idea."

Seymour watched her for a moment. "We could try a smaller branch. Shutters are expensive: they won't fit them everywhere."

She looked up, grinning. "Of course!"

"I take it we're not actually bothered how much cash we can get away with?"

"No. I don't even want to keep it."

"What shall we do with it?"

She shrugged. "How about the Children's Hospice? They have a charity shop along West Gate."

He grinned. "We could donate a bag of cash."

She chuckled. "You don't happen to have a sawn-off shotgun, do you?" she asked.

"I have a shotgun," said Seymour, "but it isn't sawn-off."

"Do you have a saw?"

He stared at her, horrified. "Yes, but I couldn't use it on my shotgun."

She patted his knee. "When are you likely to use it again?" she asked.

He considered the matter, then shrugged. "I guess I'm not. Okay, I'll cut down the barrels – but I'm not loading it."

They sat there a few moments longer before Harriet suggested they cruise around, looking for a suitable bank branch to attack. An hour later, she dropped Seymour off at his home.

"Nice place," she observed as he climbed out of the car.

"You must show me yours now you've seen mine."

She looked sideways at him and grinned.

"Nobody's said that to me since I was about fourteen, Seymour," she said.

He laughed.

"Shall I see you tomorrow? And do you have a telephone number?"

He searched in a pocket as he spoke and produced an old visiting card, which he handed to her. She told him her number, which he wrote on the palm of his hand with a pen.

For a moment, he stood awkwardly on the pavement, until she smiled again, and gunned the engine. He watched as the car accelerated off with a throaty roar from its exhaust and turned the corner at the end of the street. He went through the gate, up the path lined with pansies and petunias and let himself in.

He listened carefully, to see if there were any sounds suggesting either of his children might have let themselves into his house already. Only the ticking of the hall clock reached his ears. He went towards the lounge, hoping for some peace and quiet. Ten minutes later, he heard the sound of a key in the front door. He turned to see Kay let herself in.

"Hi, dad," she said as she closed the door and came towards him. Putting down her shopping bag she reached up to kiss him on the cheek.

"Hello, sweetheart," said Seymour, noting the look of determination in her eye which he guessed meant she'd decided that "looking after dad" was her new project. He didn't want to be anyone's project, including his daughter's. Still, he could hardly turn her away.

"I've come round to cook you dinner."

He looked at her askance. He knew very well that Kay's culinary results rarely lived up the promise of the recipe. He led the way into the lounge and sat himself in his favourite chair. She followed him, with the bag.

"I thought fish would be good for you," she said, patting her shopping bag.

Seymour fought hard to keep his rising sense of frustration out of his voice.

"I appreciate the thought – but we need to talk, Kay."

She put the bag down and sat in the adjacent chair, clasping her hands.

"What is it, dad?" she asked earnestly, "You know you can tell me anything."

"I'm glad you said that, love," he said, "because I need to make something clear to you – and David – that is fairly difficult." She gazed round-eyed at him and he hurried on.

"That fact is, I know you and your brother mean it for the best, but I don't need mollycoddling. I feel fine, and I can look after myself. I'm not losing my marbles, so there really isn't any need for you and David to make such a fuss – though believe me when I say I appreciate it."

She brushed away the threat of tears. "Oh, dad! It's so typical of you to say that, but we love you, and we owe you this much."

"No – no you don't!" He struggled over the words: he wanted to tell her to leave him alone, just carry on as normal, but felt that to do so would hurt her feelings. The back of his mind was filled with memories of Kay as a little girl, getting dirty when she tried to help out in the garden, blowing out birthday-cake candles, and with eyes shining at the sight of the Christmas tree loaded with gifts. All before she had grown up and become the ruthless professional career woman she was now. Her mind, he knew, was focussed on material gains, which was one reason she'd never given him a grandchild.

She was clearly not going to give up easily. She leaned forward and kissed him again, wetting his cheek with more tears.

"We know we wouldn't be where we are today if you and mum hadn't made sacrifices for us. We only have a few weeks to make it up to you."

Seymour held her away from him. "No, you don't realise, you don't have to make anything up to me. What we did, your mother and I, was what any parent in our position would have done: we tried to give you and David a good home and a good education. It was nothing we couldn't afford," he added, thinking of Harriet's very different experience of life.

Kay gently patted the back of his hand.

"Oh, dad, I love you," she said, dotting a kiss on his forehead. "You sit here and I'll grill this – it's sea bass. I thought we'd both enjoy that." She patted him again, and swept away into the kitchen.

Seymour rolled his eyes, gritted his teeth, and settled down to watch the early-evening news on the television.

His mind was busy trying to remember where he'd last seen his hacksaw.

*

In the excitement of acquiring her dream car, Harriet had overlooked the need to provide for secure parking. The builders of tower blocks in the nineteen-sixties had never envisaged any tenant having the wherewithal to buy a new car, let alone one that, she imagined, had every youth who saw it drooling over its sleek and powerful looks.

As she pulled into the small, square courtyard provided for overnight parking by residents, the exultation which followed her drive through the town centre, exhaust drumming and heads – particularly male ones – turning, was dampened by the realisation that every other vehicle around could be described as a "banger". Eddy was hanging around near the entrance to the flats. When he raised his eyes from the bright alloys and gleaming chromework to recognise Harriet in the driving seat, he slouched over to her.

"Hi, missus," he said with a gleaming white smile. "Dat's a decent bit o' wheels."

Harriet smiled back, pleased he approved. "Get in, if you like," she said.

Eddy glanced at his watch – one which looked at first glance like a Rolex Oyster, but she recognised as a cheap copy of far-eastern origin, costing about a tenner on the market.

"I got a few minutes 'fore my nex' appointment," he said.

"When are we getting started on widening your language skills?" asked Harriet, "You want to come to my flat around seven?"

She had a sudden thought. "Make that six if you'd like feeding as well."

Eddy turned his glance from the dashboard to look at her face. "You wanna feed me?" he asked incredulously.

"Is anyone else?"

"I look after myself."

"That's good," she said, "but you should be looked after occasionally by someone else."

She fired up the engine and took the car out of the parking square. She headed for the London arterial road.

"Where we goin'?" asked Eddy.

"Just there and back again, to see how far it is," Harriet replied, settling her sunglasses on her nose.

They reached the dual carriageway and she pressed the accelerator pedal. They were pushed back into their seats as the car leapt forward. She moved through the gears smoothly and soon caught up with cars in the nearside lane. Without hesitation, she signalled and moved into the outside lane, tearing past them.

Eddy glanced at the speedometer and his eyes widened. "You know you is doin' de ton, missus?"

"Am I? Great isn't it? And please call me Harriet, not missus," she added.

The car tore round a long swooping bend onto a clear road and the speedometer needle crept further upwards. Wind whipped through Harriet's hair and caused it to stream out behind her. Eddy, shorter, was not bothered by the wind. Harriet noticed his hand creep tentatively out until he was able to grip the door handle and smiled to herself.

As they approached the next junction, she slowed and took the slip road up onto the bridge across the two carriageways. She turned right and made her way to the other side of the road, selecting the slip road heading back towards town. As she did so, she saw a mobile speed camera van was parked on the bridge facing the way they had come, and figured there'd be a speeding summons in the post, but probably not until she was no longer around to care.

She hit the throttle again, and the ton, on the way back to town.

*

Seymour was aware of his daughter's eyes on him as they sat in front of the television after dinner. He'd found a channel broadcasting a classical music concert, and was listening to it. His daughter's obvious distress was distracting. He thought she might be concerned about the cremation of the sea-bass, but reflected that she had a blind spot when it came to her cooking skills, and probably hadn't realised that the fish had been ruined by too much cooking and the potatoes by too little. He gave up on the music, reduced the volume and turned to face her. She was seated elegantly in the easy chair on his left.

"Kay, about the meal," he said.

She smiled. "Glad you liked it." She hesitated. "Do you miss mum?"

He raised an eyebrow. "Miss her? Of course. You can't live with someone for the length of time we were together, share the same history, without missing them when they go."

He got up and went across to the sideboard, opening a cupboard which contained glasses and bottles of spirits.

"Would you like a drink?" he asked Kay.

"Just some tonic water, if you have any. I have to drive home."

Seymour nodded silently and poured her drink. He made himself a gin and tonic and sat down again, passing the tonic water to Kay.

"Let me say this, Kay," he said, "I don't want a fuss. You are... very good... at fussing when you see a need, and frankly I'd be glad if you saw that, in fact, there isn't one: I shall be fine."

She said nothing, simply waiting for him to continue.

"It's like this, dear. I shall potter along as ever until, one day, I simply stop... pottering. I know that afterwards, you'll be strong for yourself and David, and do what needs to be done. I want to be buried with your mother, of course. Everything you need to know is in my will."

"I wish – I wish you wouldn't talk like that, dad," she said, fighting back tears.

"Okay," he said, "there's nothing more to be said, anyway, so let's talk about something else."

She shook her head. "What else?"

"My plans for the future," he said. "Of course, these are not long term, I'm not going to try and read *War and Peace*, or buy long-playing records, but there are a few things I want to try doing before... before it's too late."

She grinned damply at his joke.

"What?" she asked.

"Well, you know, I've always wanted to try my hand at flying a helicopter."

"But you do fly," she said, "We used to pop over to Deauville for lunch when David and I were little."

"And the horse-races. I remember," he said, smiling at the recollection. "But my licence expired long ago. It was for fixed-wing aircraft anyway. You have to keep your hours up or they take it away from you. I feel sure it'll all come back to me if I can have a go."

"How will you do that?" she asked.

She was surprised when he told her he had already arranged for a short flight from the local heliport. His mouth turned down as he added, "And Harriet has booked us in for a charity parachute jump."

Kay stared at him, shocked. "But you don't like heights."

"I know that," he said, grimly, "but I have been told it's the least I can do." He glanced up at her, a wry expression on his face.

"Who told you that?"

"Harriet."

"Didn't you tell her that with almost no effort at all you could do much less?"

He chuckled. "No. Women, I've discovered, don't take kindly to being contradicted."

"That's true, of course," said Kay, "but we don't mind a bit of an argument. Just as long as we get our way in the end."

"So you agree: resistance was futile."

She giggled. "I can see you've been trained well."

"Worn down, more likely," he said, grinning. He glanced down for a moment before continuing. "I still really miss her, you know."

Kay slid off the chair and knelt by his side, taking one of his hands in hers. She cradled it against her cheek.

"Me too," she said.

They were silent for a moment. She got up.

"I'd better wash up," she said, getting to her feet and walking into the kitchen.

Seymour watched her go. As a busy GP, he'd often worked evening surgeries and out-of-hours callouts, only later realising how much he'd missed being with his children during their formative years. Changes in contracts had meant that over the last few years before he gave up, home life had become more possible, but by then his wife was becoming seriously ill and his children had flown the nest.

He pushed himself up off the settee and went into the kitchen, where Kay was already filling the sink with sudsy water.

*

That night, back home, Kay left Mark watching the television while she made a phone call from the study, down the hall a few yards from the drawing room.

"David? It's Kay."

"Oh. What's up?"

She rolled her eyes. "Why is that always the first thing you say?"

"Because you always want me to do something."

"Of course. It'll be different if you ever find a proper girlfriend: she'll have first call on you, but until then, I'm taking advantage of our relationship."

"Define 'proper'."

"One that stays around longer than a couple of weeks. You'll probably need to make an effort to smarten the place up if you ever want this to happen."

"Why? Mostly, the girls wash and dust."

"Then they realise that's why you're so keen to have them stay, and leave. You need to clean up your own mess – and I'm not talking about the rats nest of wires holding your computers together, I'm talking about the toilet bowl and the washing-up."

"Ugh!"

"And using the vac at least once a week. Why do you think we gave you one?"

"Well, I know what they're for, but I was keeping it for best."

She grinned again, despite her frustration with his lifestyle.

"I was going to suggest that you might like to hire a movie when you go round to dad's tomorrow, so you can watch it together."

"I can imagine the cosy scene," said David, "What do you suggest?"

"I leave it entirely to you. But don't forget to go. Cook him dinner, wash up. Perhaps you should practise your vacuuming skills at dad's house?"

"You don't expect me to do all that, do you? He wouldn't want it. He's capable of looking after himself, isn't he?"

"Well, yes, but David; he's very ill, however he seems. For God's sake, can't you help me look after him for a few weeks? Is it so much to ask?"

"I suppose not," said her brother, sounding like a petulant twelve-year-old. "Okay, leave it with me."

"I'm relying on you, David," she said before hanging up and returning to the Library where Mark was sprawled in front of the television, dozing. A part-empty glass of wine stood on the table beside him.

Kay picked up the remote controller from the same table and zapped through programmes, to see if any caught her interest. Failing in this, she turned the television off. Mark opened his eyes and glanced at the blank screen then round at her.

"Fuse blown?" His voice had a sarcastic edge.

"No," she replied, "but neither of us was watching, so I decided to save some electricity."

He held out his hand for the controller. She was about to pass it to him when she stopped.

"Mark, I want to ask you something."

"What?"

She looked down at her hands, fidgeting with the handset. Then glanced up at him and saw the impatience and his darting looks at the remote and her courage failed. She passed it to him.

"Nothing. Sorry," she said.

A few moments later, the television was once again filling the room with sound and pictures no-one was watching: Mark had fallen asleep again.

CHAPTER FOUR

Charley was quiet the morning after her meal with Mike English. Colin Milner was grateful because for once he could concentrate on the planning and design job he was developing. By lunchtime, however, he was beginning to ask himself if something serious had happened the night before and was wondering whether to broach the matter.

He cleared his throat.

"How was your evening?" he asked.

Charley glanced up at him, then back down to the papers on her workstation.

"Fine."

Colin mulled over her brevity.

"How'd you get on with Mike English – I take it he was the policeman you spoke to yesterday on the phone?"

"He was. It was okay. We were fine."

Colin lifted an eyebrow. "You keep saying "fine". Why is it I have this feeling it wasn't? Did he say or do something to upset you?"

Charley looked up again. "No. I said it was fine, and I meant fine!"

She glared at him.

"Okay," he said, holding up both hands in a gesture of submission, "it was so fine you haven't been able to stop talking about it."

"It's none of your business!"

Colin shrugged. "I guess not. We've spent all morning working instead of arguing. If he has that effect on you, our productivity should improve hand over fist."

"He has no effect on me."

Colin leaned forward. "Charley, you didn't sleep with him, did you?"

"No I did not! And it's none of your business anyway."

"You didn't do anything to alienate him, did you?"

"Alienate?"

"Well, you can, you know."

She stood up, furious. "Colin, you don't know what you're talking about, so –"

She was interrupted by her telephone starting to burble discreetly. She grabbed the handset and sat down.

"Milner Blythe," she barked.

As Colin watched, her anger faded and a faint glow tinged her cheeks. Her tone of voice softened, too.

"Oh, no, I'm sorry about what happened," she said, "No, I'm not upset." She listened. "Oh, has she – ? Oh, hell! I knew she'd do something stupid." She listened again. "All right. I'll come down to the police station." She glanced at the clock on her computer monitor. "Give me about a quarter of an hour, will you." She hesitated, then, "and I am really sorry about last night."

She hung up and met Colin's curious gaze.

"All right, I'll tell you what happened – but it's none of your business, really."

Colin sat back and folded his arms. "I'm all ears and the soul of indiscretion."

She looked at him twice before a small grin twisted her lips out of their firm, thin line.

"Mike and I had dinner together last night."

Colin's eyebrows rose and his head tilted on one side.

"And that's all," said Charley.

Colin retained his surprised expression. "Really? Didn't he at least ask about seeing more of you, literally or figuratively, or both?"

Her eyebrows came together. "Yes. He wanted us to go to his place for coffee – "

"And you wanted him to go to yours, and he wouldn't! I see how it was," said Colin, nodding as if he'd cracked a crossword.

Charley scowled. "No! No, no, no! That's what I told him: no."

"Just that? Just *like* that?"

She looked down. "More or less. I told him I was only there with him because I'm concerned for my mother."

"And he said?"

"Well, he realised his invitation was – was well out of place. And said he'd talk to me in future only about my mother..."

Colin peered at her. "And you replied?"

"That I was only interested in my mother, and definitely not in having a relationship."

He nodded again. "That told him, I bet!"

An expression of misery settled on her face. "Yes, I rather think it did."

"I think I've misunderstood: I thought you looked *un*-happy, but now I see it's just your version of delight. You told him you didn't want him taking a personal interest in you, and he's agreed not to. I take it after the meal you both went your separate ways?"

She nodded sadly. "But the thing is, he is rather nice, and he was very kind, and he lent me his hanky when I spilled my drink, and now..." Tears gathered in her eyes, "and now, " she sniffed, "I think he might never ask me out again."

Colin watched and waited while she mopped her cheeks.

"Be careful what you wish for," he said quietly, "you might just get it."

She looked despairingly through the folds of the paper handkerchief at him.

"I hate it when you're right," she said miserably.

"It doesn't happen very often," he said, grinning, "at least it's rare when I'm with you or my wife. At other times, in other places, I have quite a good track record."

She grinned damply. "That's because neither of us is around to tell you what's what."

"Of course," he agreed, nodding. "So you'll be off, then?"

She stared at him then at the clock.

"Oh! I'd forgotten the time. I shall be late!"

"Woman's prerogative," he said laconically, amused by her.

"Not everyone knows that," she said, pulling her coat on and grabbing her handbag. With a swift "see you later" over her shoulder, she dashed out of the office, down the stairs into the street.

Her route to the police station took her past both the Trattoria Italia and The Ten Bells, with their attendant memories. What she now saw as the disastrous end of the meal, prompted by the sight of the Italian restaurant, was overshadowed by her rosy-cheeked recollection of her wet blouse in the public house. She recovered her composure by the time she reached the police station.

Mike English met her in the small vestibule. His expression was guarded. Charley's heart sank. He took her up some stairs and into his office.

"Coffee?" he asked, going to a filter machine on the window-ledge.

"Thanks," she replied. At least he was being civil: she had feared he might not want to speak to her again. She took the mug gratefully and gulped a mouthful of the hot aromatic beverage.

"So, tell me again what my mother's done," she said.

Mike leaned back in his chair, holding his mug of coffee with both hands. She lifted her eyes to meet his gaze.

"It would seem she has bought her big red sports car – and celebrated the event by travelling at a hundred and eight miles an hour along the London road. She was photographed by a mobile speed camera, with a black youth sitting beside her."

Charley stared at him. "My mother? You sure about that? Speeding? She's the most law-abiding person I know: I shouldn't think she's driven faster than fifty all her life.

And a black youth? I'm not aware of who her friends are, but I don't think she's mentioned him when we've spoken on the phone."

Mike leaned forward, gazing deep into her eyes. Her heart thumped painfully when she thought for a moment he was going to kiss her, but he rested his elbows on the desk and leaned on them.

"Has your mother ever used drugs?" he asked.

She frowned. "Nothing that wasn't prescribed or available over the counter at the pharmacy. Why?"

"Our colleagues in Breydon seem to think they recognise the youth as a local drug dealer."

Charley's eyes widened and her eyebrows arched in surprise.

"You think my mother is into *drugs?*" she said incredulously.

Mike shrugged. "Had to ask," he said apologetically.

"Go to hell!" she retorted – and immediately wished she hadn't. "Sorry. Didn't mean that," she mumbled, feeling the blood rushing to her face again.

He gazed at her silently. She felt his eyes on her and swallowed compulsively, discovering her throat was dry.

"Do you do that a lot? Say things you don't mean?" he asked.

She nodded wordlessly, staring at the desk-top and feeling like a school-girl again.

"You really need to stop it, you know," he said mildly.

She looked at him, miserable. "I know," she said, "I'm sorry."

He stood up. "That's it, then. Just thought you'd want to know about your mother."

It was obviously a dismissal. She put the half-empty mug of coffee carefully in the centre of a beer-mat before standing. She had to make herself look up and meet his sardonic gaze.

"Thank you. I – I appreciate it," she stammered. "I realise it's nothing to do with your work here. I'm sorry to have been such a pain."

She felt her eyes sting, and quickly left his office before tears could fall. He followed her along the corridor to the security door and leaned past her to open it.

"Goodbye," she mumbled as she left him.

"Goodbye, Charley," she heard him say to her retreating back, and then she was in the street, gulping fresh air.

*

Mike English spent much of the afternoon staring at the screensaver on his computer. Every now and then the telephone would ring and startle him out of his reverie; each time he hoped it might be Charley phoning to somehow get him off the hook he seemed to be on, and each time it wasn't her he felt the weight of disappointment across his shoulders.

Normally, he thoroughly enjoyed his work, deriving great satisfaction from it, but after Charley had made it clear to him that she saw him only as a means to an end, he couldn't concentrate. When he'd first seen her in the Ten Bells, he realised he still fancied her and within a short time of speaking to her he'd known that he wanted to spend more time with her. A half-day later, he'd been tentatively contemplating a real future with her – until she'd made it plain that she didn't want that.

That had been a shock, since her demeanour and body-language from the moment he'd met her had told him she liked him. Obviously, he'd got it wrong.

For once, he finished work early and went home to spend the evening slumped in front of a televised football match, feeling very unloved and unwanted. His team lost.

*

Harriet's phone rang in the middle of Eddy's latest "lesson". It was Charley.

"I'm rather busy at the moment, dear," she said, watching the young man struggling to read a book aimed at ten-year-olds.

"I want to know how you got a speeding ticket," said Charley sternly.

Harriet rolled her eyes. "How did you find out about that?"

There was a slight pause before Charley replied, "The police told me."

Harriet frowned.

"Why would they tell *you?*"

Another hesitation. "The point is, what are you doing, getting a speeding ticket – and I gather you've been out and bought this big red sports car you were on about!"

"My goodness," said Harriet mildly, "I never knew our police forces were so forthcoming with information – especially to disinterested parties."

She heard Charley suck in breath. "I am not a "disinterested party" – I'm your daughter."

"Forgive me, but you are not responsible for me, Charley, and that makes you very definitely disinterested."

Eddy had turned the page and was tracing words with a finger as he read them. His lips were moving, Harriet noted.

"Look! You're my mother – *my* mother – "

"I know who I am, dear," said Harriet, trying to sound more patient than she felt, "so please don't treat me as if *I* were *your* daughter!"

There was silence in Harriet's ear for a moment before she heard a distinct sob. She frowned.

"Charley! Listen to me! You're to stop crying at once. You've done nothing wrong, but I am definitely old enough not to need looking after. Everything's sorted out that has to be. Seymour reckons that the cost of the sports car will be expunged from the credit card after – afterwards, so it won't be a charge on the estate. Bless him, he was going to put it on his card, but I made him bring me home so I could pick up mine."

There was another long sigh and a sob.

"I'm going to have fun," she finished.

"How can you have *fun* when you're dying?" asked her daughter.

Harriet smiled to herself. "How do I have fun? Let me count the ways..."

"This isn't Shakespeare, it's real life," moaned Charley.

"And I'm not giving up on it easily, love. Tell you what, I've always wanted one of those make-over things: let's go together and spend a day being pampered and primped."

Charley sniffed. "If that's what you'd really like to do. Okay. Shall I arrange it?"

Harriet detected the onset of yet more mothering instinct. "No, it's my idea, so I'll make the arrangements. I'll give you a ring when it's sorted."

"What are you going to do afterwards?" wondered Charley.

"You know, I hadn't thought. I might try and fix a night out with Seymour. Somewhere grand. Wonder if he's got a dinner jacket?"

"Mum, do you *know* anywhere that grand?" asked Charley.

"No, but I'll think of something," she said vaguely, recollection of a particular event having occurred to her, not being one she wished to tell Charley about.

After hanging up, she made Eddy and herself a mug of tea. Sitting opposite him, she took a sip of the hot brew, and smiled.

"You seem to be coming on by leaps and bounds, Eddy," she said, "and that's a metaphor. Metaphors are very useful..."

She kept him interested in both reading and writing for nearly an hour before they began to flag from the effort. She was impressed with Eddy's determination and persistence, and hoped it would continue.

After he left her flat, she tidied up and washed the mugs before surveying the contents of the fridge and larder for something to eat. After her meal, she took the tablets she'd been prescribed by the hospital and waited for them to take effect. She'd felt the pain begin to break through while she'd been talking to Charley and put off taking the pills as long as she could, in the illogical hope that it would go away by itself. She'd shunned drugs all her life, as much as was consistent with common sense. Now, as she waited for the pain to lessen, she studied the boxes they came in.

An hour later, she arrived outside the door of Eddy's eighth floor flat and knocked. Climbing the stairs to the eighth floor had proved quite exhausting, and she hoped he would let her in so she could get her breath back.

The door was solid timber, but scarred as if something heavy had been thrown at it repeatedly. There was a spyhole in it. She heard chains being loosened and locks being turned. In a moment, the door opened enough for Eddy's face to fill the crack. He looked worried.

"What yo' want, missus? Harriet?" he added, correcting himself.

Harriet's sensitive nose had detected the sweetish, dampish smell of cannabis in the air. She smiled tentatively.

"I wonder if you could provide me with some, er, dope," she said.

His eyes opened wide, the whites standing out.

"What yo' want it for, miss— Harriet?"

"I want to see – "

She stopped as he opened the door wider, reached out, and pulled her into the flat, closing and locking the door behind her.

As he fixed the last chain in place, he came to join her in the living room.

"I doesn't do business on de landin'," he explained.

The room was only moderately untidy, Harriet thought, as if it had been quite tidy a few hours ago, but had gradually become cluttered during the day. On a small glass-topped table in front of a threadbare chair was an ashtray containing the ends of old joints, a scattering of tablets and drying cannabis leaves. Beside them, a small pile of sealable plastic bags waited to be filled, and a tiny balance was there to weigh out equal quantities of the drugs.

Eddy waved her into the chair while sitting opposite her on an old kitchen one.

"Now, Harriet, you's to listen to me," he said, "When I come to your place, I listen to you and do what you tell me. Now you's in my place, you should listen to me and do what I tells you, ain't dat right?"

Harriet nodded meekly. Inwardly, she shuddered at the thought of what the substances before her on the table might do to the people who used them, whilst knowing perfectly well, with another part of her mind, that she was in the flat precisely to buy some drugs for herself – and probably enough for Seymour. She supposed that would make her a "supplier" in the eyes of the law, and she was glad she wouldn't be around long enough to have to answer for it.

"Well, you can't have none," Eddy continued.

"Why not?" she asked, surprised at his refusal.

"Because dey bad for you, Harriet. You a nice woman, dese drugs will wreck your life."

A chuckle rose in her throat too quickly to be repressed.

"You're trying to tell me that drugs – these things you sell to anybody who has the right money – are bad for my health?"

"Dat's right!"

There was a pattern of taps on the door. Eddy got up and peered through the spy hole. He glanced over his shoulder at Harriet.

"Sorry, Harriet," he said, "dis is one o' my better customers."

She shrugged. He loosened the chains, unlocked the door and opened it. A young man Harriet estimated at around eighteen or nineteen slipped into the room and paused to stare at her.

He turned to Eddy and spoke in an accent Harriet readily identified as London. "You di'n't say you 'ad your mum wiv you, Ed."

Eddy came into the room and stood between the young man and Harriet.

"What you want, Ronny?" he asked.

"You got E's, man?"

Eddy glanced round at Harriet, who was taking a great interest in the transaction, for all he was trying to shield her from it. He turned back to his customer.

"How many?" asked Eddy.

"How much?"

They agreed a price.

"I'll have ten – no, make it a rahnd dozen, Eddy."

The customer felt in his pocket and pulled out a roll of cash, beginning to pull notes from it as Eddy went into his bedroom, judging by the smell which emanated from it, returning a short time later with a small plastic bag containing the tablets.

There was an exchange of money for tablets.

"How abaht Roofies, Eddy? Couple?"

Eddy looked at Harriet. The look in her eyes told him she knew perfectly well what Roofies were, and why they were popular. He shook his head at his customer.

"No, I ain't any o' them. Now if dat's all...?"

Harriet speculated from the shocked look in the customer's eyes that Eddy's haste to eject him from the flat was unnatural. As soon as the door was open, he left, bestowing on Eddy a very old-fashioned look as he passed him.

The door locked and chained again, Eddy resumed his seat opposite Harriet. He was apologetic.

"I's sorry, missus, but it's my livelihood. I ain't got another an' it pays well."

Harriet nodded, tight-lipped. "I really hope you'll move on to something that won't get you put inside, Eddy."

"Are you going to tell, Harriet?" he asked, and for the first time she really understood how much he had trusted her simply by letting her into his flat. She shook her head.

"No, of course not. I don't want to see you sent down – but I don't approve of anyone dealing in illicit drugs. That's one reason why I'd be delighted if we could find you something else to do that paid reasonably, and gave you the chance you need to finish your education."

There was another coded knock on the door. With an apologetic glance at Harriet, Eddy got up and peered through the spyhole. This time he didn't open the door.

"What you want?" he called.

"E's and speed," came the reply.

"How much you got, man?"

"Fifty."

Eddy calculated. "Ten tabs and a gram."

"Okay." The purchaser sounded disappointed.

"Wait," commanded Eddy, and went through into his bedroom again. He re-emerged with two of the two-by-one-inch plastic bags. He flipped open the letter box. The exchange of cash for drugs was effected smoothly and Eddy returned to his seat, pushing the banknotes into his pocket.

"Sorry, Harriet," he mumbled. "Look, you should go. Wouldn't do if de filth were to raid dis place and fin' you heah."

She gritted her teeth.

"I want some cannabis, please, Eddy, like I said."

He stared at her and slowly shook his head.

"Harriet, you's straight, girl. You don't wanna start doing drugs *now!*" he said.

She smiled, a trifle lopsidedly. "I can't explain it, Eddy, but I really want to, and I don't have time to go down town and find someone there who'll sell me some."

"What you gonna do wiv it? You don't even smoke."

She nodded. "I know," she said wryly, "but rolling a cigarette – I mean, spliff – can't be so difficult, can it?"

Eddy shook his head, his eyes closed. "Oh, it very difficult. I should give up de ideah right now."

She grinned at him. "Eddy! You could show me how to do it."

"I ain't got no skunk on de premises, missus," he said, shaking his head and folding his arms.

She leaned forward, smiling and tapped him playfully on the knee.

"Liar," she said amiably, "the place stinks of it."

"How would you know?" he asked.

"I used to teach at the High School. I know what skunk smells like."

"Dat place is one den of iniquity," said Eddy. For a moment, he adopted an expression of righteous indignation, but couldn't retain it. He grinned.

She realised at once why he looked so pleased. "Good word! Where'd you find it?"

"In de Bible."

She stared at him incredulously.

"When did you start to read the Bible?"

He looked away from her. "It was jus' lying around. I ain't got many books an' I wanted to practise my readin', so I used de Bible."

She felt sure that under his dark skin, he was blushing.

"That's a real toughy of a book to start with, Eddy. If you want something more challenging than we've been looking at, I've got some with a bit of adventure in, which you might enjoy."

He grinned. "Dat sounds good, Harriet."

"But first, show me how to make a spliff."

The smile disappeared from his face. He stood up and disappeared briefly into his bedroom once more, bringing back a large plastic bag full of dried plant and some cigarette papers.

He put the bag on the table, careful not to disturb the things already on it.

"Dis is skunk, missus," he said. "Skunk is named for its smell."

"I think I'd got that," she said. "It looks horrible."

"We don't use it for its looks," he admonished. "Now, watch, and do what I do."

He pulled two cigarette papers out of the little cardboard packet containing them, and handed one to Harriet. He followed it by tearing off a strip of cardboard about three-quarters of an inch by a quarter.

"What's that for?" she asked.

"Cannabis burns hot, so you have a filter to put a bit o' distance between you an' it."

He took some of the skunk from the bag and crumbled it along the crease in the cigarette paper. Harriet copied.

"Isn't that going to be not very big, as cigarettes go?" she asked.

He looked at her, leaned over her and pushed his hand down the side of the cushion on which she was sitting, retrieving an opened pack of hand-rolling tobacco.

"Okay. We'll put some tobacco in wiv it," he said, suiting his actions to his words. She copied him, bulking out the joint with the ordinary tobacco – at least as harmful as the cannabis, she reflected, but enjoying the respectability of being legal.

They rolled up the cardboard "filters" and held them in place whilst folding the paper round both filter and tobacco-skunk mixture. A quick lick of the adhesive edge to seal the paper into a tube, and a final twist of the unfiltered end of the joint to prevent the somewhat loose contents slipping out and it was ready.

Harriet held hers in the palm of her left hand and looked at it uncertainly.

"What now?" she asked.

Eddy looked at her sideways. "What you fink? We smoke it," he said.

Harriet kept her eyes on the joint. "This is what people with MS use to make their pain more bearable?" she asked.

Eddy nodded. "Yeah. It's good at it, apparently. Arfritis, too."

She felt better about that: better to picture herself as the victim of a government policy that denied people the beneficial effects of cannabis in order to protect them from its more harmful aspects, than as a user of illicit drugs, which seemed so much more sordid. After all, she was in pain.

Eddy produced a lighter and she stuck the marijuana cigarette between her lips. As he held the flame, she sucked experimentally, and her throat filled with acrid smoke.

It was all she could do not to drop the spliff as she began to cough hackingly.

Eddy watched unsympathetically. "I think you should give up bein' a druggy right now," he said, "You's obviously not cut out for it."

"I will" – coughing again – "be okay," she wheezed. "Just need to work on it a bit."

He lit his own joint and drew the smoke in appreciatively, expelling it slowly through his lips.

Harriet tried again. She had another coughing fit, and began to feel sick. She was sure her complexion had turned green: it felt as if it had. She took another puff and, when she'd finished getting her breath back after the coughing fit it induced, became aware of a feeling in her brain that was like a buzz. Something seemed to be going along steadily in the background, and she thought of warm, summer days, and sweet balm. Eddy's room seemed less untidy, more a place of comfort. She took another puff. The coughing fit was shorter, and the feeling that she was going to be sick had faded.

Eddy looked at her through half-closed eyes. "Dis is good stuff," he said. "Built my rep on it."

"It's certainly fast-acting," Harriet said.

He nipped his joint to put it out and stood up.

"I t'ink you better go now, missus," he said. "Here." He pushed a couple of tablespoonsful of the weed into a small plastic bag and gave it to her.

She put it in her handbag.

"How much do I owe you, Eddy?" she asked.

He shook his head. "Dis one on me – for de lessons."

He ushered her out of the door and she seemed surprised to find that outside, there was a cold wind blowing along the landing outside the flats, and it was quite dark. She was glad it was downhill back to her place. She was going to sleep like a log, she could tell.

CHAPTER FIVE

Charley's cross-country journey to see Harriet was long and tedious. She arrived on Monday afternoon and took a cab from the rail station to the tower block where her mother lived. As she got out of the taxi, clutching her weekend bag, her gaze was irresistibly drawn to the gleaming Mazda which was undoubtedly her mother's. A few local youths were clustered around it, but none laid a finger on the polished bodywork or shining chrome.

The lift, for once, was working, and Charley travelled up to the third floor, making her way along the landing to Harriet's flat. She put her bag down while she searched for her own key, but the door suddenly opened to reveal her mother looking quite smart in a black woollen top and tailored black trousers.

"Come in, dear," said Harriet.

As Charley stepped inside past her mother, she became aware of a cloying, dampish smell, which seemed familiar from university days. Recognition was sudden and a shock.

"Mother!" she exclaimed, staring at Harriet, "you've been smoking pot!"

"So have you, if you know what it is," said her mother.

"But mum! It's illegal!"

"Yes, dear. Now, how was your journey?"

"You can be arrested for possession."

"Yes, dear," said Harriet calmly, "now, did it take long to get here?"

Charley looked fiercely at her. "I want to talk about your use of cannabis not whether my journey was okay. It was shit, as usual, only worse because of the maintenance works, when they put ridiculously low speed limits in place. Now, where did you get the dope?"

"I have a friend who looks after me in that department. I look after him as a *quid pro quo* in another."

Charley goggled at her. "You're not... sleeping with someone for dope, are you?"

Harriet laughed. "You really think someone might find sleeping with me is worth supplying me with an illicit substance? I'd be flattered – if only it was something worth a bit more than a fiver."

Charley looked relieved. "So you haven't had much, then? You're not an addict?"

"No, I don't think I have time to develop any dependence on the stuff."

Charley suddenly remembered her mother's condition and shut her mouth on what she had been going to say.

"Is it this man you met in hospital who's supplying you?"

Harriet shook her head. "No. Why don't you sit down and I'll make us a mug of tea."

Charley sat. "I don't know how you can be so dismissive. It's criminal!" she exclaimed.

Harriet didn't answer. She poured hot water on teabags and stirred them. She brought the mugs through from the kitchen and sat opposite her daughter.

"How would you like to go shopping with me as well as having a massage and a facial at a health club?" she asked.

Charley looked at her askance. "Why do you want me to go shopping with you?"

"Well, it's for clothes, and I want to get something special. Thought you might like to be my adviser on matters of *haut couture*."

"How *haut?*"

"Very. I thought I'd go down to London and trail around Harvey Nicks and Harrods."

Charley blinked at her. "That's a bit up market for you isn't it?"

"I know. I'm being terribly wicked, but Seymour says the balance on one's credit card is covered by a free life insurance which clears it in the event of the cardholder's death." She paused. "So you needn't worry that there'll be a huge debt after I've gone."

Charley's face turned scarlet. She couldn't meet her mother's eyes. Harriet waited for her.

"I'm not like that, really," Charley said, forcing her gaze to meet Harriet's. "You must think I'm a right cow!"

Harriet put her mug down and went to her daughter, holding her close. She looked down onto Charley's head, her eyes misting.

"You're my beloved daughter," she said, "and I'll fight anyone who says otherwise."

It was too much for Charley. She burst into tears. Harriet stroked her head and gentled her until she stopped, when she passed her a tissue to mop her face.

"Now: come shopping with me?"

Charley dabbed her nose and nodded.

Seeing the crisis was over, Harriet sat down to finish her tea. Charley watched her for a moment.

"I want to ask you something," she said.

Harriet put her head on one side.

"You've never protected yourself from me," she began.

"Do I need protection?"

"Sometimes. I know when I was younger and still living here, I was sometimes quite horrible to you. I did a few things I shouldn't. I took advantage. I felt sure you knew, but you never said anything."

Harriet smiled. "You mean, stuff like all that graffiti on the underside of your bookshelves?"

Charley stared at her. "How long have you known about that?"

"Probably since soon after you did it. I never realised you were so keen on football."

Charley shook her head, grinning. "Not football: foot-ball*ers*," she said.

"Quite," said Harriet. "You kept quiet about your first boyfriend as well, if I remember correctly."

"You once told me that if I was ever unsure about a boy, I was to consider whether I'd bring him home to tea. Eric – I think that was his name – was not 'bring-home-to-tea' material." She blinked away the memory and met Harriet's gaze. "He was good to practise on," she added.

"I don't want to know, thank you."

"I know," said Charley. She screwed up her face. "I wonder if it's the same for boys?"

Harriet shook her head. "I don't think so. Girls approach relationships differently." She smiled. "We have more to do."

Charley grinned.

*

The following day, while Charley and Harriet were delighting in the wonders of Knightsbridge and Oxford Street, Seymour was ticking something off his list by driving an old World War Two Sherman tank. Kay took the opportunity of his absence to clean his house, while her brother, David, went to the office currently buying his services and fiddled with their computer network.

Mike English had a busy morning: a gang had stolen a new kitchen, bathroom and Jacuzzi from the weekend home of a London-based entrepreneur. It was the end of a very busy day before he could think of anything but work. His subconscious mind, he realised, had been chewing over the matter of Charley all the time. Detective Constable Jane Jenkins had been with him all day, dealing with the usual work-load of a big crime. She passed his office door and noticed him still sitting at his desk.

"Mike – want to come for a drink?" she asked.

He thought about it then nodded, standing up and grabbing his jacket and anorak.

They walked the short distance to the Ten Bells and went inside. The high table they'd been sitting at when he'd seen Charley and Colin was unoccupied. Jane waved him to a seat.

"I'll get these. What would you like?"

"Scotch and soda, please," he said.

He studied the people in the bar. They were the usual crowd, mostly people like himself, relaxing over a drink on the way home from work. One or two had probably been 'relaxing' for quite a while, judging from the way they were beginning to behave. Even as he watched, four of these noisier ones at one table rose from their seats and left.

Jane put his drink in front of him. She'd bought a glass of white wine for herself.

"Thanks," he said.

She sat opposite him, casually graceful, one foot resting on the rail fixed to the stool for the purpose, the toe of the other touching the floor. Not for the first time, he found himself wishing she was not a colleague. On the other hand, now Charley had appeared in his life again, maybe it was irrelevant. Jane leaned on one elbow and studied him.

"You've been very quiet today, Mike," she said, "got something on your mind?"

"Nothing to do with work," he replied.

She blinked at him slowly, grinning. "Can't be anything important then, to the man who lives for his job."

He looked at her sharply, as if about to argue, but gave a little shake of his head.

"You don't know me as well as you think," he said.

"Well," she said thoughtfully, "How's this for a stab at the out-of-hours Mike English: I know you're not Colin Firth, but you make a fair stand-in for Mr Darcy. You're single, a detective-sergeant, so not at the bottom of the income ladder by any means, and to paraphrase Jane Austen, any man in that condition must be regarded as prospective husband material."

"What's that to do with anything?"

"I expect like the rest of us, you find it difficult to maintain a relationship, due to the erratic hours and the need to break dates at very short notice – or none. And yet, also like the rest of us, you want someone at home."

"Yes, everyone knows that. It's part of the cross we bear as police officers."

"Just knowing about it doesn't make it easier to cope with," she replied, and looked down at her glass before looking up at him again. "I guess you're between relationships just now, and maybe you'd prefer to be in one."

"Are you trying to ask me out, Jane?" he asked, a grin slightly curving his lips.

She shook her head, smiling. "Not while we work together," she said, "I was thinking with someone else."

The faint grin was still there. "Got anyone in mind?"

Jane looked down at her glass again.

"I was wondering about that girl who came to see you – Charley."

Mike pursed his lips wryly. "What gives you the idea I might like her?"

Jane sipped her wine. "Just saw the way you behaved with each other the other night, in here."

"You couldn't have. You left just after she arrived."

"But I'd already seen your response, the minute you saw her. You looked round and saw her, and liked what you saw."

He sipped his drink and grinned ruefully. "I didn't realise I was that obvious. We actually went out with each other for about a month, once," he said.

"Oh? What happened?"

"Usual things, like you said." He held his glass between the tips of his fingers, studied the bubbles swirling round the lumps of ice. "You're correct that I really like her, but I don't think she realises that."

"Have you told her so?"

"Not in so many words."

"No matter. I'm sure she knows – though it's nice to be told, too."

He shrugged. "But how would she know. You're right: I should have told her. I thought it would be better in the beginning to keep things low key, you know. Not overwhelm here with serious stuff. I tried to be subtle. Took her out for dinner." He kept his gaze on his drink, not used to baring his feelings in this way.

She grinned at him. "That's about as subtle as being hit over the head with a traffic light!"

"Whatever! Anyway, things didn't work out, and she's just another client now."

She gave him an old-fashioned look. "Really." She lifted her glass to her lips.

"We had dinner together afterwards," he explained, "but that hadn't been planned or anything. It was just convenient for us both."

She looked at him askance. "And it came as a surprise to you when she seemed to think you were after renewing your personal relationship? After having dinner together?"

He shrugged evasively. "Well, we didn't talk about personal things – except her mother, of course."

Jane looked pityingly into his eyes. "Maybe, but *how* did you talk? Was there much eye contact? Were you concentrating on her to the exclusion of everything going on around you? Can you describe anybody sitting at one of the other tables? I'll bet you can describe her, in minute detail."

He looked confused. "Well, uh..."

"We'll take it that the answers are yes, yes, no and yes, so you'll not be surprised that she thought you were interested in her personally. You've done the course in body language; you know what messages such behaviour gives."

"I suppose so," he said. "The truth is, I *do* like her, as I said. She's feisty. And I thought she liked me. Her body language was quite expressive, too."

"Then maybe there's hope for you. Though, Detective Sergeant, you know it's ever so slightly unethical to be having a personal relationship with a client?"

"She's really interested in something going on in another police area, so she's not a client in the usual sense," he said.

"Hmm."

He drained his glass. "Want another?"

"No thanks, but don't let that stop you."

He went to the bar and bought a refill, returning to the table.

"For what it's worth," Jane said, as he slid back onto the stool, "I'd be tempted to go and visit the mother."

"Why? She lives miles away."

"It's just a thought. If you ingratiate yourself with her, maybe the daughter'll see you in a different light. Girls like a man with a bit of drive and determination about him, and she'd see you were taking her seriously. I'd guess that's a big worry of hers, because she almost certainly knows that the reason she's given you for her concern is a bit thin. So let her see you *do* take her seriously. Go and see the mother."

Mike sipped his drink thoughtfully. He made up his mind. "Okay, I agree. I'll go – as soon as there's an opportunity. The Case of the Stolen Spa Bath is taking number one slot at the moment."

"Don't leave it too long," she said as she drank the last of her wine. "Well, I must be off. See you in the morning."

He watched her stride out of the bar and disappear from sight. A few minutes later, he left the bar himself and went home.

*

Seymour reached home still feeling elated from his afternoon of tank driving. The house was empty, and he went upstairs to shower. He came down twenty minutes later, feeling refreshed, and went into the kitchen to make a start on his evening meal. For once he felt hungry and looked forward to it. He wished Harriet was there so he could tell her about his day, but she'd phoned him early in the day to tell him she and her daughter were going shopping in London.

That was bad enough, but she'd also booked them into a Health Farm the next day. It took the edge off Seymour's enjoyment.

He sat down to eat at the kitchen table. Halfway through his meal, he heard the front door open, and looked round expecting to see Kay, but it was David who stood in the doorway.

"Got any food to spare?" he asked.

Seymour shook his head.

"If I'd known you were coming, I'd have made more. See what you can find, if you're hungry."

"I'll order a takeaway."

Seymour shrugged. Everything was too easy for the young, he thought.

"Did your sister tell you to come round?" he asked.

David shrugged. "Yes. Not that I wouldn't."

"Of course not," said Seymour, not believing him. He knew his son.

"It's not necessary, David," he said, "and frankly, I'd rather you didn't keep coming round. Once a week is fine: just try and come for family dinner on Thursdays."

David grinned sheepishly. "No problem, dad."

"Good. So you can go home, duty done."

David's brow knitted. "Just like that? Go home?"

"You don't want to be here, and I don't go along with Kay's plans for the pair of you to look after me. Maybe one day I'll need looking after, but not yet. Go home. I'll see you on Thursday."

David's mouth turned down and he shrugged again. "Okay, if that's what you want."

He turned towards the front door.

Seymour watched as David left the house. "It's what we both want, son, admit it," he muttered, sotto voce.

As the door closed behind him, he bowed his head, wishing the relationship with his son was somehow closer, but recognising that both of them needed space. Life was better for them when they were apart than when David was in his home unwillingly. It was so obviously a chore for him to be there that Seymour was glad when he'd gone.

He raised his head and went upstairs to where he kept his shotgun. Over twenty years before, a patient who'd become a friend had invited him to a grouse shoot a couple of years running. At first, Seymour had used a borrowed gun, but then disbursed around two thousand pounds on the acquisition of his own weapon before the following season's shoot. No sooner had he bought it than the patient had died of a heart attack whilst on holiday, and the gun had never been used.

He sat on his bed and looked at it. The walnut stock needed a polish and the barrels cleaning, but otherwise it seemed in good condition. He had no intention of firing it. He took it downstairs and out into the garage.

He clamped it in his workbench vice and lifted his hacksaw down from the nail on which it hung. It seemed almost sacrilegious to take the rusty saw to the shiny barrels and for a while he contemplated what he was about to do. But as Harriet had said, when was he ever going to use the gun again?

He lined up the blade against his thumb and pulled it back to score the first mark.

It took him less than half an hour to desecrate the gun. After shortening the barrels, he'd taken a file and some emery paper and smoothed the cut edges before wrapping it in an old plastic carrier bag and taking it indoors. In the lounge, he put it on the floor beside his favourite chair and switched on the television, but moments later the telephone close to him rang and he answered it, muting the television sound.

"Have you had a good day, Seymour?" asked Harriet.

"I got to drive a Sherman tank," he said with a hint of pride.

"It sounds as if you enjoyed yourself."

"I did. How about you?"

"Charley and I have worn a groove in the pavement outside Harrods and Harvey Nicks. It's been wonderful."

"Did you venture within these august temples to capitalism and retail trade?"

"Of course," she said. He could hear the smile in her voice. "Wait until you see what I've bought. Charley pushed the boat out as well, and looks absolutely gorgeous in her new dress."

"I'm glad you both had a good time."

"Tomorrow, we're both booked in to a major pampering session at Greaves Hall."

"I've heard of it," said Seymour. "Hot baths, cold showers and birch twigs, I gather."

Harriet chuckled. "Emollients, herbal drinks, massage, swimming, and cucumber slices," she said.

"I guess those are not for sandwich filling."

"Very therapeutic they are, Charley says."

"Well, have a good time. I'm sure you will."

She cleared her throat. "There's just one little thing, Seymour."

"It's not about paying for it all, is it? I still think that won't be a problem."

"No, no. But now I've bought some finery and I'm having a make-over and so on, I'd really like to show it all off somewhere."

"Okay. I'll see if I can think of anywhere."

"Thanks." She hesitated. "Seymour, are you a Mason?"

"No," he said, wondering where her question was leading. "Why?"

"Because they're having a Masonic Ball this week."

Seymour pursed his lips. "So?"

"Well, I wondered if you could get us tickets."

"I don't even know if they *issue* tickets, Harriet," he said. "Isn't it all secret and hush-hush? How could we possibly wangle an invite?"

"I don't know," she replied, "I thought you might."

"I'll have a think," he said, "but I really don't hold out much hope."

"Don't you know someone who *is* a Mason?"

He thought for a moment. "Possibly. Someone who used to be a patient – if he's still alive."

"Are many of your former patients dead, Seymour?"

He stared at the handset for a moment. "I have no idea."

"I was only joking," Harriet said. She hesitated again. "How's the other thing we have planned going?"

"I, uh, used the hacksaw tonight. I'm glad I wasn't very attached to the – the gun."

"Sshh! Someone might be listening."

"There's nobody here."

"I was thinking GCHQ or MI5, tapping the phone lines."

"I think Government Communications Headquarters and the Secret Service have bigger things to worry about."

"Well, anyway. Why don't you come over tomorrow evening and see Charley and me with our makeovers."

He grinned. "Okay. See you then."

Harriet extended the invitation to include joining them for dinner and they fixed a time.

He got up and went in search of the telephone directory, returning with it to his chair. He made half a dozen calls before he went to bed.

*

The following day Seymour spent at the Flying School learning the theory and basics of controlling a helicopter. He felt jittery but elated when at an appropriate moment, the Chief Flying Instructor led them out of the line hut to the helicopter, a Bell 206 Jet Ranger. Seymour found that his ancient knowledge of fixed-wing flying was of use in the classroom and theory part of the training, but the flight controls of a helicopter were quite different.

The early training was aimed at controlling the helicopter in the hover, before moving on to mastery of take-off and landing. The tricky part, he found, was something called the collective, which, in conjunction with the pedals, made the helicopter move up or down, and cyclic pitch, which made it move forward, back or sideways. Then there were a few more things to remember when the machine was actually travelling rather than hovering.

It all made his head spin, but by the time he returned home, he felt a real sense of achievement. The CFI had not been surprised when Seymour had asked for lessons as often as possible – he was used to people who'd landed jobs flying to the North Sea gas and oil production platforms needing immersion training. As a result of his request, Seymour now had a busy programme of training, in flight theory, aviation law, and practical flying.

Meanwhile, Harriet and Charley were being pampered and cosseted by experts at Greaves Hall. They'd spent the morning being depilated by the application of hot wax, followed by a swim in the warm waters of the pool, and, after a light lunch, a leisurely Hawaiian massage and facial treatment. Finally, side by side in front of a bank of mirrors, coiffeuses, manicurists and makeup artists applied their skills, so that by the time they had to leave, both were looking like film-stars.

"I can't believe how good that's made me feel," said Harriet.

"Seems a shame simply to be going home," said Charley.

Harriet, behind the wheel of her beloved sports car – driving steadily and with the hood down so as not to blow away their hairstyles – glanced quickly at her daughter.

"Why don't you give that nice policeman a ring and tell him that you're sorry about what you said?"

Charley had told Harriet about her regrettable last encounter with Mike English.

Charley felt a flush of embarrassment. "I can't. I spent ages telling him that I wanted a business relationship, and he's accepted it. He was very... coldly professional," she said after she found the words she wanted, "when I left him."

Harriet rolled her eyes. "And you've regretted it ever since?"

Charley turned to her. "Don't you start! I had Colin bending my ear about it the morning after."

Eddy, realising that Harriet had company, stayed away from her flat that evening. Charley was planning on spending one more night with her mother before returning home in the morning.

She stood at the sink washing salad leaves. Suddenly she grinned and turned to Harriet who was carving some ham.

"I suppose this seems perfectly normal to you? Not at all incongruous? Two women in full war-paint, and we're messing about in the kitchen of a high-rise flat in stocking feet, making a salad."

Harriet smiled. Charley was looking very glamorous, even without her shoes. Her reddish hair was pinned up, and her maquillage put a pale glow in her cheeks, liner and green eye-shadow emphasising the almond shape of her eyes, while her full lips, gleamed with the lightest silk colour.

"You're right," she said.

"Seymour will be round soon to admire your appearance," said Charley, spinning the lettuce in a centrifuge. "I'm looking forward to meeting him."

"Oh – I'd forgotten I'd invited him," said Harriet, "I wonder if there's enough salad?"

Charley curled her lip. "I'm sure we'll make it go round," she said.

Harriet thought for a moment then nodded. She sliced some cheese and placed the slices on the plates. Charley added the other parts of the salad and they carried the plates to the dining table.

Seymour arrived some fifteen minutes later. She opened the door to let him in. He stared at her and uttered a low whistle.

"Never let it be said that one of these makeover things is a waste of money," he said, "You look... amazing. Stunning!"

Harriet couldn't keep an unladylike – but very womanly – smirk off her face. She beckoned him inside.

"Wait till you see the real family beauty," she said, standing aside to let him admire Charley, who had turned a deep plum colour at her mother's compliment. Seymour smiled and held out his hand.

"I've heard a bit about you," he said, "it's a pleasure to meet you at last."

Charley, who up to that moment had been inclined to dislike Seymour for the influence she felt he had over her mother, promptly changed her mind and decided he was quite charming. She could even be generous and acknowledge that he was quite good looking, considering that the relationship wasn't going anywhere with only a short time left to both him and her mother. The thought brought her back to earth and she waved Seymour to a chair.

"You're just in time for food," she said, "Hope you don't mind salad."

"Not at all, not at all," he said.

She watched as he speared some lettuce.

"Would you like some wine with that, Seymour?" Harriet asked.

A strange expression settled across his face. He sniffed the lettuce, then ate it. Harriet's eyebrows went up. Seymour glanced up and caught her eye.

"Uh, no thanks," he said. She realised his expression was one of bafflement.

"Did you want some mayonnaise, or salad dressing?" she asked, pointing to the items in the middle of the cloth.

Seymour smiled, hesitantly. "Uh, yes, I will, thank you," he said. She passed him the jar and he spooned mayonnaise onto the side of his plate.

"Is there something wrong?" Harriet asked as she watched him.

"I'm sorry, Harriet, I don't mean to be rude, but are you using air freshener in here? There seems to be a strange smell."

Harriet stared at him as realisation dawned and her lips formed an O of understanding. She blushed.

"Oh, Seymour, I'm sorry," she said, "it'll be the skunk. It hangs around."

"I didn't realise you had a pet," he said.

"No, no. Not an animal: weed."

"Wee – ! Oh! Skunk! Dope? Marijuana?" he exclaimed.

She nodded. "Yes. I'm finding it quite good for pain," she said.

Seymour stared at her. "I didn't know you were into drugs."

"It was just something on my list," she replied, "and then I found out it was useful."

Seymour dragged his eyes from Harriet to her daughter.

"Don't look at me," said Charley, "I was shocked when I found out as well. After all those warnings she gave me when I was a girl!" She grinned at her mother who shrugged, wryly.

"To which you no doubt paid a great deal of attention – I don't think!" she said.

Charley grinned, dropping her gaze.

Later, when the dishes had been cleared away and they were sitting on Harriet's battered three-piece with coffees to hand, she felt under the settee and pulled out a *Golden Virginia* packet. Inside was tobacco, Eddy's bag of skunk, and cigarette papers.

"Anybody want one?" she asked.

Charley's mouth dropped open. Seymour eyed the paraphernalia with curiosity.

"All right," he said, "but I don't smoke and it'll probably make me sick."

Harriet pursed her lips. "You're right. I hate smoking it. Let's try cannabis tea."

"How do you make that?" Seymour asked.

"I don't know. Just chuck it into the teapot and add boiling water, I suppose." She took the cannabis through into the kitchen, boiled the kettle and suited her actions to her words. After it was brewed, she brought everything back into the lounge on a tray and they stared at the pot as if some mystical – and stoned – genie was going to emerge from the spout on a cloud of steam. After a minute, Harriet lifted the lid, inhaled and gave the infusion a stir.

Another minute passed before she declared the concoction as possibly worth trying. She half-filled each mug with liquid that was yellowish and aromatic, the scent of the powerful drug filling the room. She passed mugs to both Seymour and Charley before picking up her own.

They each looked at the others as if wishing to synchronise their sips. Slowly, the mugs were raised to their lips, the aroma inhaled, and the hot drink drawn over their tongues.

Seymour wrinkled his nose. "I don't normally take sugar," he said, "but I could use some in this."

Charley agreed. "Unless you have a shot of whisky."

Harriet nodded and went to her sideboard. A bottle of Bell's stood between a bottle of vodka and another of gin. Harriet handed Charley the bottle.

"Here," she said, "help yourself."

Charley poured a rough measure into the cannabis tea and sipped it. She looked up at her mother.

"I'd say," she said slowly, "it's an acquired taste."

Seymour took the bottle. "Almost anything's better than its actual taste," he declared, and poured a good slug into his cup.

"That's better," he said after taking an experimental sip, "but it's a waste of good scotch."

"When you've all done criticising!" Harriet interrupted. "I'm interested in its medicinal qualities, not its flavour. It's got to be better than smoking it."

She sipped her unadulterated cannabis tea and resisted the natural reaction to screw up her face at its taste.

"I believe you can also make cannabis cake," Seymour said. "A friend of mine went on a stag weekend to Amsterdam a year or so back, and spent most of their time, as far as I can tell, wandering around the red light district. In the course of this, they visited one of the coffee shops where you can buy small amounts of cannabis for smoking or baked into a cake."

Harriet raised her eyebrows. "Maybe I should try it. It's probably better than trying to smoke it, and I certainly don't like the taste as tea."

"Instead of using just the cannabis in the pot, why don't you mix it with ordinary tea leaves?" asked Charley.

"Could try that, too," replied Harriet, "but the idea of doing a spot of baking sounds interesting. If I make cupcakes with strongly-flavoured icing, you'd never know what you were eating."

Seymour watched her. "How much pain are you in?" he asked quietly, putting his mug down.

"Honestly?" she asked.

"Honestly."

She pursed her lips. "A fair bit. It seems to be getting worse."

"Do you still take your prescription?" he asked.

She shrugged. "Of course, but the cannabis seems to help a lot. The prescription drugs don't take all the pain away."

"Wouldn't it be safer to ask your doctor for something stronger rather than supplementing them with dope?"

She shrugged again. "Maybe. All right, I will."

Charley was gazing round the room. Harriet noticed.

"Are you all right, Charley?"

Charley dragged her attention back to her mother. "Hmm? Oh, yes, I'm fine," she said.

"You look a bit spaced out," Harriet said.

Charley looked at her blankly. "Do I really?"

Harriet nodded. "Yes, dear. I don't think you should have a second cup." She turned to Seymour. "How about you, Seymour?"

He frowned. "Can't tell the difference," he said. "I'm fairly sure it's not having the same effect on me. If I recall correctly, cannabis works better on some people than on others. Some people," he glanced at Charley, "are more susceptible than others."

Charley had drained her cup. Harriet studied her for a moment.

"Do you think you should have an early night, dear?" she asked.

Charley peered at her, then shook her head slowly and deliberately.

"It's a long time since my mother tried to get me into bed," she said. She stood up and weaved her way towards the small bedroom she was using. At the door she turned round. "Long time since *anybody* tried to get me into bed. G'night." She went in a closed the door behind her.

Seymour and Harriet looked at each other.

"These youngsters," said Harriet, "they can't hold their dope."

Seymour shook his head. "Not like the older generation," he agreed.

Harriet looked at him fondly. "Do you fancy your chances at getting me into bed?" she asked.

"How much of that stuff have you had?"

Harriet looked at her mug and found it was mysteriously empty. She refilled it and sipped.

"Can't let it go to waste," she said.

"I suppose Charley'll be all right?" he said.

Harriet took another swig from her mug before answering. "A chip off the old block, I reckon."

"Which means... she'll be all right or she'll be zonked?"

Harriet rested her hand on his arm. She was having trouble focussing as she looked into his eyes. She'd never realised how kindly they were and with what warmth Seymour looked at her. She felt a little scurry of interest.

"I think it's time I was going," said Seymour, standing up.

"You don't have to," she said softly, rising with him and keeping her hand on his arm.

"Actually, I do," said Seymour, patting her hand. "Things to do, early tomorrow." He moved towards the door, turned back. "Actually, I meant to tell you: I think I might have figured out a way into the Masonic Ball on Friday."

As he watched her, expecting a response, he became aware that Harriet's eyes were closing and opening, like someone fighting off a powerful urge to fall asleep. Suddenly, gracefully, she slipped towards the floor.

Reflexively, he grabbed her but he was at an awkward angle and couldn't stop her progress though he made sure she didn't hit her head on anything hard. She seemed to be asleep. He checked her breathing and pulse quickly, and found them to be normal. He walked round her until he could take hold under her arms and drag her inelegantly towards her bedroom. He hoisted her inert form onto the bed, swinging her legs up and rolling her in the quilt.

He was panting heavily when he'd finished, not used to such strenuous exercise, and leaned against the wall, watching her. She seemed perfectly comfortable, and he considered leaving her and returning home, but was worried and thought it would be better if he stayed and kept an eye on her. His decision made, he slipped off his shoes and suit and lay next to her on the denuded bed, covering himself with a sheet. He listened to her steady breathing and reached out to turn off the bedside light, meaning to keep watch over her, but in a few minutes, despite his best intentions, he fell asleep.

At first light, Harriet's eyes flickered open. She became aware of the fact that she was enveloped in the quilt, and was feeling very warm. Her next realisation was that she was still fully clothed, and couldn't remember how the previous evening had ended, but concluded she'd been put to bed. As she cast off the folds of the quilt she realised that she was not alone. Rolling over, she saw Seymour, asleep, still wearing his shirt.

Carefully, she slipped out of bed and removed her crumpled gown. She glanced again at Seymour and gently spread half the quilt over him before slipping under the other half. She was suddenly wide awake: Charley, she remembered, was in the spare room. It seemed important that Seymour should not be discovered beside her. She glanced at the clock: half past five. Oh well, she thought, he could have another half-hour or so, but then she'd really have to get him out of the flat.

She lay there quietly, glancing at the clock every now and then. Beside her, Seymour was finally prompted awake by her movements.

Suddenly, he scrambled out from under the quilt and made a grab for his trousers. Harriet turned to watch. He noticed her look, and a blush spread to his cheeks. Harriet smiled.

"I love it when you're embarrassed, Seymour," she said softly. "Did you put me to bed last night?"

"Yes," he said, "I didn't go home in case you might be suffering from something more than a mixture of cannabis tea and scotch whisky. Hope you don't mind."

"Would that be 'don't mind' being put to bed, or taking the whisky and tea, or finding you still here in the morning?"

Seymour looked distressed. "I'd not thought I could have done so many things that might upset you."

She smiled at him and shook her head. "You've done nothing to upset me. I'm grateful to you for being here when I needed you. You should have shared the quilt."

He blushed again. "I didn't think that would be quite proper," he said.

"I shouldn't have minded. But speaking of 'quite proper', I think it wouldn't be a good idea for Charley to find you here."

"No, by gosh," he said, slipping on his jacket and shoes. "Probably best if I leave now."

She nodded. "Thank you. I know it seems poor reward for what you did – sending you off without breakfast – but I'll make it up to you."

"No need, no need," he said, another blush threatening to appear. He got to the door before turning back to the bed.

"Bye, Harriet," he said.

She propped herself up on her elbows. "Bye, dear Seymour."

He hesitated for a moment, then leaned down to kiss her. He aimed for her cheek, but she turned her head until her lips met his. He only broke the kiss when his back complained loudly and he had to stand up.

"See you later," he said, and quickly slipped out of the room.

A moment later, she heard the outer door click shut behind him.

CHAPTER SIX

"How is the old boy?"

Mark pushed his laptop computer aside to speak to his wife.

"He seems to be all right," said Kay. She had arrived home from work and picked up a duster. There was a collection of Coalport figurines which needed attention from time to time in a display cabinet along the wall from their television.

"Not looking ill, then?" he asked.

Kay stopped dusting and sat opposite him.

"No. He seems fine at the moment, but the degeneration is progressive."

"So he'll become more and more dependent until he falls off the twig?"

She frowned at him. "Yes, if you must put it that way."

He leaned back against the squab of the settee. "Come on, Kay, you know the old boy's living on borrowed time. It's not as if we've spent much time with him since we got married, so I don't see why you're pretending to be upset now."

She stared at him. There was enough truth in what he said for his remark to hurt. She looked down at her hands.

"That may be so, but he's my dad, and soon, he won't be around for me to talk to," she said.

"So? It won't make a difference."

She took a deep breath, fighting for control: his words brought tears to her eyes, and she didn't want to break down in front of him.

"It's difficult for me to explain," she began, getting to her feet, "but knowing he has only a short time to live... it's made me think." She gripped her fingers tightly, then walked over to the display of figurines and made small adjustments to their positions. "It's almost like being given a second chance."

"Huh?"

"Well, you know: you know how after people have died and you sit there thinking, I wish I'd told him this, or I wish I'd said that to her? Well, in a sense I have the chance now to say what I've always felt about my dad to him, *before* he dies."

Mark grinned. "You're not going to tell him what a dry old stick he is, and what a bore, are you?"

She looked at him through tearful eyes. "Mark! How can you say that? He isn't a dry old stick, and he isn't really boring, if you listen to him. He's had a very interesting life. He used to talk to me when I was a child and tell me stories about what it was like when he was a boy." She began to pace round the room. "Then he stopped. I guess I grew up and wasn't around so much, so we never went on with our little chats."

"And since we've been married you and he have had virtually nothing in common," said Mark.

She studied him.

"That's not true. We just haven't had time to be together."

"You could have made time."

"I was doing what I've have always done, working."

Mark nodded. He stared at her speculatively before a crafty smile curled his lips.

"How much is the old boy worth?"

Kay shrugged. "I don't know."

He chuckled. "Come on, Kay! I bet that's why you're spending so much time round there: you're taking inventory."

She stared at him, shocked.

"Mark! Do you really think that that's all I'm interested in?"

He raised a sceptical eyebrow. "Well, isn't it? You don't need to answer that: I know it's not something anyone would want to admit – but all the same, I wonder what he's worth. There're some oil paintings that might fetch a few quid. And of course the house itself must be worth – "

Her mouth fell open. "Mark! How can you think about such things? This is my father we're talking about – *my dad!* I don't care about the value of his things. It's not as if we need the money."

"Good speech," he said drily. "Of course the money's important. I know you believe that because you've put so much effort into spending it, despite the fact that, as you say, we didn't really need more – thanks to my mother."

"I thought your family's wealth was earned by your Victorian ancestors," she said, "not your mother?" She took her seat again, her back straight and rigid.

"Who cares where it came from. Mother controls it now."

"Your mother likes to control everything."

His eyebrow lifted again, this time in amusement. "Getting a bit waspish, aren't we? Just remember, my mother hasn't sat on her wealth like your father. We owe our standard of living first and foremost to her, for setting us up in this house when we were married." He leaned forward. "And don't forget, it was my wealth – my family's wealth, if you like – that got you interested in me in the first place."

Kay knew there was some truth in what he said, but it wasn't the whole story. She would not have married him unless she had seen something in Mark himself which she loved. They had seemed very much birds of a feather at the time, soul-mates even. The fact that Mark was the heir of a wealthy family had been comforting and nice to know, but it wasn't the reason she'd married him. Just now, listening to him talking as if nothing else mattered but money and the accoutrements of wealth, she found herself wondering just what that reason had been. She stood up and looked down at him.

"Think that if you like, but it's not true – not entirely true. Anyway, a person can change."

He lounged back to look up at her, still grinning knowingly.

"You can believe that if you like. I've known you for a very long time."

She stared at him, then turned on her heel and strode out of the room, up the stairs to the comfort and security of her bed. There, with the door locked and the curtains drawn, she indulged in a bout of tears.

*

Later that day, Seymour and Harriet met up at a small private airstrip. This was nothing to do with Seymour's flying lessons, but was where they were due to take their parachute jump. He was nervous.

"Look, Harriet, this isn't me. I don't do parachutes."

"I'm sure they'll look after you," she said.

The instructor greeted them as they went into the office.

"Either of you ever jumped before?" he asked.

Harriet and Seymour both shook their heads. The instructor beamed.

"Well, absolutely nothing to worry about," he assured them.

Seymour was not convinced, but followed him through a door into a room furnished by four desks shoved together in the middle and a dozen chairs spread around them. Four people sat at the table already.

"Welcome, everybody," said the instructor. "There's a certain amount of training we need to do before we start jumping out of the aircraft. Two of you," he nodded at the couple of very fit twenty-somethings nearest him on his left, "have jumped before, but I'm afraid you still have to go through the safety procedure."

They nodded, shrugged.

"But for the others, this is all new," he concluded, "so we won't be rushing anything. It's important that you feel as confident as you can that you will be able to deal with the drop."

Harriet glanced quickly at Seymour and saw the tension in his neck as his jaw muscles clenched. Below the table, she squeezed his hand.

By lunchtime, they were feeling like a couple of very inflexible old people. Joints were sore, and muscles which hadn't been used for a long time were aching. The instructor was smiling and he seemed to be happy.

"I think we're ready to go," he announced, "so Saturday if you're all available."

Seymour was about to protest when he caught the instructor's eye. The man looked at him, and Seymour felt sure there was a hint of disdain – even pity – in the look, as if the instructor was sure he wouldn't go through with it. Seymour straightened his back and stuck his chin out.

"If anybody's really scared of jumping out of a plane two and a half miles up, this is the moment to say so, and you can walk away," said the instructor.

Seymour, and the rest of them, kept silent.

"Good. Then Saturday, nine o'clock. I'll run through the procedures again, before we take off," he assured them.

Harriet glanced up at Seymour and smiled encouragingly.

The practice had taken several hours and involved much learning to fall without breaking bones, and how to control a parachute by pulling on particular cords.

Now, it seemed, the die was cast.

*

Harriet recalled the early morning, just after Seymour had left, when she'd heard Charley's bedroom door open, and got up herself.

Charley had a quick breakfast, intending to catch the early train home. She hadn't said much over breakfast, but she'd kissed Harriet goodbye when she left, and recovered much of her usual disposition when, quite deliberately, Harriet had warned her against any more drug-taking.

"After all, it's obvious you're too susceptible to them," she'd said.

Charley had bitten her tongue to keep the retort she would have liked to make to herself. In fact she'd enjoyed herself greatly, both shopping in London, and the Greaves Hall make-over. And she had a beautiful new dress which she planned on saving for a special occasion. It had taken a lot of self-control not to reply in kind, but she'd managed. Harriet's remark brought her down to earth and helped her reassert her common sense and usual manner. The journey home provided her with plenty of time to calm down.

*

"You'll be okay, Seymour. Anybody can find their way back: you won't get lost."

Saturday had arrived all too quickly for Seymour. The instructor was cheerful, deliberately so, he thought resentfully. He was sure the man had seen through his pitiful bravado and was making him pay the price for being frightened of what they were about to do. They were crouching uncomfortably in the back of a small aircraft which had had its seats and the rear door removed. The rip cords of the chutes were clipped securely to a steel wire fixed to the cabin roof.

The pilot started the engine, which drowned Seymour's reply.

"Remember what I told you," the instructor shouted over the engine noise, "make sure you jump clear of the aircraft. There's a tailplane out there will have your head off if it gets in the way."

"Thank you for that comforting thought," muttered Seymour. The instructor glanced at him but appeared not to have heard.

"You keep your hand on the ring pull for the emergency chute until the main one has opened, and then you transfer both hands to the cords and steer like I showed you earlier." He went through a pantomime showing how to steer the parachute.

The aircraft reached the runway and began to crack on speed. Seymour glanced down at Harriet and saw how she was enjoying herself. He would not have chosen this form of madness had it been left to him, but he'd felt obliged to keep her company – after all, they were in this together, and if either of them wasn't going to survive the jump, it should be neither. He had to be with her.

She was ahead of him in the queue. She turned and studied his face.

"You'll feel great when you hit the ground," she said, "I imagine."

"That's a real comfort," he shouted in her ear.

She grinned. The aircraft climbed for several minutes then steadied itself on course. A red light went on over the open doorway. The instructor, who was the only person not attached to the steel wire by his rip-cord, took station next to the door.

"Okay, please stand up and pull your goggles down." He waited while all the passengers scrambled to their feet. He beckoned the twenty-something young woman to the door.

"You've done this before, yes?"

She nodded.

"Okay. Good luck. See you back in the bar."

They waited a moment before a green light came on next to the red one.

"Go!" yelled the instructor, giving the girl a push. She disappeared out of the door way, her rip-cord suddenly released, blowing horizontally aft in the slipstream. The young man who was her companion took her place at the doorway.

"Go!" Push. Gone. Second rip-cord whipping in the wind.

Harriet shuffled forward.

"You okay?"

She nodded. "I think so."

"You'll be fine. If you forget what to do, it won't matter, we'll come and find you."

"Right. thanks."

He nodded. "Go!" And she was gone. Seymour stepped into the breach.

The instructor grinned at him. "Just like stepping off a bus," he said cheerfully. "Go!"

Seymour looked down at the ground over two miles below as he felt the push in his back. He muttered a prayer as he stepped out into the void.

There was wind noise, then a loud crack. He looked up and saw the parachute canopy beginning to unfurl above him. The aeroplane roared away on its course. He'd lost the ring-pull for the emergency chute, but the main one opened fully and his rate of descent was checked. He looked down again. The ground was just there... below his feet, his whole life depending on the webbing and canopy which kept him in the air. He felt a physical ache as his bowels cramped and for a moment he closed his eyes. Wind whipped past his face and he was glad he was wearing goggles when he forced himself to look again. He tried to pull experimentally on the cords he'd been shown to control direction. The parachute swung so that he was facing back the way they'd come.

Harriet's parachute was a few hundred feet below him. He couldn't pick out the ones which had gone before her against the pattern of fields and distant houses. He realised the plane had been turning in a wide circle so everyone was being dropped roughly equidistant from the airstrip. Vehicles about the size of a pea were down there. Seymour found he could speed up and slow down the rate of descent as well as turn left or right, so on the whole had a fair bit of control. He wished he could have appreciated the vast panoramic view he had of the Norfolk countryside, but his whole body was tensed and he felt sick.

A few minutes later, he realised that that same Norfolk countryside was coming up to meet him at what seemed to be an alarming rate. He pulled on the control cord which was supposed to slow his descent, and tried to pick out a suitable landing site.

It was suddenly too late. A field rushed towards him. At the last minute he remembered the instructor's guidance – either run forward, or curl yourself into a ball and roll. The speed was too great, he felt, for him to do the running thing, so at the last minute, as his feet hit the ground, he tried to curl up and roll.

The landing jarred him severely. When he opened his eyes he was flat on his back. Three curious Friesian cows were bearing down on him, reaching him before he could free himself from the parachute harness. They nudged him with their snouts, and one tried to lick his face. He brushed the animal away, finding and twisting the quick-release that let the harness fall from him. He sat up and the cows backed off.

A Land-Rover pulled up by the entrance to the field and a young man got out, climbed over the gate and came towards him, grinning.

"You okay, squire?"

Seymour suddenly realised that there was something wrong with his legs and feet. They didn't want to obey him. His blood ran cold at the thought that the landing could have jarred something that brought on the symptoms of his condition. He grinned at the man, without humour.

"I seem to be having a problem standing up," he said. A totally irrational feeling of shame was causing his colour to rise. He did not want to become dependent on others like this! It was anyway too soon: he wasn't expecting it.

"Let me see if I can help," said the man. He squatted beside Seymour and slipped his arms round him. "Let's try for standing," he said, and carefully lifted Seymour to his feet. As he straightened out, Seymour experienced a sudden pain shooting across his lumbar region, and the feeling returned to his lower limbs. At first there was pain which made him gasp, then the feeling subsided and he was able to take his weight.

"I think I'll be all right now," he said shakily.

The young man studied him. "Best let me give you a hand over to the Land-Rover," he advised, looking concerned. "Bad landing was it?"

Seymour nodded. "I guess so."

He walked with difficulty to the edge of the field, grateful for the man's support, but thankfully aware that he was recovering. The man opened the gate, closing it behind them, and opened the door of the Land-Rover. Once Seymour had slid into the seat, largely unaided, the man hopped over the gate back into the field to retrieve the parachute.

Seymour watched him, thinking that this had been a hint of what the future held for him. He gritted his teeth, trying not to feel sorry for himself. There had to be a positive side to it all, he thought. Stephen Hawking was the shining example of a man who had exceeded all expectations, not only in respect of his insightful studies of cosmology and physics, but also of how long he might have been expected to live when he'd first been diagnosed with Motor Neurone Disease, ALS. So a useful future, of sorts, was possible, Seymour told himself.

The difficulty walking had eclipsed his earlier feelings of dread arising from the jump. His innards were slowly recovering, but the recollection of those few minutes in the air remained fresh in his mind, and threatened to cause a relapse. God! he thought, he'd never used to be like this, but as he'd grown older, the terrible, gripping fear of having nothing beneath his feet had worsened, the fear that however secure he might be, something dreadful would happen and he would fall to his death, conspired to wake him from his sleep, shaking and sweating after a nightmare in which the floor of a lift dropped out, or he was atop some tall building and somehow fell hundreds of feet to the ground. It was completely irrational, he knew, but that precisely described a phobia. He searched his mind for the word: acrophobia – an irrational fear of heights. Perhaps, like having to rely on others for mobility, he might have to get used to admitting that he did not enjoy high places.

He waited for his driver.

The young man arrived shortly, the parachute rolled up on his shoulder as he climbed over the gate. Watching him, Seymour felt a pang of regret that he could apparently no longer do things like that, and certainly not with the young man's insouciance. During the short drive, he forced himself into a lighter mood. No point in giving Harriet an excuse to fuss over him: that time would come soon enough, he thought.

Harriet was waiting for him when they got back to the Portacabin which was the airstrip operations room and flying club bar. He noticed her cheeks were flushed and her eyes bright. She pushed a cardboard cup of coffee at him.

"Got you a coffee. How'd you like that?"

"Just as it comes – white, without," he answered dourly. Everything still ached.

"I meant, the parachute jump. Something else we can tick off."

"Oh, *that*," said Seymour, "I keep trying to forget *that*."

She sipped her coffee. "Didn't you find it exhilarating?"

"I found it very painful," he grumbled. "How was your landing?"

"Think I'll do better next time."

"Next time! Please God, never again!"

"We'll see. I mean, it's not as if we know precisely how long we've got. Anyway, do I take it you had a rather rough landing and it's rubbed your temper up the wrong way?"

"There's nothing wrong with my temper," he growled.

She raised her eyebrows. "Oh, so this isn't bad-temper I see before me, it's just Seymour Whittle being polite and charming. Sorry, I didn't appreciate —"

"That really will do, Harriet!" he said. One or two heads turned towards them. "All right," he continued in a softer tone, "my landing was what you can call rough. Landed in a herd of cows."

She stifled a laugh with a hand, shaking her head. "Oh, you poor thing," she said with an absence of sincerity he noticed. His frown deepened.

"If you're going to carry on like this, I won't tell you about — " He dropped his voice to a dramatic whisper, "the Masonic Ball."

Harriet emptied her cup and threw it in a waste bin. "Ooh! Come outside, Seymour, where we can be private."

He leaned forward to whisper again. "It's a long time since a woman said that to me. You should be careful: a man could get the wrong idea."

She led him outside, turning to face him.

"It might be the idea I want him to get," she said.

Seymour harrumphed.

"Now, how do we get into the Masonic Ball?" she asked, grinning at his discomfiture.

*

Mike English got something of a break when a lorry was stopped for having a non-working brake-light. The driver had been apparently philosophical about it, until the traffic officer asked to see the paperwork for his load, and when that couldn't be provided, the load itself. The back of the truck contained kitchen and bathroom fittings and a large Jacuzzi, which rang a bell with the officer. The driver was promptly arrested on suspicion of burglary, and the lorry together with its load taken into police custody.

At Breydon police station, the Custody Sergeant pointed out that the driver was entitled to an obligatory rest period of at least eight hours. Mike reckoned there was nothing he couldn't leave his highly competent DC to do in the time it would take to follow her recommendation to go and see Charley's mother.

He would have phoned ahead, if he'd known Harriet's number, but he didn't, so he was quite unexpected when he arrived on her doorstep at seven o'clock after a two-hour drive.

He heard some laughter through the door, a woman's and a man's deeper voice. He was telling himself he should never have come when the door opened, exhaling a strong aroma with which he was perfectly well acquainted.

Harriet stood in front of him, the remnants of a smile still lingering on her lips.

"Hello," she said, with a lift of her eyebrows.

Mike's nervousness returned. He still didn't have a plausible explanation for his visit.

"Hello," he replied, "I'm Mike English. Are you Harriet Blythe?"

The smile had slipped off Harriet's face as he identified himself. Mike was beginning to wonder if gone to the wrong address.

"Yes," she said. "You must be the policeman Charley's been telling me about."

"Oh! Has she mentioned me?" That was good news. Must mean that he'd made a bit of an impression on her – hopefully a good one.

Harriet's smile had been replaced by an expression of alarm. She stepped towards him, pulling her door shut behind her and making him move back until he was leaning on the balustrade overlooking the parking square below.

"Um, it's lovely to meet you," she said anxiously, "but quite honestly this isn't a good time. I'm doing a little community service for a boy who lives upstairs."

Mike wondered what she might possible be doing for someone further up the tower, but it offered a way out of his dilemma.

"Ah, perhaps it's his cannabis I can smell."

"Cannabis?" she repeated faintly, "Can you smell cannabis? Are you sure?"

"I was on the drugs squad for two years. You get to know these things."

She gave a nervous laugh. It was on her breath too, he noted.

"I've spent the last two hours getting here," he said, "Do you think I could use your bathroom?"

He saw the alarm in her eyes give way to resignation. She turned and led the way.

Eddy was in the lounge, Harriet stood in the doorway, blocking it, and pointing Mike at the bathroom door.

"It's just down there, Detective Sergeant," she said.

Mike almost smiled at the banality of her warning. By the time he returned from the bathroom, Eddy had gone, the lounge had been quickly tidied, and Harriet had been round with the air freshener.

She was sitting on the settee, smiling as he came through the door.

"Eddy had to leave," she said.

"I thought he might," said Mike. "Was he the person with you when you were clocked at a hundred miles an hour by the speed camera?"

She blinked. "You know about that?"

"Charley was concerned about you. She thought the police might be able to help."

"I wondered how she knew." Harriet looked down at her knees.

"I should apologise," said Mike.

Harriet looked up. "What for?"

"Well, really I abused the system. You're no official concern of mine – not directly anyway – since you don't live in the area covered by my force. I made a low-level enquiry, mainly to get your daughter off my back."

"Charley can be a bit determined at times."

He raised an eyebrow and nodded in agreement.

"Would you like a cup of tea?" Harriet asked.

"That would be very welcome."

"Come through into the kitchen if you like," she said.

He followed her and watched as she filled the kettle. The teapot was on the drainer, and she rinsed it out, tipping leaves that were the wrong colour for tea into the strainer. She had her back to him and couldn't know that he was watching.

"So the fact that you work in a different police area, does that mean you're not here to arrest me?" she asked.

Unseen by her, he smiled ruefully. "I probably should," he replied, "but it's a lengthy amount of paperwork, interviews, getting the local police to take you away, and at the end of the day, you're likely to get off with a caution."

"So… not, then."

"I don't think I'd hear the end of it, and Charley would probably never speak to me again."

Harriet, having filled the kettle and switched it on, turned to face him.

"Does that matter to you?" she asked.

He looked down briefly before meeting her gaze. "A great deal," he said.

She smiled thinly. "Do you have plans for Charley?"

"Maybe," he said. He really didn't want to talk about them because if he did he'd have to admit them to himself, and at the moment he wasn't sure what he wanted to do.

Harriet made a point of ensuring that he saw the tea-bags taken out of a Tetley packet before she popped a couple in the pot and scalded them. They took the pot, a jug of milk and two mugs back into the lounge.

When they were sitting opposite each other again, Mike leaned forward.

"Can I suggest something to you without giving offence."

She regarded him suspiciously. "What?"

"Air-fresheners containing synthetic scents won't get rid of natural smells, they only mask them for a while. You need to ensure that you buy sprays containing natural scents which actually do get rid of the smell of dope." He smiled tightly. He wanted her to know the gloves were off.

She nodded. "Thanks. I'll bear it in mind." She poured the tea and passed a mug to him. "So why are you here?" she asked as he took it.

"For a bit of advice," he said.

"About Charley?"

"Yes."

"She know you're here?"

"No. Just at the minute she doesn't seem to want to speak to me."

She listened while he summarised the meal he'd shared with Charley, when her body language had seemed to indicate that she liked him, and the brief meeting in his office at which she had made it clear she was only interested in him as long as he agreed to have her mother put under some sort of surveillance.

"That's just not a possibility," he said, "we don't have time to put innocent – or nearly innocent – people under surveillance. And in any case, I couldn't do that to Charley's mother because then two members of the same family would probably never speak to me again."

Harriet sipped thoughtfully.

"You like Charley. I think she likes you – maybe – but won't admit it to herself," she said.

"That's about it," he said.

"And that's why you've landed yourself with an long round trip to see me."

"'You're my only hope, Obi-wan Kenobi'."

Harriet laughed. "Nobody would take you for Princess Leah, nor me for a Jedi Knight."

Mike smiled. "Maybe the other way round."

She laughed again and shook her head. "I'll have a word with her, if you think it would help," she offered.

"No, thanks," he said, "I'll argue my own case."

She cocked her head at him. "So what do you want from me?"

"I'd like to know something about her. Why, for instance, she might be keeping her distance."

Harriet swallowed some more tea. It was cooling rapidly. She held the mug with both hands and stared down at the floor.

"I think it may be something I did," she began, speaking in a soft monotone. She looked up into his eyes. "I met her father at a dance. We had a pleasant evening, dancing and drinking and what-not. Then we disappeared out the back of the dance-hall. Ten minutes later, I was pregnant, and I never saw him again." She took another deep swallow, and looked down again. "I'd thought he seemed such a nice bloke. He was a Yank from one of the Suffolk bases – I never knew which. When I found out I was expecting, I tried to find him, but no-one seemed to know where he was."

"What was his name?" asked Mike.

"Richard Kinnear."

"Rank?"

She shook her head. "He was in civvies. And I don't know his number either," she added. "When he never contacted me – and he had my parents' phone number – I lived with them then – I realised that I had been a one-night stand for him, maybe not even warranting a mention to his mates at breakfast the next day. I didn't spend any more time looking for him, and brought Charley up myself."

"Does she know?" he asked.

Harriet glanced at him as she refilled their mugs. "Yes. I've never kept the circumstances of her conception secret."

Mike hesitated over the next question. "Did Charley ever have a step-father?"

"No. Until she went to school, I stayed home being a full-time mum. Later, I had to take any job I could get while she was growing up. I couldn't afford childcare, and

I wanted to be home when she was. Believe me, no man would have volunteered to take that sort of burden on."

Mike sat back. "Thanks for telling me," he said, "Is it possible that she might measure all men by her absentee father – at least subconsciously?"

"Possibly," said Harriet, "If so, it's my fault because I never found a better role-model for her."

"I think you did a terrific job of bringing Charley up single-handedly."

Harriet waved away his praise.

"I only did what I had to, to make up for the fact she didn't have a father, and I should have been more careful. But then, quite a few girls of my age believed you couldn't get pregnant either your first time, or if you did it standing up. I'm afraid we were wrong, on both counts." She smiled ruefully. "On the plus side, I got Charley, and I wouldn't swap her for all the tea in China," she added.

"I feel a bit that way myself, though I have a bit of work to do."

"I think you might just have to lay siege to her for a while, then carry her off on your white charger," Harriet advised. She shrugged. "You never know, it *might* work!"

"I'll let you know," Mike said, rising to leave.

"Will you let me have your number," asked Harriet, "I'd like to keep in touch."

He gave it to her.

"Are you driving all the way back at this time of night?"

"Got to, I'm afraid. I have a prisoner to interview about a Jacuzzi. He'll be upset if I'm not there to wring a confession out of him."

Harriet's eyebrows arched, and she grinned.

"Of course, I'm joking – about the wringing thing," he added as he left the flat. Harriet put her hand on his arm and he turned towards her. She reached up and kissed him on the cheek.

"You'll make someone a wonderful son-in-law one day," she said, "and I shall tell Charley so."

He looked alarmed. "No, please don't or I won't see her for dust."

"I'll tell her to stay put, or I'll come back and haunt her."

Mike suddenly recalled that Harriet was supposed to be dying. He opened his mouth, but she put a finger across his lips.

"Goodbye, Mike. It's been really nice to meet you," she said, and before he could reply, she had slipped back inside her flat and closed the door.

He felt bad that he'd forgotten her terminal diagnosis all the time he'd been with her. He turned and made his way slowly down the staircase, taking it for granted that the lift wouldn't be working – he'd never found a functioning one in a tower block yet.

He reached his car, checking round it for damage but finding it intact. He hoped he would stay awake for the whole of the journey home.

CHAPTER SEVEN

The hotel was set back, hidden away in a tree-lined parkland. Once it had been the home of a rich aristocrat and his family, but death duties and inheritance tax had had their inevitable effect on his personal wealth, and the property had been sold to satisfy the Treasury's demands. A company had bought it and added it to their successful chain of five-star hotels, and the cost of renovation, so far beyond the means of the aristocrat, were the basis for huge reductions in Corporation Tax. In effect, the Treasury was paying back the tax taken from a private pocket into the cash register of a commercial business.

Such musings filled Seymour's mind as Harriet drove them into the car park. The aristocrat in question had been Seymour's patient, and a member of a Masonic Lodge. He and his Lady were intending to be present at the Ball, as guests of the organising Lodge, but had arranged to arrive late. Seymour and Harriet were to try to slip in and occupy their places for a while.

His Lordship had been sceptical when Seymour had spoken to him on the telephone.

"For goodness' sake, Doctor, they have all sorts of tricks to identify strangers. You won't last five minutes."

"Maybe, but I have to try. Harriet is dead keen. She bought this new outfit and apparently feels obliged to flaunt it somewhere special in public."

"Good lord! If she's really got the bit between her teeth, I can see you really don't have an option," said his Lordship, glumly.

Seymour could almost see his former patient shaking his head.

"Obviously, I can't tell you any of their secrets," his Lordship continued, "I can only suggest you look out for coded questions, like 'are you on the level?' and 'is everything all square with you?' Any question that might have been aimed at a stone mason in the past."

"Right," said Seymour, "and how do I answer them?"

"Well, if you say no, you're telling them plainly you're not a Brother. If you say yes, at least you can claim later it was the innocent answer to a question."

"Aye. I see," Seymour nodded.

"But be warned, there are other ways of spotting a fake. It takes less than five minutes usually," said his Lordship, "and be careful how you shake hands. Go for the thumb on the knuckle bone of the third finger, or better still, try to avoid it. No problem for your lady friend, of course."

"Aye, right," said Seymour again, "and what are they likely to do to me when they find out we shouldn't be there?"

"I expect they'll show you the door, politely. You can always say you got the night wrong, or the location, and were expecting to be somewhere else. Me and the lady wife will be there by nine, anyway, in time for the sit-down, so I'd like you out of the way by then." He paused. "Are you sure it's worth it for perhaps an hour or less?"

"Needs must," said Seymour.

"When the devil drives," his Lordship completed.

"And Harriet," added Seymour, to himself.

He climbed awkwardly out of the low-slung car and closed the door, moving smartly round to the offside to open Harriet's door. She swung her legs out and stood beside him.

She had faithfully re-applied the make-up she'd been given at Greaves Hall and managed to put her hair up in the same style. Beneath a black velvet evening cape she wore a classically styled electric blue silk ball gown, with tailored bodice and a full floor-length skirt. In one hand she clutched a small purse by Fiorelli in creamy white leather with a gold clasp and trim. Her shoes matched the colour, with three-inch heels.

He took station by her shoulder and they walked towards the door through which other guests were arriving. The Ballroom had its own entrance, separate from the hotel's reception. Beside him, Harriet suddenly stiffened, then moved off at a tangent towards a group of two couples heading for the same door. One of the women looked up and saw her, and in minutes, they were deep in conversation. Seymour felt in his pocket and slipped a finger-stall on his right hand before he approached them. As the women greeted him, their men approached holding out their hands to shake. Seymour waived the finger-stall at them and ducked his head apologetically. One man shook his left hand with his right, but there were no unusual fumblings with Seymour's knuckles.

Harriet had been startled at first, but covered her surprise at the sight of the stall quite well, and it seemed no one had noticed him put it on. The group of six slipped in through the ballroom door together, Harriet deep in conversation with one of the women, from whose company she parted when they were safely inside. Men on the door had scarcely given the group a glance.

A waitress, smart in her black skirt and white blouse, offered glasses of sparkling wine. Harriet took hers and said 'cheers', sipping some gratefully. Seymour was about to do the same when he noticed some of the men were looking his way, each with a glass of wine, none drinking from them. Seymour put a warning hand on Harriet's wrist.

"I think we might have to wait before we drink this."

"What for?" she asked, looking round carefully.

He leaned close to her ear. "I don't know," he said. They stood close together, trying not to attract attention. In front of them was the dance floor, at the far side of which a small quartet occupied a dais. The floor was filled with small groups of people, and much hand-shaking was going on between the men. Seymour tried hard not to catch anyone's eye. He still had the finger stall on.

"What's supposed to be wrong with your finger, if anyone asks?" asked Harriet in a low whisper.

"A suppurating pustule that might burst at the slightest pressure," replied Seymour.

"Ugh! Sounds horrible," she said, screwing up her face.

"It's meant to keep would-be hand-shakers at bay," said Seymour.

"It's going to keep *me* at bay!" Harriet muttered.

"That's my girl," said Seymour. "Oh-oh! That woman you were talking to earlier is dragging her husband over here."

"Old school friend," was the only explanation she could manage before the woman reached them and smiled at Harriet.

"Haven't seen you for, what is it now? It must be..." she screwed up her face while she did the arithmetic, "thirty seven years." She glanced up at Seymour. "And is this your husband?" she smiled and held out her hand. Seymour shook it with his left. He held up his right hand with the finger stall and dipped his head in apology.

"Pleased to meet you," he said.

"Mary, this is a friend of mine, Seymour Whittle. Seymour, Mary Campbell."

"Mary Storridge these days. Pleased to meet you, Seymour," said Mary. She looked at his hand. "That looks as if it might be painful," she said.

"It's fine if I don't touch it," he said.

Mary laughed. "Must be a bit of a problem in here," she said, looking round the groups on the floor, "they're all at it – shaking hands, that is." She giggled. Seymour grinned: he'd noticed.

"This is my husband, Graham," said Mary.

Seymour nodded and smiled. "How d'you do."

Graham smiled, looking a little puzzled.

"Which is your Lodge, Brother?"

"Uh, well, it's just a little one, over by the coast."

"I'm in Tallman's, myself."

"Do you have a minimum height?" asked Seymour with his wide-eyed innocent look.

Graham looked at him from under his brows, then grinned. "Hah! Very funny."

Someone, the crown of whose scalp was innocent of hair, like a tonsure, surrounded by thinning grey locks, rapped on a table and the guests fell silent. He picked up his glass and began to sing. The words were quickly taken up by the men present – except Seymour, who didn't know them. Beside him, Graham was giving lusty voice to what sounded like a eulogy to food and drink and stones and mortar. Seymour tried opening and shutting his mouth and hoping that no-one would notice.

Harriet had, and was trying hard not to laugh. The song ended and everyone raised their glasses.

Harriet pulled at Seymour's arm.

"I think we should circulate, Seymour," she said, pulling him away and waving a hand at her friend. "See you in another thirty-seven years, Mary." She smiled graciously, as the band launched into a quickstep.

Seymour put his right hand on her waist, held her right in his left, and they set off round the dance floor. They were both long out of practice, and while natural turns weren't too difficult, Seymour's attempt at a reverse turn almost ended in catastrophe when he stepped accidentally on Harriet's foot.

"Ouch!" she muttered through gritted teeth. Seymour apologised then over her shoulder noticed Graham steering Mary towards them, his expression moderately angry.

"Get moving, Harriet, I think they're after us," he said in her ear.

"It's easy for you to say that," she said, hobbling on her injured foot. "I think you may have done me permanent damage."

"I'll check as soon as we get out of here," he promised, "now *dance!*" He almost dragged her round the dance floor towards the door. At the edge of the dance floor, Graham and Mary caught them up.

"You never did say which Lodge you're from, Seymour," he said.

Seymour ignored him. Harriet's foot was his main concern.

"Sit down, Harriet. I'll have a look at it now." He grabbed a chair and helped her into it. A small crowd had gathered. Seymour knelt down and slipped Harriet's shoe off. Her instep was badly bruised. He was feeling the bones of her foot when Graham appeared at his shoulder.

"You're not a Brother, are you Seymour?"

"Harriet," said Mary, "is it true, that Seymour isn't a member?"

Harriet and Seymour looked at each other.

"I got my dance, Seymour," she said, "so it's okay."

A florid man with a large nose bearing the scars of erysipelas pushed through the crowd.

"What's going on here?" he asked.

"He's not a Brother," said Graham, pointing at Seymour, who was trying to ease Harriet's foot back into her shoe.

"Nothing broken as far as I can tell," he said to her, "just a bad bruise." He looked round and stood up.

"Well?" asked the florid man.

"Well what?" Seymour asked tiredly.

"Are you one of us? How simple do you need me to be?"

"You're simple enough as far as I can see. We're leaving now."

"So, you're not – " Graham started.

"No, we're not staying for the meal," said Seymour.

"Yes. No. But are you a brother?" asked the florid man again, his rising temper evident in the pitch of his voice.

Seymour held Harriet tightly as he took much of her weight. They got as far as the door out to the car park before he turned.

"That's for me to know and you, apparently, to wonder about," he said, turning away and helping Harriet outside. After they'd managed a few yards towards the car, the door opened behind them.

"Sorry about that, Harriet," came Mary's voice, "let's hope it won't be so long before next time."

Seymour and Harriet continued on their way.

"It didn't seem as though you'd parked so far away when we arrived," he muttered.

"Let me try walking on it, Seymour," said Harriet. She tested her weight gently and hobbled a few steps. "Come on."

They reached the car. He held the door open.

"Are you sure you wouldn't prefer me to drive?" he asked.

She thought about it. "Oh, all right," she said. "Just be careful with it."

He helped her into the passenger seat and went round to the offside. It took a few minutes to adjust the seat and mirror to cope with his greater height, then he twisted the key in the ignition and listened as the powerful engine sprang to life.

"Please try to curb any residual boy racer or second childhood tendencies you might be feeling," she said.

He grinned at her. "I shall treat it like glass," he said, letting in the clutch so quickly the wheels sprayed gravel over the flower beds and adjacent vehicles. In a moment, he swept past the ballroom door, outside of which the tonsured man and two others had appeared, standing either side of the florid one and watching them go.

"What's the opposite of a reception party?" Seymour asked.

Harriet smiled, saying nothing until they reached her tower block.

Seymour climbed out and held out a hand to steady her as she stood up. He closed and locked the vehicle, handing her the key.

"Well, I'd better go," he said.

"Won't you help me up to the flat?" she asked plaintively.

"Of course."

The lift, remarkably, was functioning. They rode up to the third floor. Harriet kept her arm tucked in Seymour's as they walked to her door.

"Come in for a coffee," she said.

"Thank you." He followed her in and helped her to her settee.

"You sit there, I'll make it," he said. He went through into the kitchen and found mugs and makings. When he returned to the lounge, holding two steaming mugs of coffee, Harriet had taken off her shoes and the velvet cape, and was leaning back against the settee cushions.

Seymour put one mug near her and took the other with him to the easy chair opposite. He looked up at her and smiled.

"I don't think I mentioned it before," he said, "but you were by far the most beautiful woman in the room."

She smiled. "Seymour, do you think you could come over here a minute?" she asked, patting the seat beside her.

He moved as she wanted. She took his hand in hers.

"I don't think I mentioned it, either," she said, "but you were the handsomest man."

He smiled, feeling the blood rush to his face. "We'll be a great loss to the world when we're no longer here."

She laughed. "Do you think they'll notice?"

"If you're talking about the Masons, I expect they'll still be congratulating themselves on not having given away any secrets to outsiders."

She smiled again placidly. "Do you think you could pass me my painkillers, they're behind you," she asked.

Seymour reached over the back of the settee and found he could just reach the packet on Harriet's sideboard.

"I should take an extra one," he said, "it's not likely to do you any harm, and it'll help with the foot. I am truly sorry I stepped on it."

She rested a hand on his arm. "Don't worry about it, and don't mention it again," she said. She washed two of the powerful tablets down with a couple of mouthfuls of coffee.

"The thing is," Seymour began, "we weren't there very long, and we only managed two circuits of the dance floor. Was it all right?"

"To be honest, Seymour, I didn't expect you to be able to fix it at all. I really thought I was asking for the impossible, but you did, and put yourself through a lot of hassle because of it. Nobody has ever done anything like that for me before. I can't tell you what it means." Her eyes misted as she spoke to him. As she finished, she took his face in her hands and kissed him slowly on the lips.

"Oh, it was nothing, woman," he said gruffly, "I've always wondered what Freemasons get up to. I don't think we'll have time to think of a way of getting into a Masonic Temple – and anyway, my face is probably going up on Wanted posters in every Lodge in the county. They'll be on their guard against another attempt at infiltration."

She kissed him again. She was fascinated that he blushed.

She pulled the long skirt of her dress up to her knees.

"Could you just check my foot over again, please, before I go to bed."

Seymour nodded and knelt on the floor so he could reach. His examination of her foot suggested that apart from discoloration of the skin where his shoe had left its mark, the swelling was subsiding and the foot looked as if it would be all right by the morning. As he held her foot gently in both hands, she lifted her other leg, and rubbed the side of his cheek with her toes before dropping the foot to his thigh.

He gazed into her eyes which smiled an invitation at him, while trapping her wandering toes with one hand.

She pulled both feet free and stood up, holding out a hand to him. He took it and rose to his feet.

"Seymour," she began.

He shushed her. "Remember the rules, Harriet."

She shook her head and smiled.

"Did anyone say anything about love, Seymour? I think we agreed we wouldn't fall in love."

"Exactly," he said.

"Never said we couldn't have sex, or even just sleep in the same bed."

"No."

"It seems stupid for you to have to go home at this time of night."

Seymour glanced at the clock. Turning back to her, he rested both hands on her shoulders.

"Harriet, let's not be too ambitious here and push the boundaries we set ourselves," he said.

She tilted her head and studied him. "You're a real, old-fashioned, gentleman, aren't you? I'll bet you've not had a girlfriend since your wife died."

"No."

She slipped a hand round his shoulder and pulled herself close to him.

"You're secret's safe with me," she said, grinning.

He pulled his head away and looked down into her eyes. "What secret?"

"That you're a gentleman. You can use one half of the bed while I use the other, and we can be quite respectable – nearly!" she said. "Now, how about another drink?"

They looked into each-other's eyes for a moment before Seymour sat down again on the sofa.

"If you're sure..."

Harriet smiled. "I still have some scotch and soda."

She mixed the drink and brought it over, sitting next to him.

"Aren't you having one?" he asked.

"I'm okay with the coffee. I haven't finished mine."

Seymour sipped his drink. Harriet watched him quietly.

"I have a little surprise for you," he said.

She looked up at him. "What?"

He felt in an inside pocket and pulled out a paper folder bearing the logo of one of the local airlines flying from the regional airport near Breydon. He checked the name on the ticket and passed Harriet's to her.

"Hope your passport is up to date."

Harriet's eyes widened with surprise. She opened the ticket: it was for a flight the day after next to Paris.

"It was a deal. Special rate as long as we stayed at least one night in Paris, so I thought we'd have two."

"That's wonderful!" she exclaimed, "what a lovely idea. I've never been to Paris." She leaned forward and kissed him again. "Let's go to bed, Seymour," she said.

Seymour stood up. "I'm not sure I should..." he said.

"Don't worry about my reputation," she grinned, "I don't care what the neighbours think. Half of them have their boyfriends round anyway."

"And what about the other half?"

"They're visiting their girlfriends."

He smiled. "It'll be a bit of a giveaway when I leave this place in the morning, still in my dinner jacket."

She shook her head, amused. "I'll just tell people I found a box of Milk Tray on my pillow."

He rolled his eyes. "If they're under forty, they'll never understand the reference," he said, "I only just remember the advert."

"One thing you can do, dear Seymour, is unzip my dress if you would, please."

When he'd done so, she held the bodice in place while she turned back towards him. He looked at her, the sight and feel of her warm flesh beneath his fingers bringing back old memories. She held out her hand. He clasped it in one of his and she led him into the bedroom.

He averted his eyes while she slipped out of the gown and her underclothes, and removed only his jacket, trousers and footwear. Then while she slipped her nightdress on and settled herself comfortably down the left side of the bed, he gingerly lowered himself onto the right and lay still, facing the window. For a moment, Harriet contemplated touching him; she lifted her arm, but then, with a little sigh, she rolled over, turned out the light and waited for sleep to claim her.

*

Seymour's house was silent and sepulchral when Kay let herself in the following morning. She'd expected to find her father at home and felt disappointed when she discovered he wasn't. She'd not slept well, annoyed with Mark for thinking what he did of her. He seemed to think she was interested in the value of her father's wealth, whatever it was, and in the light of their argument, she strongly suspected that he was only concerned by how much Seymour's estate would swell the family coffers. She felt physically sick when she remembered his face, pinched and sharp with avarice. He'd changed a lot since they'd married.

She made herself a cup of coffee and sat on the settee in her father's favourite place. She felt in her handbag and pulled out a packet of cigarettes and a smart brushed steel lighter. She'd open the windows later to let the smoke out: no-one knew she'd started to smoke the occasional cigarette, but she found it helped just at the moment.

There were no ashtrays so she fetched a saucer from the kitchen to stand in for one. She took a deep drag and expelled the smoke through her painted lips. She'd left home at the usual time, as if going to work, but a hundred yards away from the house, she'd stopped the car and phoned the office to tell them she was taking the day off. They'd manage without her. She'd wondered what to do next. Mark worked at home, preventing her from going back there, so she'd come to her father's house.

She was finishing the cigarette, still deep in thought, when she heard the key in the Yale lock on the front door. She scrambled to her feet, knocked the impromptu ashtray off the chair-arm, and was trying to brush the ash back onto the saucer when Seymour came in.

She stopped and stared at him.

"Bit early for dinner jackets, isn't it?" she said.

"Oh, hello, Kay," he said, surprised to find her in his house. His nose wrinkled. "Can I smell cigarette smoke?" he asked.

Colour flooded her cheeks. "It's me. I have the occasional one. I just knocked the ash onto the floor."

"Oh," he said, nodding.

"I'll open a window," she said.

"Right. I'm gasping for coffee. Would you like one?"

She looked over her shoulder as she pushed a window wide. "I've a cup of instant here, but if you're making the real thing... Please."

When he'd gone into the kitchen, she quickly continued cleaning up the spill and threw it and the remains of the cigarette into the fireplace. She drained her cup and took it and the saucer to the sink and washed it.

Seymour was counting off five seconds after the water had boiled before pouring it into a cafetière.

"What made you start smoking?" he asked, "Trouble at t' mill?"

"I was just feeling a bit down," she replied. She knew she couldn't describe herself as 'depressed' to him, because he saw it as a rare clinical condition, rather than its common use to describe unhappiness.

He pressed the plunger to filter the coffee and poured it into mugs on a few tablespoonfuls of cold milk. She picked up her mug and walked ahead of him back into the lounge.

He sat in an easy-chair, letting her resume her place on the settee he usually occupied.

"So what's making you unhappy?"

She snorted. "As if you have to ask! I'm not looking forward to losing my father!"

"But I'm fine at the moment. Not dead yet," he said. He sipped, studying her over the rim of his mug. "What else?"

She looked at him, wanting to unload some of her worries, but it would be disloyal to Mark. She shook her head.

"I can't tell you."

He sipped again. "Okay. Let's talk about something else. Mark, for instance. How is he? He never says much when he comes round here – how are things with him?"

"Just fine," she said, keeping her face blank. There were times when her father's seeming prescience almost unnerved her.

Seymour stared out of the window. "Do you mind if I'm a bit blunt?"

She shook her head, staring at the floor.

"I think you were quite lucky to marry him."

Kay stared. It was not what she'd been expecting him to say. She had a shrewd idea that her father knew just what Mark was like.

"I thought so too, at the time," she said.

He nodded. "But since then..."

"Since then?"

"I have this feeling that you and he aren't quite in tune as much as you once were."

"People change," she said.

He tilted his head. "And not always for the better."

She pursed her lips.

"How long is it you've been married now, Kay?" he asked.

"You should know," she replied, "you gave me away."

"Five years then." He allowed his eyes to slide down her body to her flat stomach. A blush spread through her cheeks.

"I know what's going through your mind!" she snapped, "but Mark and I agreed we wouldn't have any children. We decided that before we were married."

He gazed up at the ceiling as if thinking. "Well," he said, "there's plenty of time to change your mind - you're only twenty-eight."

The blush deepened. "Why should I change my mind?"

He looked at her mildly. "Because, as you said yourself five minutes ago, people change. One of my patients found herself in the same predicament – oh! I'm sorry, we haven't established that you're in any predicament, but please, just go with me on this one – where, when she was nineteen, she'd married a chap who was a fair bit older and had a previous wife and children. He didn't want another family and at that time, neither did she. The marriage went ahead. Five years later, she started getting broody," he grinned at her, "which, incidentally, is what I diagnose in your case, and changed her mind. Unfortunately, whilst nineteen-year-old girls grow up to be twenty-four or more, in the process changing their ideas, older people have a clearer idea of what they do and don't want. Her husband hadn't changed his view, with the result that they divorced. She found another, younger, man, and within eighteen months was happily pregnant. They moved away before her confinement."

She gazed at him evenly for a moment, her lips thinning. "Good story, dad, but as you said, I don't have a predicament, so it doesn't apply."

Seymour looked down, chastened. "Of course. It was foolish of me to think of that particular matter as analogous." He looked up, hopefully. "Forgive your old dad?"

She smiled, but it didn't reach her eyes. "Of course."

"Just as well I'm not your GP, dear."

CHAPTER EIGHT

Harriet enjoyed Paris. Seymour had booked them separate rooms at a comfortable hotel. For their evening meal, they found a restaurant near the Pompidou Centre. There was a queue made up entirely of locals, which Seymour took as a sign that the place must be good. They had to wait half an hour before they could get a table, but the food proved worth it.

The following day, they'd taken a trip on a *bateau mouche*, seeing the city from the River Seine, followed by a visit to the Louvre and a quick tour of Notre Dame Cathedral. They completed their last evening with a ride up the Eiffel Tower from where the whole of Paris, sparkling like a jewel, was spread out before them. If Seymour gripped the rails until his knuckles whitened, Harriet chose not to notice. Later, alone in her room, with its massive four-poster bed, she felt suddenly lonely.

Seymour was the best thing that had ever happened to her, she realised. If she was honest with herself, she would have to admit that she'd known this for some time, and, despite her own stricture on the subject, she strongly suspected that she had fallen in love with him. Which was plainly ridiculous at her time of life: fifty-five but feeling thirty-five. There had been men-friends before – actually, quite a number, she reminded herself – but she'd never felt about them how she felt about Seymour. He might have a tendency to grumpiness – all right, he could grump for England, she acknowledged – but it was part of his charm. So could she if she'd a mind to. He was also courteous, and resourceful: hadn't he got her – in fact, both of them – into a Masonic Ball, where they'd had no right to be? And she knew deep down that he hadn't wanted to make the parachute jump. He should have said he didn't like heights.

Then, even after she'd become certain that he hated them, he'd taken her in the elevator up the Eiffel Tower. On one of the decks, they'd walked to the rail at the edge and she'd felt the tension in him as they looked down to the ground a hundred metres below, but he hadn't complained. He'd even asked if she wanted to go up the Montparnasse Tower, which was higher than the Eiffel, but she could see all she wanted through the ironwork of the older structure. The coloured floodlights which illuminated it in gold and silver made her gasp with its sheer beauty and elegance. There was still an air of Edwardian 'belle époque' about it which filled her mind's eye with recollections of paintings by Renoir and Toulouse-Lautrec.

There was something very magical about Paris at night, and Harriet knew she had to thank Seymour for the opportunity to enjoy it before she died. She felt a strong need to share her happiness with him and got as far as picking up the telephone to ask him to join her when she reminded herself of the dangers of, if not falling in love – it was too late for that, she had done so already – at least letting Seymour know how she felt. It would screw up not only his last few days, but also there were their families to consider. Charley, she suspected, wouldn't mind, but she had a feeling Kay might not be too thrilled – might feel her nose being pushed out of joint.

So, she decided, putting the telephone down gently, she would deny herself the pleasure of Seymour's company. It was better that she did.

*

When she arrived back in her flat, Harriet felt somehow let down. She'd enjoyed Paris and was sorry the visit had ended after so short a time. She had her memories: she would have had more if she'd remembered to take a camera with her.

"Damn!" she muttered when, in the middle of unpacking, she realised she'd forgotten it. Never gave it a thought, if the truth be told. Still, the memory of the wonderful time they'd had, that moment, some distance up the Eiffel Tower, when she'd known that if Seymour had kissed her, or more, she would not have resisted. Had there been other people about? She scarcely could recall. She'd wanted to give herself to him, and the effort it had needed later, when she'd stopped herself telephoning his room, had left her weeping for all the things she could now not have. According to the hospital's guidelines, she would be dead all too soon.

She thought of Charley. Of course she'd manage: she was a fine, independent woman, well able to look after herself. She'd have liked a grandchild... and the image of Mike slid into her mind. She grinned. He was the kind of man who'd stand up to Charley, she felt. Maybe, if there had been more time! It all came down to time...

*

Mike English was feeling moderately triumphant: over the weekend, they'd wrapped up the investigation into the theft of the Jacuzzi and other fittings when the lorry driver had decided he wasn't taking all the blame himself and gave up the rest of the gang. Most of Tuesday had been spent putting them up before magistrates and getting them bailed to the Crown Court. The case was now in the hands of the Crown Prosecution Service and the pressure was off him. He wanted to celebrate, and Jane was this evening going out with some friends to a hen night.

The person he'd quite like to celebrate with was Charley. She intrigued him, challenged and annoyed him, and he enjoyed being with her. He looked at the telephone on his desk, and put out his hand, but then withdrew it. No, he thought, she wouldn't... He got up and took his mug over to the coffee maker. There was still a little very stewed coffee in it. He emptied it into his mug. There was no milk left and without it, it tasted foul.

Dammit! He drained the mug and picked up the telephone while the bitter taste was still strong in his mouth. Dialled. She'd have gone home, he knew. He was about to hang up when he heard her voice.

"Milner Blythe Associates."

He licked his lips. "Charley?"

There was silence for a moment before she spoke. "Mike?"

"Uh, yes. Hope you don't mind my phoning you."

"Is there a problem? Is it my mother? What's wrong?"

He had an idea. "Will you have dinner with me again this evening – like we did before, the Trattoria Italia, just so you don't think I'm trying to have a date with you."

"Well..."

"Only you know your mother is not really a topic I can talk about officially, not on the premises, so to speak." Please don't recall the fact that we have talked about her in this very office, he silently begged.

"Just tell me this, is she all right? She's not... dead?"

He shook his head. "No, Charley, she's fine. Believe me, if it were as serious as that, I'd tell you now, rules or no rules." And there were no rules.

"Okay," she said, "when shall I meet you?"

"Would you mind if we ate a little later, say half-seven or eight? There're just a few things I need to do." Like dash home, shower, shave, change clothes. But let her think it was business.

"Yes, okay. I wasn't doing anything this evening as it happens," she said.

He hung up after making the final arrangements and stared at the phone for a moment. Then in a rare display of emotion, he punched the air: "Yes!" which caused a few heads to lift among the night shift in the CID office.

He almost ran out of the building, anyone seeing his grin left scratching their heads, while the Custody Sergeant looked sideways at his constable and said, "I bet there's a woman caused that. I know the signs, son, I've been there, got the T-shirt."

Mike arrived outside the Trattoria Italia with about five minutes to spare. He'd changed from his work suit into a pair of tailored tan slacks and a sports jacket in a dog-tooth check, with a yellow shirt open at the neck and brown Oxford Brogues. He looked around to make sure Charley wasn't waiting somewhere nearby, then went in to ask Young Bill if he could lay a table for two.

"Ah, Michael, it is a very busy night," Guglielmo explained, "if only you had called me, but I have had to let your table go."

"Damn!" muttered Mike, desperately thinking where he could take Charley without her becoming suspicious. There was another Italian restaurant round the corner and up the hill, about two hundred yards. If they weren't fully booked as well. He reached for his mobile phone. The old man was still talking, waving his arms and sighing gustily through his moustache.

"... The lady was most insistent that she wanted the same table she had when she last came here. I felt sure you wouldn't mind."

Mike suddenly stopped his frantic activity and stared at the proprietor.

"Why would I not mind?" he asked.

Guglielmo shrugged. "Because you let her sit at your table last time you were here."

Mike stared at him then edged his way further into the restaurant until he could see the table he usually occupied. Charley sat there, watching him, amused.

"See, signor, I could not refuse the lady."

Mike turned to him. "I understand – you are as putty in her hands."

"Si."

"You had me going then."

The old man smiled delightedly. "Si."

Mike walked past him and stood beside the vacant chair opposite Charley.

"Mind if I join you?"

"I thought that was the plan. Sorry about the table, but I remembered from last time that it is usually laid only for one, and I asked Young Bill if he'd mind adding another place. He was happy, he said, to oblige, and gave me his most ingratiating smile."

Guglielmo had remained within earshot, and turned to them, raising his arms.

"Is love, no? I know these things." He winked and tapped the side of his nose, beaming at them.

It was too much for Charley, who blushed delicately.

"I think for that, you owe us a drink," said Mike to the old man.

"Okay. I have a bottle of nice Chianti. I bring you a glass."

"That'll be fine," said Mike.

"I'll throw in two straws so you can share it," said Guglielmo, his expression blank.

Mike turned to look at him in exasperation. "Could we just... get on?" he asked.

Guglielmo smiled and nodded. "Of course, Mike. It was just a good joke, yes?"

"Yes, but now it's wearing thin. I have things to say to this lady in private."

Guglielmo's face lit up again and he went over to the small bar whistling *Que Sera, Sera.*

Mike turned to Charley and smiled. "I might just have to arrest him one day for bare-faced cheek."

She smiled at him, but then her expression became more serious.

"What was it you wanted to tell me?"

At that moment, a waitress arrived to take their orders. She was carrying two glasses of the red wine.

"I'm not having a starter," Charley said, "you carry on. I'll just have a main course."

Mike was quite hungry. He ordered an antipasto of red and green peppers, then looked at Charley.

"What main course?" he asked.

She scanned the menu, finally pointing at something.

"Conchiglie alla tonno," she said.

Mike looked down the menu until he found it.

"I'll have the same," he said. He looked at Charley. "Shall we get a bottle of the Chianti as well?"

"I think I'll just have this glassful," she said.

"Oh, okay, I'll stick with it, too," Mike said, turning to the waitress with a smile.

After she had gone they were left, looking at each other in the flattering light of the candle, the gentle sounds of Italian love-songs playing in the background. For a moment, they stared into each-others' eyes before Charley spoke.

"Well?"

Mike cleared his throat which had suddenly gone very dry, and took a sip of wine to alleviate it.

"Just about sorted the stolen bathroom case," he said.

"Good," she said, "Now, what's happened to my mother?"

"She's fine."

Charley looked at him, her head tilted slightly.

"And that's it? That's what you couldn't tell me on the phone?"

"No, no, it isn't that," he said. He was glad nobody from work could hear him. This hesitancy was unusual.

"She was fine last time I saw her," he amplified.

Charley looked at him narrowly.

"You've seen my mother?"

The waitress reappeared with Mike's antipasto. She arranged additional cutlery beside his plate, wished him 'buon appetito', and left them. Mike picked up the knife and fork she'd provided, keeping his eyes on his plate but aware that Charley was waiting for his answer.

"Yes. I was in the area and... decided to drop in," he said.

Charley folded her arms and sat back.

"What made you think of doing that?" she asked in a cold tone of voice.

He shrugged. "I was just in the neighbourhood, and I remembered what you said about her when we were, uh, going out." He ate a mouthful of the peppers.

"What did I possibly say that was so important you remember it after all this time?"

"You just talked about her. I thought she sounded to be an interesting lady." He couldn't divulge the fact that he was blessed with total recall, and could have told her everything they'd ever said or done together. He'd discovered that other people, faced with his formidable memory of events, thought of it almost like having been bugged and weren't at all comfortable with being reminded – often months later – of something they'd forgotten ever saying or doing. He did not want to make Charley feel uncomfortable, but she was already unhappy with him. He felt as if he was on very thin ice with her.

"And she was – more interesting than I'd ever have thought," he said.

She stared at him still. "And that's it, is it? My mother interests you."

"I think your mother is very interesting, yes. I'd like to get to know her better."

She looked at him coldly. "You won't have time."

Mike gripped his hands, and looked down at his meal. "I know that. I shall be sorry when she's no longer with us." He looked into Charley's eyes.

Charley was having to fight the urge to fling herself into Mike's arms, so strong and protective, and comforting at this time when her mother was nearing death. She had to be strong, and anyway, the time wasn't right to be thinking about herself and a possible future with Mike English. The only way she could maintain a distance was by being business-like and professional, and trying to ignore those little ripples she felt in her tummy every time he spoke.

Fortunately, what he was telling her helped stoke up the fires of indignation. How dare he go and see her mother behind her back? Why hadn't her mother said anything about it? She repeated these questions over and over again and found it helped. And now he was looking at her with hurt eyes. The trouble was that she thought there *might* be a possible future with him – just not now. She'd already sent him away once, and she didn't want to do it again, in case he never came back.

If there were a 'back burner' for men, she would desperately want to put Mike on it, so she could just put him aside temporarily, for a few months, then when she knew she'd need picking up, resurrect him and welcome the comfort and care he was sure to lavish on her – she thought. But another thought crashed into that: what if she'd misread the signs and he wasn't as interested as he seemed. After all, he was a policeman, and they could be deceptive – had to be sometimes, to catch the baddies. And if he worked with that DC Jenkins all day, wouldn't she be more available to him? She was certainly attractive (if you liked your women tall and brunette, which she sincerely hoped Mike didn't but held out little expectation of his being that fussy).

She held his gaze. Damn, it was difficult not to succumb to temptation. She had to work hard at her indignation.

"I don't see why. Visiting her once doesn't mean you know her."

"She's a woman of great character. I wish we did have longer."

Charley pouted. It was galling to be in complete agreement with him when she would have preferred an opportunity to give him a set-down.

Mike finished his starter and sat back while the waitress cleared the space for the main course. Charley decided to try a different tack.

"Did you know my mother had a boyfriend?"

Mike looked up, slightly incredulously. "No. Who?"

"He's called Seymour Whittle."

"I've not heard of him."

She grinned wryly. "You might. He's been told he's dying, too, like her, and I think they're planning to live it up a little together before they do."

She stopped suddenly, a lump filling her throat, causing her to gasp for breath while at the same time her eyes brimmed with tears. It was odd, she thought, because she was furious with herself for appearing to be so weak, and she couldn't normally weep when she was furious.

Mike offered her his clean folded handkerchief. She dabbed delicately at her eyes, not wanting to smudge the makeup she'd so carefully applied. She held the linen over her nose and gazed at him in mute appeal. He opened his hands, grinning.

"Go ahead and use it. I've got others."

She cleared her nose, dabbed her eyes again, and cursed herself for a weakling. She folded the handkerchief and offered it back to him. He held up his hand.

"No, that's okay, you keep it."

She grinned and put it in her handbag.

"I'll wash it and let you have it back," she said. "You're the only man I know who has a proper handkerchief."

He grinned. "It's just as well you know me then. You're the only girl I know I'd offer it to."

She pursed her lips and narrowed her eyes. "Are you accusing me of being a cry-baby?"

"No, not at all. The last time I was able to help you out, you weren't crying: you'd just tipped some wine over yourself." His eyes, unbidden, focussed briefly on her breasts.

"Yes, well, you made me nervous," she said.

"No longer, though, I hope."

"Well I know you could lock me up if I did anything wrong. So you do still make me nervous."

He raised his eyebrows. "Surely you don't think I'd do that?"

She looked away. "Why not! It's your job."

"Charley! I'd never do that!"

She stared at him.

"What I'd quite like to do is take you into custody," he continued.

"Why?" she demanded, "what have I done?"

Suddenly he broke eye contact, and seemed confused. "I – I didn't mean at the police station," he mumbled.

"What are you talking about?"

He shook his head. "Sorry, I shouldn't have said that."

Charley was confused. For a moment, she'd thought he was suggesting something quite personal, yet he seemed to have backed off. She tilted her head and studied him. What if, she wondered, he actually liked her – *still* liked her – despite the fact she'd ended their relationship two months ago? A little frisson of excitement slithered down her back. Maybe it was that which caused him to retract and re-trench. Oh sod it! she thought. Maybe it would be fairer to both of them to find out.

Hesitantly, she reached across the table and rested her hand on his, watching his face.

"Mike?" she said softly.

He looked into her eyes, then down at her small hand resting on his large one.

"I'm only going to say this once," she said, "so pay attention, please."

He stared at her.

"Mike, I quite like you, and occasionally I think we shouldn't have stopped seeing each other. I think that's what makes me nervous when you're around."

She bit her lower lip and waited, conscious of his scrutiny and the blood rushing to her face. For an age, he stared at her deadpan, before a smile tilted his lips and rushed to his eyes. Suddenly her hand was trapped between both of his, and her heart started to pound against her ribs.

"Makes me nervous, too," he said, "but I want us to write off the past and start again."

The waitress appeared at his elbow with the steaming pasta dishes balanced precariously on her arm. They quickly withdrew their hands until she'd placed one in front of Charley and the other in front of Mike.

"Would you like some pepper, sir?" she asked, wielding a very long pepper mill.

Mike glanced at her. "Please."

Charley had some, too, and then they were left alone. Mike took Charley's hand again in his.

"Well?" he asked.

But Charley was not going to be drawn so easily. "What do you think we should do?"

He hesitated a moment, running the ball of his thumb against the tips of her fingers. "I'd like to say some things up front."

"What?"

"As you know, it isn't easy for a person to have a personal relationship with someone in my line of business," he began.

She nodded.

He went on: "You'll remember when we were going out together before - our last date particularly. I had an urgent call to deal with, and if I'm honest, I was so caught up in it, it was a long time before I remembered to let you know. When I realised, I felt dreadful, and you – well, for you it was just one time too many. I don't want to lose you again, Charley, but I can almost guarantee that there'll be times I let you down. I really, desperately, want you to believe that I don't do it to hurt you, I don't do it intentionally. Please, Charley!"

She looked down at her enfolded hand and rested her other on top of his. Her eyes were misting, but for quite a different reason from the last time. She looked up.

"If you're asking me to be your girl again, I will," she said.

He lifted her hand and brushed it with his lips. "I'm asking."

*

Kay had had a bad day. She felt alone in her concern for the fact that her father would live only a short time. She wanted to watch over him, alert for the first signs of his ultimate collapse, but knew he wouldn't be happy about that. With her husband offering no support, seemingly interested only in how much her father's estate might be worth, she could only confide in her brother, David.

She'd left work early and gone round to his flat. He'd made some attempt to tidy the place after she'd phoned to say she was coming, but he hadn't been able to hide the scent of neglect and rotting food. She wondered how he could live in that environment: it made her feel sick.

David pointed her at the second-hand leather sofa positioned in front of the gas fire. She scanned it automatically for signs of anything that might come off on her skirt before sitting down. There was something colourless dried onto one arm of the sofa, which she carefully avoided.

He sat on the almost new Aeron swivel chair positioned in front of his state-of-the-art computer on its workstation. The only other furniture in the room was a tall bookshelf and a chest of drawers, positioned against adjacent walls, a widescreen plasma television and home theatre sound system. Under the television was bundled the handset controller for a video game console. Cables ran between television and computer, and extended from the theatre system to the surround-sound loudspeakers positioned around the room. Curtains were hung across the window, permanently closed – they were drawing-pinned to the frame. Kay longed to be able to tear it all out and start again, beginning with a new carpet and a large tin of emulsion.

"What's up, sis?"

"It's dad, of course. I don't know what to do for the best."

"He seems happy enough."

"Just because he *seems* happy, doesn't mean he *is*," she said.

"If he seems happy, surely you've just got to accept it."

She wrung her hands, staring down at her lap. "I know I should, but I can't get over the thought that he's going to die – soon, according to the doctors. It brings back my memories of mother."

He looked away, impassive.

She decided there was no point trying to make him understand her sense of loss and loneliness if he wasn't feeling it himself. She turned to face him, smiling brightly.

"And how are you, dearest brother? Got yourself another girlfriend yet?"

He grinned. "Yes."

"Tell me about her."

"I reckon you'd like her. She's into cotton print dresses and keeps her hair in a French pleat."

Kay's eyes opened wide in surprise.

"Has she ever seen the inside of your flat?"

His eyes narrowed. "Yes, once, so far."

She looked at him askance. "But you tidied the place up?"

He nodded. "Yeah, most of it."

"And have you seen her since?"

He scowled at her. "Look! Why do you keep on about it. This is me," he waved at the room, "it's what I am. I'm not obsessive about tidiness like you are."

She looked at him mildly. "You seem to have no concept of tidiness, let alone any idea of keeping the place even moderately clean," she said. "I bet if I looked in your bathroom I'd come out feeling sick. Come to that, the smell in here is overpowering – how often do you empty your waste food bin?"

"Every week, when I put the waste out for the bin-men."

"So have you actually seen this girl again, since she was here."

"Yes I have. Mind your own business, sis."

Kay bit her tongue on the verge of asking if it was to apologise or listen to the girl saying goodbye. David was a person of scruffy habits and poor personal hygiene. How could he have come from the same womb, the same family, as she did?

"Will you arrange the funeral?" she fired at him suddenly.

"What fu – Oh, dad's you mean?"

"Of course, dad's," she snapped, "It's the most important thing after trying to make sure he is comfortable in his last days."

"Dad's very comfortable. He told me. He said he didn't want us fussing around."

She stared at him. "So I suppose you've kept away?"

"It's what he wanted."

"He didn't tell me that."

"Wonder why! Figure it out."

She stood up. "I'll ask him about it. Meanwhile, why don't you find out what sort of funeral he wants."

"Why don't you do it?"

She stared at him. "Am I hearing you correctly? You've done very little for him since you were fifteen. This is absolutely your last chance."

"Why should I do anything for him? I mean, I didn't ask to be born."

She went to the door and opened it before turning back to him. Her eyes were brimming.

"I just don't understand you any more, David," she said, "we're *family*, for God's sake. We should stick together. You are... appalling."

She pulled the door closed behind her.

For some minutes, he stared at the door, his bottom lip thrust out before he turned and brought his computer back to life.

CHAPTER NINE

Eddy had been round the previous evening, a few hours after Harriet had returned from Paris. She told him about the place, and how easy it was to get there, in the hope that he might be encouraged to lift his awareness beyond the Abbey Farm estate into the greater world that lay out there, so far undiscovered by him. They'd spent their usual hour dealing with reading, writing and pronunciation, then he'd gone back to his flat, leaving another ounce of skunk on her living room table.

Her recollections, over breakfast, were interrupted by the letterbox flap. She went to the door and picked up a brown manila envelope from the doormat. She opened it with a puzzled frown and read the single sheet inside. Then she got on the telephone to Seymour.

"Have you had a letter from the hospital?"

"Yes," he replied.

"Why would they want to do more tests?"

"I don't know. Maybe they thought of something else."

She stared at the letter. "It says, 'as soon as possible'."

"Are you doing anything today?"

"I thought you and I were..."

"Ah, yes. Well, we can still do that."

"I'll come over and pick you up."

"Okay, thanks," he said.

After hanging up, Harriet went into her bedroom and stared at the contents of her wardrobe. She didn't need to think about clothes much: slacks, T-shirt and anorak would be adequate.

Twenty minutes later, she waited at the kerb while Seymour lowered his length into the seat beside her. He was wearing an overcoat and a tweed hat.

"Good disguise, Seymour. They'll never be able to recognise you with that on," she said.

He glanced at her sharply but her face was deadpan – until he turned away and looked ahead, when a small smile lightened her expression.

She parked in the multi-storey outside the hospital and they made their way into the outpatients' department.

"How are you feeling? I forgot to ask," said Seymour as they took their seats after registering their presence with the receptionist.

"Fair to middling," she said.

"You still supplementing your prescription?" he asked softly.

"Just occasionally."

"No ill-effects?"

"Just the opposite. I have really bad pains when I don't use the stuff."

He shrugged. "Let's hope these new tests help."

Harriet pursed her lips. "Let's hope they help – in time!"

Seymour did not reply, his eyes cast down, studying the shiny toe-caps of his shoes.

"Harriet Blythe!" a nurse called from a doorway. Harriet go up and followed her, leaving Seymour in the waiting area. The nurse showed her into an examination room.

"Can you take off your clothes and put this hospital gown on, please," said the nurse, showing her where the article of notional modesty was hanging. "You can leave your panties on."

"Thank you," said Harriet politely and waited until the nurse had left before getting out of her clothes. There was a locker in which she could place them and keep the key until she was ready to change back. When she'd finished, she sat on the one chair, next to the examination table, and waited.

Around the time a young man who appeared to be about seventeen, in a white coat, came in and told her he was the doctor who would be carrying out the first of a series of comprehensive tests, the nurse who had earlier collected Harriet from the waiting area returned and led Seymour into another examination room.

It was lunchtime before both Seymour and Harriet were finished with the hospital. Harriet was strangely quiet and did not encourage conversation. Seymour, who had undergone a CT scan, decided she did not want to speak of her appointment, and so didn't. Instead, he decided to behave as if they had never been asked to return to the hospital.

"Before we go back to the car," he said, "why don't we get a bite to eat?"

"Okay," she said brightly.

He heard the edge in her tone, but did not respond to it. He led the way to a coffee shop.

"Coffee and sandwiches all right?" he asked.

"Fine, thank you."

They found a seat in a corner away from most of the other patrons, and Seymour fetched the food and drink.

For a few minutes, they got on with their meal without talking. At last, Seymour couldn't refrain from asking.

"Are you all right, Harriet? Were the tests okay?"

She stopped chewing and shook her head, then swallowed.

"Don't mind me, I'm just being silly. It's just that having to go through all these tests again makes it all seem very real."

He nodded sympathetically. "I think I understand. It's human nature to try to ignore the sort of stuff we've been told – after all, nobody in truth can predict the future, and when doctors say you've only got weeks or months to live, it's just their best guess. There could be some miracle cure between now and then that'll leave us alive till we're well into our hundreds." He grinned.

Harriet returned the smile. "I know what you say is true, really. But there isn't much time between now and then for them to come up with the miracle cure."

Seymour took another bite of his sandwich and chewed reflectively.

"Do you think it might be time to put our swan-song into operation?"

She studied him for a few moments.

"I've never done anything really bad before," she said.

He nodded. "Me neither."

"I know I suggested we rob a bank, but are you quite happy to do it?"

"We're in this together," he said, "we're going to die together, and before that, we're going to *do* together. Do and die, together."

Harriet gazed at him. Her eyes suddenly filled with tears. She stood up and grasped his hand.

"I need to go outside," she said, "please!"

He went with her to the door, and she pulled him along the pavement, stopping after a few paces.

"Sorry, I couldn't talk in there," she gulped.

"What's the matter?" he asked, concerned. He slipped his arms round her without thinking.

She looked up into his eyes. "Oh, Seymour! I try very hard to be philosophical about – our – situation," she said miserably, "but the idea of being dead in a few days or weeks, when I don't feel that bad at the moment... it's difficult."

He held her head gently against his chest. "I understand," he said. "All the things we wanted for ourselves and our children, which we won't be around to see."

He held her until her tears ceased. "Come on, let's go back to the car. Tell you what, I'd like it if you'd come to dinner tomorrow evening – the children come round on Thursdays to be fed, one more for place setting won't be a problem. Besides, you can meet my family – and I think they'd like to meet you."

141

She looked up at him again. Impulsively, she raised herself on tip-toes and kissed his cheek.

"You are a dear, sweet man, Seymour. I wish I'd met you years ago."

He grinned. "Years ago, I was a dear, sweet, *married* man."

"I would have been happy to be your 'bit on the side'."

"How interesting! I never had one of those."

She chuckled and shook her head at some private thought. They strolled arm in arm back to the multi-storey carpark.

At the car, she got in first, while Seymour ran his hand over the gleaming paintwork.

"You know, this car is not the most discreet of vehicles," he said.

"Being discreet was not in my mind when I bought it," Harriet said.

He grinned as he got in. "They're going to spot us, casing the joint."

"Let them," she replied, "I don't care. What's to worry about as long as they don't interfere with our getaway. Just what is our getaway plan, Seymour?"

He placed his fingertips together. "Well, I reckon we set a day and time."

She nodded in agreement.

"And then I book a pleasure flight in the helicopter, for the two of us."

"Okay," she said, nodding again.

"Then, we, uh, knock over the bank – I think the term is – and drive off to the heliport, pausing only to drop the money off at the hospice shop."

"And then?"

He shook his head.

" I'll get rid of the pilot of the chopper, and we'll take it."

"How will you get rid of him?"

He raised an eyebrow. "I'll still have my shotgun. Should be easy."

"And then?"

He sighed deeply. "Then we take a trip up to the north coast, turn round over the sea and come back ... I figure a hundred-mile-an-hour smash into the cliffs will see us both off, with no likelihood of either being left alive." He swallowed.

She looked at him. "Will you be able to do that, Seymour? Will you be able to drive it into the cliffs deliberately?"

"Think of the alternative. I will do it, somehow."

She was silent. "I don't know if I could accept that," she said.

"What do you mean?"

She spoke with difficulty, tears running down her cheeks. "Well, it seems to be me that's suffering more," she said, "I have all these aches and pains. I might be due to die before you are. Somehow, I can't cope with the idea that you will kill yourself because of some stupid agreement you made with me."

"You're overlooking the fact that I'm getting quite clumsy as my muscle control fails. I'm not afraid of death," he said, "I believe in an afterlife. Afterwards, apart from you, I believe Sally – my wife – will be waiting for me."

She mopped her eyes and chuckled damply. "So I may yet be your 'bit on the side' – just not in this life."

He smiled.

"It still seems wrong to me," Harriet continued, "that you should die when you could last a bit longer. Why can't you do something else, which will only kill me?"

"Because, my dear, there is no way I could do that. I couldn't kill you and not myself. It's either both of us or neither, and if it's neither, we're condemning ourselves to a lingering and possibly painful death. It wouldn't be a pleasant experience."

She thought about this for a moment.

"Look," he said, "if you want to leave our deaths to nature, we can do this. We don't rob the bank, and we carry on much as we are. Nothing is set in tablets of stone."

"You're making me responsible for your death as well as mine."

"You know the arguments for and against. I will go along with whatever you decide. You should consider the best outcome for both of us."

She stared ahead, then turned the key in the ignition. The engine sprang to life with a throaty roar, which echoed around them from the concrete walls and floors. She backed out of the parking space then headed towards the exit ramp.

There was a look of calm acceptance in her eyes as she drove.

"We'll go and take a look at the bank," she said.

*

Mark heard Kay's footsteps echoing down the hall. He found her in the kitchen, making a pot of tea.

"Is there enough for me?" he asked.

She nodded.

"You're home early," he observed.

"I wasn't concentrating too well. Things on my mind."

"Thinking about your dad?"

She stirred the pot and poured into two mugs.

"He's the last of my relatives."

"I have enough for both of us."

"A couple of uncles and a handful of distant cousins, besides your mother – but they're yours, not mine."

She sat at one end of the table. Mark picked up his mug of tea and sat opposite.

"Does it mean nothing to you that you married me, and you're now part of the Edwards clan?"

"I never thought of it like that," she said, sipping the hot drink.

"I suppose that to anyone used to a small family, we can seem a bit overwhelming - especially when we all assemble at mum's for Christmas."

Kay held her cup in both hands and tapped its patterned surface with her finger nails.

"Has your mother been around again?"

"What makes you think that?" asked Mark.

"There's a cup in the dishwasher with her shade of lipstick on it."

"So what if she has?"

She shrugged. "Oh, nothing special. She just seems to spend a lot of time in our house."

"We talk."

Kay daren't look at him: she kept her eyes on the table top. "What about?"

"Things. Whatever."

"Not about us, then?"

"Sometimes."

She looked up at him. "What do you say to her?"

"Depends what there is to say."

She looked down again. "Do you talk about us? Do you say things to her you don't say to me?"

A patch of colour appeared in his cheeks. "Sometimes."

Kay felt a mixture of shame and anger. "Why? I don't want to be discussed by you and your mother in my absence! What have you said to her about me?"

"Nothing much."

"What?" she demanded, glaring at him.

He shrugged again. "Nothing very serious. I simply observed that I'd seen you peering into prams and push-chairs."

"And what did she say?" Kay studied her cup again.

"She said she thought you were getting broody."

She looked up at him again. "And what did you say to that?"

"That we'd agreed when we got married that we wouldn't have children."

"Is that still how you feel? And please be honest."

"I am always honest with you."

"So – how do you feel?"

He shrugged. "I'd like to know if that's still all right for you."

Kay found she'd been hoping he would announce a change of heart. "Oh," was all she replied. Something cold gripped her heart.

Mark watched her for a moment. Then he smiled and leaned forward, taking her hand.

"What would you say to the idea of us having a baby?"

She stared at his face and its hopeful expression. She felt a pulse of excitement pass through her, then stop.

"I didn't know you'd changed your mind," she said.

He shrugged, keeping the smile. "Well, you know."

"What? What do I know, Mark?"

"Time marches on."

"We said we wouldn't have children. Wasn't it clear enough that time would march on. Are you now saying that you changed your mind?"

He stood up and walked round the table to stand at her shoulder, resting his hands on her.

"Well, I guess I am."

She didn't quite believe him; there had been no hint from him that he was beginning to regret their agreement.

"What would your mother say?" Kay asked, invoking the name of the one person he seemed afraid of. She looked round at him, expecting to see some sign of hesitation, but he simply smiled down into her eyes.

"I'm sure mother would be delighted."

A thought occurred to Kay. "Does your mother already know you were going to bring this matter up?"

He shifted uncomfortably, and returned to his seat.

"She thought it would be a good thing – to have an heir."

Kay's eyebrows rose. "And did she think this was the right time, not too early, not too late, to think about getting on with it?"

He nodded. She thought his smile was nervous.

Kay felt anger rising in her. "You want to get on with it now?" she asked, standing up. "Come on then, you won't mind if we go upstairs only I don't want carpet burns on my back and the kitchen floor's too scratchy."

He looked momentarily shocked, then started to get to his feet. She pounced on him and pushed him back down.

"Don't you dare!" she hissed. "Mark, you are a coward and a mummy's boy! Do you realise how often you accept your mother's edicts? How you always seek her opinion of things and then go round spouting it as if it was yours? I think you are an empty bottle, Mark, and as everyone knows, empty bottles make a lot of noise but have nothing to offer of themselves."

"Look," he said holding his hands face up, "if you don't want children, just say. We made an agreement, I can live with it."

She tilted her head. "Despite what your mother might say? Is she expecting you to report back that your mission is accomplished?"

"No!"

"So she'll be content simply to wait until my pregnancy is announced?"

"Yes, I expect so."

"Well, that's tough! If it had been your idea, and only your idea, I might have agreed to it, but I will not be treated as some kind of... of *project* by your mother."

He shrugged unhappily. "I don't think she intends to interfere. It's just that she's used to having her own way."

"What she does in her own house is her business, but you and she - especially you! - should not be discussing a matter which should be private to the two of us with *anyone* else, including and especially your mother!"

Kay turned and stormed out of the kitchen. A moment later, she put her head round the door and glared at him.

"And from now on, you get to sleep in any of the other bedrooms bar mine."

She made her way up to their bedroom - hers now - and threw herself on the bed, sobbing into the pillow.

Mark stared at the kitchen door as it closed behind her. It wasn't the kind of reaction his mother had warned him he might get. He felt anger rising in him. So she thought he was a mummy's boy, did she! He felt minded to go up to their bedroom - his and her bedroom - and sort her out.

Realistically, he knew he probably couldn't: Kay was no six-stone weakling, she worked out regularly and could pack a punch. Anyway, he thought, you don't solve arguments with women by physical force, you needed a good, strong reason. He realised now it was stupid to have mentioned his mother's interest in a grandchild. If she hadn't said what she had, he would not have dreamt of bringing the matter of children up with Kay. And now she'd banned him from sleeping with her. Well! His mother would have something... He stopped his thought in its tracks. No, mother would not be getting him out of this mess! He would not seek her advice or opinion on anything connected with himself and Kay, ever again.

There was no hurry over the business of having a child - Kay's biological time-out was years away. The best thing, he decided, was to let the matter cool off. Maybe in a few months' time, she'd feel up to discussing it. For a moment, he wondered why they'd ever made the agreement in the first place, but then he recalled his mother telling him it would be a good idea. At that time, it appeared she'd thought that once Kay had an Edwards child, she'd use him or her as a bargaining chip to acquire Edwards assets for herself. From what he'd learned of his wife since their marriage, he knew that such behaviour would never occur to her.

Sometimes, she seemed to have a knack of knowing just what he wanted, and she coped well with his short temper. Time and time again, he'd told himself just how lucky he'd been after he'd done or said something crassly stupid, when she would set him back on his feet, figuratively speaking, with scarcely a mention of whatever he'd done or said. Usually he was very grateful to her for that. Quite often he was also ashamed of how he'd behaved, but she seemed not to notice.

And now he was in deep trouble with Kay; it was all his mother's fault.

*

In the end, so as not to attract too much attention, Harriet had parked her car at some distance from the bank and she and Seymour had reconnoitred on foot. The branch had at some time in its history been an ordinary shop, but the interior had been cleared out and remodelled, producing a small banking hall with just four tills. A door at the far end provided access to the interview rooms, and beyond that into the back office. The banking hall itself was bisected on a diagonal by the one-piece counter, and just inside the street door was a table and two chairs, situated beside a rack containing leaflets advertising the bank's services. All this was visible from the street through the plate-glass windows left over from the building's days as a shop.

It was relatively easy to see what was going on. Harriet and Seymour took a leisurely cream tea in a small tea shop opposite. It was the kind which normally catered for tourists, and consequently neither of them had ever been in it before.

Their conversation was desultory, anxious not to give anything away through careless talk. They'd been there some time, and were on their second cup of tea, when Harriet spoke in a low voice.

"I've been thinking, Seymour," she said.

He looked at her in a sort-of 'rabbit-in-the-headlamps' way.

"What about?"

"Well, you're quite distinguished-looking," she said.

Seymour smiled and inclined his head graciously. "Can't argue with that."

"No. Well, you wouldn't. But I was thinking, when you go into the bank next week –" She leaned close to him to whisper in his ear " – you might consider wearing a wig."

He drew his head back and stared at her. "I don't need a wig: I've got all my own hair – well, most of it."

She smiled. "I was thinking of those fun wigs – you know, the fluorescent green and yellow ones."

"People will think we're Norwich City supporters," he whispered. "We could be arrested."

"I don't think there's a match on early next week, so we should be safe."

"Not if there are any Ipswich fans around at the time."

"Real fans don't embroil themselves in fights, so we'll probably be all right," she assured him.

He sipped his tea.

"Why would we need to worry about disguising ourselves?"

"Mainly so our families don't get hassle from the filth."

"Filth? You mean the police?"

"It's what Eddy calls them."

"It sounds non-PC to me."

She grinned at him. "And non-sergeant, non-DI, non-Chief Superintendent."

"Ha-ha!" he said, his lips twitching.

"I expect he picked the term up from some of his friends. At least he can spell and pronounce it properly now."

Seymour gazed at her wonderingly. "Somehow, I get the feeling that your lessons in English wouldn't pass muster with Her Majesty's Inspectors?"

"All in good time, Seymour. Just for now, the aim is to make them interesting enough that Eddy will keep coming back for more. He's stopped laughing so much when I drill him in proper pronunciation, so I'm making progress."

He smiled and nodded. "That's good. Well done."

She smiled at him sadly. "If only we were going to be around long enough really to do some good."

"Harriet, apart from the act of desecration on my shotgun, we haven't committed ourselves to anything. We don't have to do this."

She shook her head tiredly. "Don't start that again, Seymour. We thought about it earlier, and we have made a decision." She put a hand on his arm and looked closely into his eyes. "Unless you want to change it?"

He took both her hands in his and held them together, shaking his head gently. "No."

She disengaged her hands. "That's all right then. Now where's the local fancy-dress hire shop? The last time I needed one of those was – well, maybe I'll tell you about it sometime, when I know you better." She smiled and they got up to settle their bill.

CHAPTER TEN

Seymour woke early on what he thought of as his last Thursday. He hadn't slept well. If he was honest with himself, he didn't feel on the verge of death, and whatever he'd said to Harriet about it, it was going to require every bit of courage and determination he could summon to drive the helicopter into a cliff. Only the powerful belief that Sally, his dearly beloved wife, would be waiting for him had eventually allowed him enough peace of mind to fall asleep.

As he stood in front of the bathroom mirror over the wash-basin, he studied himself. His face was lined and looking tired. His eyes, usually such a good guide to the condition of the inner person, were clear and bright, almost the same colour as the sky whose reflection he could see through the window behind him. He'd been blond when he was younger, but over time, his hair had become more sandy, and now it was greying, and worse, getting thin on top.

His belly sagged, no longer held in by the abdominal muscles which had once kept it firmly in place, but it scarcely amounted to a paunch, let alone a beer-belly. His arms were thinner than they had been when he was younger, and his chest was – actually, he thought, sucking air in and tightening his tummy muscles to make it stand out, his chest wasn't bad for a man of his age. Nothing a whalebone corset round his middle wouldn't cure, anyway, he thought, dourly. A smile passed across his lips.

Reality imposed itself when he tried to shave: he suddenly lost his grip on the razor, which fell from nerveless fingers into the soapy water in the basin. For quite a long time, he couldn't control the movements of his right hand,

and had to continue to shave with his left. He finished his ablutions, dressed in t-shirt and jeans, and went downstairs to see about some breakfast.

After he'd eaten, he sorted through his collection of compact disc recordings, and selected half a dozen favourites and put one on the music system. It was Mahler's first symphony in a recording by the Berlin Philharmonic Orchestra. He settled back and let the broad sweeping sounds and elegant harmonies sooth his fears about the following Tuesday. Nearly an hour later, as the last chords shimmered their way into silence, he roused himself from his comfortable position, lounging on the sofa, to go into the kitchen and consult his cookbooks. He'd had to learn to cook when Sally became ill, and now could turn out a respectable meal from most recipes, though he had his favourites. He calculated how many were likely to turn up for dinner this Thursday: there would be himself and Harriet, Kay and Mark, and probably David, who might bring a girlfriend if he currently had one. So, he thought, best cater for six to be on the safe side.

He decided to braise some beef in red wine. That would be sufficiently elastic, when one added potatoes and green vegetables, to provide for all those who might turn up. The preparation complete, he sat at the table with a notepad and pen and set down a few suggestions for his funeral.

It was an odd feeling, and he was reminded of Mark Twain who was reported to be dead somewhat in advance of the event. There was the scene in *Tom Sawyer* where Tom turned up at his own funeral, the preacher rapidly changing from downbeat memorial mode to upbeat 'praise the Lords' for resurrecting him.

Seymour bloody-well hoped that God would resurrect him! It is when death is near that faith is most strongly tested, he observed. So he chose some hymns; he even penned a few biographical notes that might fill in some of the things few people – especially his children – knew about him, and then shoved it all in an envelope addressed to Kay and left it in the top of his bureau.

*

David was the first member of the family to appear that evening. A choir's voices soared through the air from Beethoven's *Missa Solemnis* on the music centre, filling the house with thrilling harmonies of the familiar anchor points of the Christian Eucharist, albeit sung in Latin.

"Hi, Dad."

"Hello, son," said Seymour from the kitchen, where he was working on the meal. The meat was already enclosed in a casserole in the oven, bubbling gently in a gravy consisting of most of a bottle of red wine flavoured with marjoram, bay, garlic and tomato purée. "On your own?"

"Dorothea decided to go late-night shopping." David leaned against the kitchen door.

"You know where the drinks are if you want one," said Seymour.

"Yeah, thanks dad." David pulled out a stool at the breakfast bar and watched his father preparing vegetables.

After putting the potatoes in a microwave steamer, he turned to David. "So she's called Dorothea. How long have you known her?"

"A couple of weeks. What're we having?"

"I'm doing a casserole of beef in red wine. Got the recipe out of the book - you know, our local celebrity chef. At least her recipes come out well first time, if you follow her timings and quantities."

David smiled and ran his gaze over the clutter of plates, dishes, and chopping boards. "It smells nice. You're really quite impressive in the kitchen, dad," he said, "Do you miss mum's cooking?"

Seymour shook his head and grinned. "Your mother was a good cook. These days, so am I. I live quite well enough. Cooking is one of life's few joys."

"I'd have thought you'd have taken up golf after you retired."

"I tried to play golf at one point in my life. They said it was easy: all you had to do was strike one small ball in the right direction, using the tiny head of a club five feet long. I found that if I did it would either go in the wrong direction, or roll about two yards and stop – sometimes both." He stopped peeling a potato and looked up, smiling. "One day, I was out there with John Davis, who was showing me how to play, round about the twelfth hole, when the heavens opened and rain and wind descended upon us. It was like one of the seven plagues of Egypt, the rain horizontal, and the wind threatening to send the ball in any direction but the right one, even if I did manage to hit it. I figured I didn't like getting wet that much."

"That's the thing about golfers though, isn't it," said David, "they play in all weathers."

"Which is probably why I'm not a golfer."

David grinned, then his face became more serious.

"Kay says I should ask you about your funeral arrangements."

Seymour looked up at him, a wry expression on his lips.

"The only arrangement you need to worry about is to make sure she reads the little note I've left her in my bureau. I hope you're not disappointed, but I've asked her to sort things out."

He couldn't help but notice how his son's expression lightened as he spoke, and knew he'd made the right decision.

"I'm not disappointed, dad. She'll do it much better than I would."

Seymour straightened up. "And how do you know that? Badly organised many funerals have you?"

"No, of course not. I've not done any, that's what I mean."

"Neither has your sister."

"No, but she'll do it better than I would. I'll help her, of course."

Seymour smiled tightly and bent over the green vegetables. Outside of his own area of interest, he knew, David was quite useless. He'd used to think it was a boy thing, but David had grown into a man and remained as tightly-focused. Seymour wondered if there was any way he and Sally could have brought him up better, but always the question went unanswered. You did what you could, you tried your best. He was on his own now, thought Seymour, and was quite likely to stay that way if he didn't improve his people skills.

The front door opened. He heard Kay's footsteps on the polished timber flooring of the hallway as she came towards the kitchen. She checked when she saw David, and gave him a brief smile before turning to their father.

"Dad, I've brought one extra for dinner. Mark's mother, Violette. Hope you don't mind, I didn't have time to phone you."

Seymour shrugged, left what he was doing and rinsed his hands, drying them before going into the living room to greet his unexpected guest.

Mark was standing attentively beside a woman who was settling herself into an armchair. Seymour recognised her vaguely from Kay and Mark's wedding. She'd been introduced to him at the time, rather formally, as Mrs Edwards, so it was fortunate that Kay had reminded him of her name, because they had never met since. As Seymour watched, she turned to the music centre and caught Mark's eye shaking her head and inclining her head towards the machine, in a clear indication that she wanted it turned off. Without hesitation, Mark acted and the sound of the *Sanctus* was cut off. As he stood up he realised his father-in-law was watching him.

"Oh, hello, Seymour," he said, colouring slightly. "Hope you don't mind, but mother didn't want the music."

Seymour shook his head, his eyes turning once more upon Violette. She was a buxom woman with iron-grey hair tightly permed. Below it, her face was lined, but her eyes and lips were made up, and her cheeks powdered. The lipstick was a slash of bright red against her sallow complexion and made her look stern and unforgiving. She looked up at him very appraisingly.

"Doctor Whittle. How are you?" There was no hint of warmth in her voice.

Seymour, conscious of Kay's eyes on him, attempted a smile of welcome.

"Very well, thank you, Mrs Edwards. Please call me Seymour. How are you?"

"I am well, thank you."

Seymour wondered what had brought her, after all this time, to his house. He studied Mark, who was wearing a faint air of embarrassment, and Kay, whose colour was heightened and who was avoiding his gaze. Trouble at t' mill, he thought.

"Well, if you'll all excuse me, I have to get back to the food," he smiled brightly round the room.

The doorbell rang, and he remembered that Harriet was also invited. What, he wondered, would she make of Mrs Edwards? He went to the door and found her on the step.

"Come in, welcome," he said, standing aside to let her pass him. He took her coat and led her through into the living room. Four pairs of eyes focussed in on Harriet.

"David, Kay, Mark, Violette – Mrs Edwards: this is my friend Harriet Blythe. Harriet - my son David, daughter Kay, her husband, Mark; and this is Mark's mother. Coincidentally, she's here on her first visit, too."

Mrs Edwards regarded him stony-faced, while their children greeted Harriet in a friendly way.

"I was not aware you would have such a houseful of guests," said Violette.

"The children usually come round on Thursdays. It's a leftover from when they were young and single, and poor," Seymour said. "Once they'd left home, Sally and I used to feed them at least once a week to make sure they got at least one square meal, and one they didn't have to buy. The habit stuck, I'm glad to say, though these days they have to put up with my cooking."

Kay smiled at him. "It's not so bad, dad," she said, "Nobody's died of it yet."

She bit her lip at the sudden realisation that their meals with her father might cease quite soon. The smile disappeared from her lips, and she put her hands up to her face, feeling the tears suddenly sting her eyes. Seymour went to her and put his arm round her.

"And nobody's going to die from my cooking tonight," he said softly in her ear. "Tummy aches are possible, but nobody is going to die."

She chuckled damply, and eased herself out of his grip to find a paper tissue. "Sorry, dad," she muttered.

He felt his own eyes moisten and turned away to return to the kitchen. He felt Violette's eyes on him all the time.

Harriet followed him into the kitchen.

"Is there anything I can do, Seymour?" she asked.

He felt grateful for her presence. "Not really," he said, "but please stay and talk. I just have to finish cooking some vegetables then we can all sit down."

She dragged a bar stool out from under the peninsular unit.

"Mrs Edwards wasn't expected," he explained.

"Is there a particular reason why she's come?"

"Not that I'm aware of, exactly. I'd guess there's a problem between Mark and Kay, but why that should be a matter for parents of adult children, I don't know."

He glanced up and caught sight of Violette standing behind Harriet.

"Ah, hello, Mrs Edwards," he said. Harriet turned her head to see. "As you can see, I have all the help I need with dinner." He waved his hand in Harriet's direction.

"I came because I think we need to talk," said Violette, suggesting that she'd overhead his remark.

Seymour paused in the middle of slicing carrots. "Oh? A problem?"

She looked at Harriet for a moment. "In private, if you don't mind."

Harriet jumped. "Sorry. Let me leave you two alone," she said, easing her way past Violette and returning to the living room. Violette closed the door behind her.

Seymour turned back to the carrots. "How can I help you, Mrs Edwards?"

"My son and your daughter are at a low point in their relationship, and I think you should have a word with her."

He felt the first stirrings of anger and fought to control his behaviour.

"What good might that do?" he asked, "and what sort of 'low point' are they at?"

"It would seem that your daughter is not prepared to bring to the marriage the things a wife usually brings."

Seymour smiled thinly. "Do you think you could be a bit more specific? What in your view is she not 'bringing to the marriage'?"

Violette studied him, her expression blank. Her brown eyes came to rest on his.

"A child, Doctor Whittle. The purpose of marriage is to provide a secure environment for two adults to procreate and bring up a family."

"Been there, done that, got the t-shirt."

She pointedly ignored his flippancy.

"Your daughter is refusing my son's reasonable request to have a child."

He shrugged. "Both my children have previous for refusing 'reasonable requests' for all sorts of things. What's the problem now? Anyway, hadn't they decided before they were married not to have children?"

"Five years ago, I certainly was opposed to them breeding," said Violette.

"Now, you've changed your mind?"

"Yes."

"But she hasn't changed hers?"

"Apparently not. It would appear she threw Mark out of their bedroom last night."

Seymour choked and thumped his chest. Violette's forehead darkened and her brows dropped.

"You seem not to be concerned about your daughter's marriage."

"It's got nothing to do with me. They both signed up for better or for worse, and the matter of having a family is up to them. If they have differences of opinion, they have to settle them," he said, "I'm sure you would not advocate bringing a child into a family where the parents are at loggerheads about the child's very existence."

She sighed. "I can see I shall have to deal with the matter myself. I realised that I should be unlikely to receive any assistance from you."

Seymour moved towards her and looked down at her determined face.

"I would strongly advise you to leave well alone. Let them sort out their own problems - they're both adults, and Kay is a sensible girl. I'm sure she had her reasons for throwing Mark out of their bedroom. Probably just one of those arguments married people sometimes have."

"This is easy enough for you to say," she said, drawing herself up to her full five feet four. "You do not have the responsibility for furthering a dynasty."

Seymour tilted his head incredulously. "I beg your pardon? A dynasty? Do you see your son as Rameses the Great?"

"My son is the last male heir of the Edwards line. It is incumbent upon him, and therefore his wife, to have children to ensure the succession," she said.

"I see where you're coming from," said Seymour, nodding. He looked down at her. "It's still nothing to do with us. Mark perhaps needs to make Kay care about – about the 'succession', as you call it, and frankly, I think he'll have an uphill struggle."

She stepped back from him. "Why?"

"I'm only guessing, but I'd say that she won't share your view that it's so important. It's no basis for a decision whether to have a child or not, which is something I'd advise her not to enter into lightly."

"I'm sure when she realises the financial benefits that will come her way when a child is born, she will think again."

"You might be right, though I don't think she will make a decision on that basis. Not if we got her upbringing right."

"She brought nothing to the marriage. My son and I have provided her with all her material benefits, and if I know poor people at all – and I do – she will be keen to acquire all she can."

"She brought love and loyalty to the marriage, Mrs Edwards," said Seymour sternly, "And as far as I can see she's been a good wife to your son."

"She undermines me at every opportunity."

"How?"

"When I suggest to him what he should be doing, she tells him not to listen. The poor boy doesn't know who to believe – his mother, or your daughter, with whom he appears besotted. It's driven him to drink."

Seymour turned back to his chopping board and put the carrots into a microwave dish.

"He shouldn't have to choose between his mother or his wife," he said.

"Of course not!"

"If you continue to interfere – and I've never heard of anyone trying to control their son's life like you are – you will force him to make that choice," said Seymour, "and if he's the man I think he is, he will choose her." He turned to face her again. "My children were brought up to believe that. once they're married, their spouse is their number one priority, bar none. After all, you choose your spouse, you don't choose your parents."

"Perhaps it's different for girls," she said huffily.

"I brought up both son and daughter with the same values," he said.

"And I brought my son up to respect his parents."

"I hope both our children do," said Seymour, "but let's not confuse respect with obedience."

"It's different for a mother. You wouldn't understand."

He smiled at her incredulously. "Did anyone ever tell you you're very manipulative?"

She stared at him. "I see we do not think alike, Doctor Whittle, which saddens me. I can see I shall be alone in trying to make your daughter see sense."

"You'll certainly get no help from me in that," he said.

"Will you actively oppose me?"

"I believe in not interfering between husband and wife, provided they're not trying to harm each other. But obviously, if Kay looks to me for support, what would you expect me to do? I can only advise her, and she can take it or leave it. She knows her own mind."

"Well, thank you for your time, Doctor Whittle." She looked at the ingredients laying around on the worktop and wrinkled her nose. "I understand that you may not be around much longer to encourage your daughter's waywardness. I'm sorry, of course. I think it would be inappropriate to dine with you. I shall ask Mark to take me home."

She turned and left the room. Seymour stared after her, his mouth open in astonishment at what he saw as the woman's gall. Glancing around to make sure everything in the kitchen could be left for a few minutes, he walked through into the hallway. As he reached the living room door, Violette marched out into the hall past him, without appearing to notice he was there. She was followed by Mark, car-keys in hand, and two patches of colour highlighting his cheekbones. He, too, avoided Seymour's eyes. They went through the front door, Mark closing it softly behind him, as if afraid to make it slam.

Seymour entered the living room and noticed that while he had been closeted with Kay's fearsome mother-in-law, David had settled in front of the television, zapping through the channels. Harriet was sitting next to him. She turned to study his face as he came in.

Seymour turned to Kay and caught her eye. He nodded towards the kitchen and returned to it himself. A few seconds later, Kay joined him. She looked apprehensive.

He chucked her under the chin and smiled. "Mrs Edwards says you threw Mark out of the bedroom last night."

"I did," she said unhappily.

"Good for you!"

She looked up and saw only the glint of amusement in his eyes, no censure. She smiled.

"I've banished him from it altogether."

He smiled more broadly. "I expect if you also begin to float around the place in something short and revealing in the right places, you'll soon make him realise that he should be listening to you more than that mother of his."

She chuckled.

"Wait till you see him drooling every time he lays eyes on you, then you'll know he's about ready to do anything you ask him."

She smiled, but Seymour noticed it didn't last.

"What's up, dear? Can I help?" he asked.

"We had a bit of an argument. It seems that Mark is suddenly of the opinion that we should have a baby." She looked up into Seymour's face. "You know we made a kind of agreement when we were married – before then, really – not to have children?"

Seymour nodded. "Obviously not the details, but I think I remember you telling me you weren't intending to have any children."

"Well, it appears that it was Violette's idea. Mark is a good man and knows his own mind most of the time, but seems to have a blind spot when it comes to his mother.

It's a case of whatever mother wants, mother gets, with him."

Seymour put the potatoes into a steamer and set the microwave oven to work.

"For what it's worth, just so's you know," he said while mixing a dressing, "I told her that she would be ill-advised to make Mark choose between herself and you, because I feel that, if he's got anything about him at all – and I think he has – he will choose you."

"Thanks, dad," she said, "What about the matter of whether we should have a baby? What did you say about that?"

"That it's a matter for you and Mark, and nobody else."

"Thanks again."

"I said I felt sure you would both make the decision that was right for you, and it's nothing to do with the rest of us. Did you think," he turned to her, "for one minute that I would support her point of view?"

Kay reached up and put her arms round his neck, kissing him on the cheek.

"No," she whispered. Tears sprang from her eyes again and she pulled herself close to Seymour. "Oh dad! I can't imagine not having you around. What will I do without you?"

Behind her, he saw Harriet emerge from the living room and come towards them. She paused when she saw father and daughter embracing, but Seymour beckoned her in with a nod of his head.

"Without me? You'll be free to order things your own way – just like you do now," he joked. "But you'll have to start cooking on Thursdays."

"Oh, God! This could be our last meal together as a family..." This time her tears flowed fast and unstoppable.

"We're all going to have to be brave in the short term," he said. He felt his own eyes watering as he held his daughter tightly. Harriet, behind her, was also mopping tears from her cheeks. Suddenly David walked in and stared at the tearful trio.

"Is dinner ready yet? I'm starving."

Kay wriggled free from her father's embrace and was surprised to see Harriet.

"Not quite, son," said Seymour, blowing his nose on a tissue, "the casserole'll take about another twenty minutes." He peered at the microwave timer. "Let's go and get everyone a drink," he said, leading the way back into the living room.

The atmosphere over dinner varied from sombre to superficial - from similarities to The Last Supper, to the ups and downs of David's love-life, which seemed to be at a low point again after Dorothea had apparently decided she wanted more out of their relationship than the opportunity to keep his flat clean.

Kay wanted to know about Harriet's life and was interested to learn she had a daughter a few years younger than she was.

"Is she married?"

Harriet shook her head. "I think she's still enjoying the single life," she said, "but I have a feeling those days may be coming to an end."

"She's got a boyfriend then?"

"Yes. He's very nice. Came to see me."

"What does he do?"

"Policeman."

"That would make for an interesting son-in-law," said Kay thoughtfully, "but aren't they a bit unreliable as husbands?"

Harriet nodded. "I think so. But love is blind, they say, so if she still wants him, I presume we can call it love."

Kay nodded. "When are they getting married?"

Harriet shook her head. "I don't think they know. I mean, I don't think they've got round to that, from what I could work out. I think they're at the stage when he's very interested, and she's keeping him at arm's length."

Kay put her knife and fork down and looked at Harriet. "So, there's still some way to go?"

"Oh, I think it's only a matter of time. If I know my daughter, she'll find it very hard to resist for long. I just wish she'd get on with it."

Kay could think of nothing to say in reply to that. After swallowing another mouthful of food, she turned to Harriet again.

"Does your daughter live round here?"

"No. She lives the other side of Cambridge."

"That must be a bit inconvenient."

"It stops her attempting to run my life for me. Also, this way, we like each other, and really enjoy being together when she visits."

Kay laughed. "I hope I meet her one day."

"I'll ask her to send you an invitation to the funeral if we don't get together before."

Kay clapped a hand over her mouth. "Oh! I'm sorry, I didn't – "

Harriet put a hand on her arm. "There's nothing to apologise for. I don't want people worrying about when I'm going to die. It'll happen. When it does, life goes on, if you see what I mean."

"I think so," said Kay, chastened.

She was beginning to feel angry about it all – this nice woman, on the one hand, and her father on the other, neither of them very old, and they were about to die. It was so unfair!

CHAPTER ELEVEN

Mike English was taking some time out to go shopping. He was looking for something he could give Charley, something appropriate, which would let her know he thought a lot about her, but not so magnificent a gift that she'd think it was 'over the top' – there would be time enough for big gestures later, he hoped.

His eye was caught by a collection of jewellery designed around brilliant green peridot. He thought it would look good against Charley's dark red hair. After trying to work out what she'd like, he chose a pair of earrings in a silver mount.

As he turned away from the pay point clutching the small parcel, he almost bumped into a blonde woman. He recognised her at once.

"Kristen! Haven't seen you for ages. How are you?"

Kristen Brook had been a girlfriend two years previously when he'd been a detective constable. The relationship typically had not survived the exigencies of police work.

"Hello, Mike," she replied smiling, her eyes on the package. She looked up. "Still a busy man at work?" There was a slight edge to her voice which he ignored.

"Very. And you? Married yet?"

She grinned wryly. "What do you think? No, I'm footloose and fancy-free," she said. She looked at the package. "Buying something for the wife?"

"No, for a friend."

Kristen moved closer until her breasts lightly brushed his arm. "So you're still footloose and fancy-free, too."

"I don't think I'd agree with that."

"But you don't sound as if you're deeply involved in a relationship, and any man worth his salt would have at least a couple of girls at his beck and call while he's not committed to any."

"You never believed me when we were going out, so I don't expect you to believe me now, but there's only one girl for me, and I'd rather like to keep it that way."

She gazed into his eyes, holding onto his arm and pressing herself against him.

"I know you won't believe this, Mike, but I've changed. I realise what a cow I must have seemed, always assuming you were with another woman when in fact you were simply having to work late." He saw her eyes moisten. "Please tell me it's not too late for me to have a second chance."

"Kristen—" he began, but she interrupted him.

"We parted so suddenly, you know... we didn't give ourselves time to consider properly what we'd already committed ourselves to."

He frowned. "I'm not aware that we'd committed ourselves to anything," he said.

She formed her lips into a little pout and looked at him sideways, under her lashes. "Well, we made love, didn't we? I know it doesn't seem to account for much between youngsters, but between adults, surely it means something more? It did to me."

Mike shook his head. "Sorry, I don't agree. Lots of people, adults included, have sex without it meaning there's a commitment."

She turned to look him squarely in the eyes. "But when they do it without taking precautions against pregnancy, surely then, we're talking long term commitment?"

Mike felt the blood drain from his face. "You told me you were on the pill."

She shrugged and smiled ruefully.

"I was when we met, but somehow I forgot to keep taking it, and to tell you."

"What are you saying, Kristen?"

"What do you think, Mike?" she said softly, her finger-nails picking at imaginary fluff on his sleeve. "We made a baby?"

"What!" He pulled himself free of her.

"I only found out after we'd – we'd broken up," she said. She sniffled.

Mike looked around them for a child. "Where is it? Was it a boy or girl?"

She reached up and kissed him on the cheek. "Bless you, Mike, for your concern. We had a little boy."

He put an arm round her. "I'm sorry, Kristen, but I didn't know. When was he born? Where is he now?"

She blinked back the tears and stepped away from him, her eyes cast down.

"I don't suppose," she said hesitantly, looking up at him beseechingly, "you've time to have a cup of coffee with me, for old times' sake."

He glanced at his watch. He could spare half an hour, but he was meeting Charley later and didn't want to be late.

"Okay. There's a coffee bar just along the street."

She smiled gratefully, and walked beside him.

They chose a table near the window where they could look out on the passers-by. It was ingrained habit for him: he always positioned himself to see what was going on nearby. Kristen had misread his purpose once and accused him of doing it so he could watch other girls walking past. He remembered that occasion now as he sipped his Americano.

"Where's our son?" he asked again, experiencing a strange sensation as he said the words. How could he have a son and not know? He felt the first stirrings of anger. Why had she not told him before?

She looked at him through eyes brimming with tears, and rested a hand on his arm.

"Oh, Mike, I knew you'd care. Believe me, I wondered whether to mention it to you, but I was frightened: I thought you'd be angry, and besides I didn't find out until nearly a month after we broke up."

"But he *was* mine?" he asked anxiously.

She smiled sadly at him. He buried his face in his hands.

While Kristen studied him through eyes suddenly cold and calculating, he saw his life having to change. The existence of a child would probably wreck any future he might have had with Charley. What an absolute mess! he thought.

"For a little boy suddenly to come face to face with a man who says he's his daddy could be very traumatic," she said, "but perhaps if you came to stay with me, like, move in, maybe he would accept it better and I could get the two of you together."

Mike sighed deeply. It was too much. If he had to choose between Charley and his son, he would have to choose the child. But he knew he did not want to resume a relationship with Kristen, and moving in with her was not an option he could consider. He shook his head.

"I can't do that," he told her, "I have a girlfriend. Why can't I simply be introduced to the boy somewhere on neutral territory – say, the park?"

Kristen put her hand on his arm again. "I could be good for you, Mike. I know where we went wrong last time. We'll – I'll get it right this time."

He shook his head again. "This isn't about you and me any more, Kristen. We aren't a couple and never will be, but you can hardly deny me the chance to see my own child and have a say in his upbringing."

She stared at him, two reddish spots of anger appearing in her cheeks. She stood up suddenly.

"Well! Mike English, if there's no future for you and me together, you'll never ever meet your son. Stay away from us!"

She stormed out of the door and disappeared down the street, leaving Mike with his head in his hands. He struggled to pull himself together and went to the counter to pay for the coffees. He was aware of the curious gaze of the waitress and several of the other customers who'd heard at least some of the conversation with Kristen, and hurried out of the shop towards home. He almost collided with Charley.

"Charley!"

She looked at him with tightly-controlled anger. "Oh, hello Mike. I wasn't expecting to see you for another twenty minutes, I was doing a little window shopping."

He looked down at her. "I was, uh... I met an old girlfriend in a shop. We were catching up on old times."

"I noticed." she said. "You seemed to be having quite a heart-to-heart."

"She wanted me to go and live with her. We used to go out a couple of years ago."

"And you were thinking about it?"

"It isn't as simple as that."

She looked a question at him.

He shook his head. "She says I have a son."

Charley's jaw dropped. "Mike!"

"I didn't know."

"Oh, lord!"

"Look – can we go to my place?" he suggested, "I need time to think about this and I can do it better indoors. Will you come with me? It's not far."

"You must be joking!" she said. "If you've got anything to say, you can say it here."

He pursed his lips, twisting them into a sad little grin. "Okay. Come into the coffee shop with me – honest, I'm cold standing around out here!"

"Okay, but this had better be good," she said, in a voice which was intended to show him that he was not forgiven, yet.

They sat at the same table he'd occupied a short while ago and bought coffee.

"Right," he said, in the manner of someone for whom the bell had tolled, "let's get this stuff with Kristen out of the way."

"Yes," she said, "let's. Just what is she to you?"

He looked at her directly. "Nothing. Nothing at all. I haven't seen her since we broke up, and she says she didn't find out she was pregnant until almost a month after we did."

She studied his face for a moment without speaking.

"It's not something I can do anything about now," he said sadly.

She thought for a moment. "You only have Kristen's word on this?"

It was his turn to stare at her. "Yes." He frowned. "Why?"

Charley rolled her eyes. "I'll let you into a secret: some women can be a bit spiteful, and have long memories. One of the easiest things we can do to a man is cause him to feel guilty."

"But why would she do that? We parted amicably enough."

She looked pityingly at him. "That's a bit more compli-cated to explain, but believe me, she might have been very pissed off with you when you split up and simply con-cealed the fact at the time."

He shook his head in bafflement. "I don't understand."

"You feel guilt now, don't you?"

"Uh, yes."

"Then she's paid you back for however much she felt hurt when you and she parted company."

Mike stared at her in dawning comprehension. "You mean, it's possible there was never a child?"

She smiled briefly. "Eureka. Road to Damascus. A new epiphany dawns."

"But there could be?"

Charley groaned. "Yeah. You haven't been listening. Did she look like a woman who is bringing up a child?"

"No."

"You ever seen the child?"

"No. She said it would be... traumatic for him to meet me, unless I moved in with her."

"But she refused to let you meet him if you didn't?"

"Yes. I told her I couldn't. I said we – she and I – had no future together, but that I wanted to meet the boy. She refused."

"You refused to live with her, even though it was the only way she'd let you meet the boy?"

He looked at her. "Yes."

"Then believe me, you're probably fairly safe in assuming she was not being truthful."

"So you think I'm not a father?"

"No."

"I was just getting used to the idea."

"Well, get un-used to it."

He gave her a sudden appraising look.

"How would you feel —"

"Don't begin to go there!" she interrupted.

He looked at her wryly. "I want us to be an item again. A proper, long-term, one. I told you that there will be times I have to put the job first. I will break dates, sometimes I might not be able to tell you, and I've no doubt you will be very angry with me from time to time. Believe me, I won't do any of these things lightly – I didn't then. If there's any way I can convince you that (a) I don't want any other women in my life, and (b) I'll never upset an arrangement or break a date if it's not absolutely unavoidable, then tell me." He took her hand in his and looked at her through guileless brown eyes.

Charley sipped her coffee again, studying him over the lip of her mug.

"Okay, Mike. The bad news is, I can be fairly possessive myself, and if I ever catch you in a relationship with another woman who is not a member of your family, you won't see me for dust. Is that okay?"

He nodded, grinning. "Fine - and just remember, it cuts both ways."

"Well, I'm glad we've got that little matter out of the way."

"So you're my girl again?"

"Yes." She smiled. "Apart from one little question."

"What?"

"You never mentioned Kristen to me last time we were supposed to be going out together. Why?"

"I didn't think you'd be interested in my old girl-friends," he replied, "and she and I were finished long before I met you."

"Maybe I wasn't," she said, conceding he might have a point. She took a mouthful of her latte.

"Good. Uh, I have something which I bought for you, burning a hole in my pocket, but I'd rather give it to you someplace private. Now we've cleared the air, so to speak, will you come to my place? It's not far."

She studied him for a moment before making up her mind.

"Hmm!" she sniffed, trying to sound severe. "All right, then, show me your castle."

"Hardly that," he grinned.

They finished their coffee and he led her to a new apartment block overlooking the river. It was, as he'd said, close to the town centre and they reached it in a few minutes. A lift, which Charley guessed had never malfunctioned in its life, elevated them to the fifth floor. He turned the key in his door and stood aside to let her precede him through the vestibule into the main living area.

She found herself in an open-plan lounge, with large windows overlooking both castle and cathedral, furnished with a large three-piece suite in white leather with oak feet and trim. The floor was polished timber with a couple of scatter rugs. In the far corner stood a baby grand piano, whilst in the nearer corner stood a large television with a flat screen, satellite receiver and DVD recorder. Loudspeakers for surround sound were attached at appropriate points round the room. Three light fittings interspaced with paintings provided interest on the long wall facing the windows, with one more fitting flanked by two more paintings on each of the shorter walls at either end of the room.

In short, Charley concluded, the room was tastefully decorated with lots of attractive space. Not much of anything, but the high quality of it all stood out. She'd glimpsed other rooms through part-open doors just inside the little vestibule, and knew he had used one room for his computer - probably a sort of 'den', she thought, while another was a sizeable bedroom. On the other side of the vestibule had been a large kitchen-dining room and a bathroom.

He waved her to a seat in the lounge.

"Let me get some coffee, then we can talk," he said.

"Okay," Charley nodded, her eye caught by one of the paintings.

He followed her gaze. "It's a print of 'The Death of Nelson' by Arthur William Devis," he said. "I could have had an original oil painting of Cambridge Science Park, somewhat nearer home, for less, but I decided that I liked the Devis picture better."

She nodded and walked over to the piano, running her fingertips across the smooth keys. "Do you play?"

"A bit. Not very well, but I find it very therapeutic."

"Will you play something for me?"

"Maybe. Coffee first. I'll see, while it's brewing."

He went into the kitchen area. Charley followed him.

This floor was tiled in textured ceramic, and at the far end the centre of the floor was taken up with a small island containing a gas hob and stainless-steel work-surfaces, together with a small double sink. Overhead was a rack with an integrated cooker hood over the hob, and hooks from which kitchen utensils dangled within easy reach. Around the walls were more cupboards and work-surfaces, these apparently made from oak, and a large American-style fridge-freezer filled the corner by a wide window which ran along much of the outside wall. It was, Charley concluded, a practical yet stylish kitchen. She wondered how much he used it.

He was filling the coffee machine with filtered water, and glanced round when she came in.

"In case you were wondering," he said, "I had some help from my parents, plus a fairly large mortgage."

"Just so I'm not too impressed with your material possessions," she smiled.

"I don't want you to get the wrong idea about me, over anything," he said as he flicked the switch. He walked towards her. "Come on, I'll see if I can impress you with my piano-playing. Any chance you're deaf in both ears? It helps, I believe."

They went back into the lounge and he sat at the piano. After a moment's thought, he played Hoagy Carmichael and George Gershwin before closing the lid and going to fetch the coffee.

Charley was suitably impressed. It occurred to her that he might well sing, too. She wondered how well they'd have to get to know each-other before he let her find out.

He brought two mugs through from the kitchen and set them down on a small coffee table between them. He took one end of the settee while Charley sat at right-angles to him in an armchair.

He felt in his jacket pocket for the small packet he'd bought in the jeweller's.

"I thought you might like these," he said, holding it out to her. She looked into his eyes, her own widening with delight, and took the packet, opening it carefully. With the presentation box in one hand and the other poised to lift the lid, she glanced shyly at him. Opening it, she sucked in her breath.

"Oh, Mike, they're lovely," she said, picking an earring out and letting the opalescent, green peridot reflect the sunlight coming through the window. "I must try them on."

"There's a mirror in the bathroom," he said.

She got to her feet and followed his pointing finger.

It was much as she expected; finely, even luxuriously, appointed. The mirror was also the door to a recessed cabinet over the washbasin. She opened it quietly and had a look inside. Shampoo and shower gel, shaving stuff and electric toothbrush. There was a strong smell of aftershave clinging to the inside of the cabinet, most probably explained by a bottle of *Opium*. No sign of condoms, so presumably he kept them elsewhere. She removed her pearl studs and popped the new earrings in, closing the cabinet door to see how they looked in the mirror. Pleased, she returned to the lounge, the new earrings catching the light as they moved.

Mike stood up as she entered. She went to him so he could have a look at them *in situ*. He slipped one hand against her cheek and the other round her waist. His eyes were fixed on hers. She suddenly felt weak in his arms and leaned against him. Heat formed deep in her, and began to spread upwards and outwards. She felt blood filling her lips and raising the colour in her cheeks.

"You look so beautiful, Charley," he said thickly before he turned his head slightly and captured her lips in his.

She felt him pull her towards him so she could feel his arousal, but didn't feel quite ready for the intimacy he seemed to be demanding. Gently she eased herself away from him.

He broke the kiss.

"What's the matter, my love?" he murmured in her ear.

"We can't!" she gasped. "I'm not on the Pill."

He lifted his head away so he could look at her.

"You're right. Stay here. I've got some condoms in the bathroom, I think."

She shook her head. "Not in the cabinet you haven't. I looked."

He looked at her, distracted. "In my bathroom cabinet?"

"Yes. Sorry. Incurably nosey."

He stared at her for a moment before shaking his head.

"I cannot believe I haven't any bloody condoms," he muttered.

"Perhaps you get through more than you think," she said in a kindly voice.

"I haven't slept with anyone since we went out before," he said, and added wryly, "and if I remember rightly, we didn't sleep together then."

"I think you're right. I feel sure I would have remembered, judging by what I detected lurking in your trousers," she said.

He screwed up his face. "Maybe I threw them out. Past their shelf-life, I think."

She stood up. "Good job we still had one functioning brain between us."

"You've been listening to the feminist propaganda that says men don't have enough blood to work their penis and brain at the same time," he accused.

"Seems to be true, doesn't it." She picked up her handbag and watched as Mike got to his feet and fastened his shirt, tucking it back in his waistband.

*

Charley took the rest of Friday off work and decided to visit her mother. Mike had had to return to the police station, still muttering about his lack of foresight. She'd been amused, and told herself that at least he hadn't really planned to seduce her. She wondered if he would be surprised when they did finally get it together to discover he was her first. She had little doubt that soon, they would. She reflected that last time they'd gone out together she'd been somewhat hasty in dumping him.

The road to Breydon was mostly dual carriageway, and she made good time. She really should have taken more days off work in the circumstances, she told herself, but work was good for her, preventing her moping about what she could do nothing to stop. Nevertheless, she might be able to make her mother's last days easier. Somewhere lurking at the back of her mind was the guilty knowledge that she had never repaid Harriet for all that she had done and sacrificed in order that she, Charley, could have as normal a life as was possible with only one parent and not much money for them to live on.

She gritted her teeth as she drove into the parking square at the foot of the tower block where Harriet lived. Her mother's car, still gleaming with polish and with a wheel still at each corner, was parked in its usual spot. It seemed to have a charmed life, probably, Charley thought, something to do with her mother's friendly relationship with Eddy, whose word seemed to be law.

Charley tried the lift call button, but there was no sign of a response. After waiting a couple of minutes she began to make her way up the stairs. On the last flight before the third floor, a man in overalls was using a long-handled brush and some chemical in a bucket in an attempt to remove some of the graffiti which adorned the walls. As she reached the landing outside her mother's flat, she became aware that there were other people in council overalls appearing on several of the landings she could see on the other side of the square. It was odd, she thought, because she hadn't noticed any council trucks or vans when she'd parked.

She knocked on Harriet's door and let herself in.

"Hi, mum," she called, looking around for Harriet.

Harriet was in the kitchen, sitting with her legs apart and her head between her knees on one of the kitchen chairs.

"Oh, Charley," she groaned.

Charley flew to her side. "Mum! What's the matter?" She crouched next to Harriet and put her arms round her.

Harriet was sucking in deep breaths. "I'm sorry, love, I just came over all funny," she gasped.

"Oh, Mum!" Charley hugged her tightly, as if this alone could make her right.

Harriet gradually sat herself up and shook her head to clear it.

"Ooh! That was a bit unpleasant."

Charley bit her lip. Was it a sign that her mother wasn't going to see the week out?

"Shall I make us some tea, mum?" she asked, wanting to be doing something which hid her face from Harriet in case it gave away her thoughts.

Harriet looked at her daughter's back as she filled the kettle at the sink.

"I've been baking, dear. Thought I'd try something a bit different. Lots of orange zest in them."

Harriet dropped her gaze and pursed her lips. "I'd keep off the ones with chocolate icing, if I were you."

Charley was sitting down again. She grinned. "So you can have all the chocolate ones yourself? Hah!"

She caught her mother's eye. Something in her expression made Charley stop and think. She looked at the chocolate-iced cupcakes, then at the pink strawberry-iced ones, then back at her mother, who was shifting uncomfortably on her seat.

"What is it about the chocolate-iced ones?" she asked.

As she finished speaking there was a loud and peremptory knock at the door.

"Police!" shouted a male voice, "Open up or we'll knock the door down!"

Harriet and Charley stared at each other, wide-eyed. Harriet answered the door.

On the step was a group of uniformed officers, wearing helmets and stab vests with the word 'Police' emblazoned across them. As Harriet opened the door, they pushed her back into the room. Another person in a raincoat, holding a handkerchief up to his face came in behind them and waved a piece of folded paper in Harriet's face.

"I've got a warrant to search this address," he told her, punctuating his sentence with a sneeze.

Harriet was staring at him, horrified, her hands up to her face.

"Wh-what for?"

"Drugs. We have reason to believe that you're dealing drugs to all the kids round here."

Charley appeared at the kitchen door.

"What rubbish," she said, " And where's your warrant card?"

The man in the raincoat identified himself as Detective Sergeant Walmsley of Breydon Drugs Squad.

"And who might you be, miss?" he asked Charley.

"Her daughter," she replied indicating Harriet.

"Both of you: sit down please." He pointed at the settee.

Charley forced herself to smile. She'd hastily sprayed the kitchen with the odour-killer her mother had bought after Mike's hint about the smell of cannabis, and now managed a quick squirt around the living room. It seemed as if the detective's cold was also working to his disadvantage.

"Do you mind if I bring our tea through, we were just having a cup – my mother's ill, you know, and has just had two nasty shocks."

"All right," said Walmsley, watching carefully as Charley retreated into the kitchen and reappeared with a tray bearing two mugs and a small plate on which were two strawberry-iced cupcakes. She carried it over to where Harriet was sitting - almost collapsing - down onto the settee. She passed one of the mugs to her mother and kept the other herself. Each of them picked up a cupcake. Charley invited the detective sergeant to sit down while the uniformed police officers were searching the rest of the flat.

"Now, what gives you the daft idea that my mother could be involved with drug dealing?" she asked.

"How many other people do you know live in a tower block and have a rather flash sports car – and associate with a known dealer."

Charley looked a question.

"Eddy Washington: black kid lives on the eighth floor."

"Is he a drugs dealer?"

Walmsley screwed up his face in a 'don't give me that' sort of look.

"Just a bit. Supplies most of the kids round here with weed and Es, and probably some other stuff as well."

"Poor Eddy," interjected Harriet.

Walmsley scoffed at her sympathy. "Don't give me that 'poor Eddy' nonsense," he retorted. "When we've interviewed you, we'll find out just how involved with him you are."

Harriet's eyebrows lifted. "But I can tell you that now," she said.

"Oh, yeah?"

"Yes. It's quite simple really."

"Amaze me with it," said Walmsley, sitting back and crossing his legs.

"I'm a supply teacher, between contracts at the moment – as my daughter told you, I'm quite ill – but Eddy has been coming to me for lessons in reading, writing and speaking. He missed out on quite a lot of school, he tells me —"

"It happens when you're put in a Young Offenders' Institution," muttered Walmsley.

Harriet continued, "...and wanted to improve his prospects. I offered to help. You will no doubt find the reading and exercise books we've been using – they're on that book-case." She pointed past the detective's shoulder.

He turned and saw half a dozen reading books aimed at very young children, and the exercise books. Picking them up, he leafed through them.

"This stuff in here: my kids read it when they were about eight. Eddy's fifteen."

"Yes, but he's at around key stage two, which is what those books are aimed at."

Walmsley stared at her. Behind the settee, the three officers who had been searching the place assembled one by one. The sergeant looked up. They shook their heads.

"Nothing, Sarge."

"Nothing," said the second. The third emerged from the kitchen, shaking her head. Charley noticed the woman had picked up one of the chocolate cup-cakes. She glanced at Harriet, who saw, too, and bowed her head, covering her face with her hands.

"Nothing in the kitchen, Sarge," said the woman, licking icing off her fingers. She glanced at Harriet and Charley. "Very nice cakes," she said, "hope you don't mind – I just love chocolate icing."

Walmsley looked back at the two women in front of him.

"Does that mean you have no evidence against us?" asked Charley.

"The car."

"I've always wanted a sports car before I die," said Harriet.

Walmsley scoffed. "Yeah, don't we all!"

Harriet bit her lip. "According to Doctor Millington at the hospital, I am suffering from a cancer and am likely to die quite soon."

"That's why she bought the car," added Charley.

"Yeah? And paid for it with what?"

"A credit card," supplied Harriet, looking down at her knees.

"Oh! I suppose the garage just swiped it through and that was that?"

"It's a Platinum card, with quite a big credit limit," she said.

"You can prove this, I suppose?"

"If you let me go into my bedroom, I can show you the receipts from the dealership."

One of the constables behind her shifted on the balls of his feet. He cleared his throat.

"What?" demanded Walmsley.

"I saw them, Sarge."

"And you didn't think to mention it?"

"Well, I thought you'd want to talk to the prisoners first."

Charley stared at Walmsley, a look which he correctly interpreted and hastened to deal with.

"They're not prisoners, Clough. Just suspects." He dropped his gaze to Harriet and Charley. "Well, they *were* suspects." He stood up suddenly. "Right, then, we'll be going." He eyed the two mugs of tea.

"I don't suppose..."

Charley shrugged. "Make yourself at home, why don't you!"

"Thanks," said Walmsley, beaming. He nodded at the officer with the cupcake. "Four teas, Mary, quick as you like." He glanced at Charley. "Any more of those cakes? I'm a bit partial to chocolate, myself."

Charley nodded faintly. "Th-there's several. Help yourself, do."

Walmsley beamed again. "It's very good of you to take our, uh, visit so well."

Harriet peered at him through her fingers. "Oh, drop in any time!" she said faintly.

"Thanks, uh, Mrs Blythe. May I call you Harriet?"

She nodded, unable to speak. Her shoulders shook. Mary, the police woman, came through from the kitchen with mugs of tea and a plate of chocolate-iced cupcakes. Walmsley and the other officers fell upon the refreshments.

"Interesting flavour," said Mary, "did you put something in the mix?"

Harriet began to choke. Charley patted her back while smiling at the officer.

"I've no idea. Bit of an experimental cook, my mother," she said.

"Tastes familiar," Mary persisted, screwing her face up with the effort of trying to recognise the unusual flavour.

"I know what you're saying," said Walmsley, "it *is* familiar, isn't it." He looked at Harriet. Charley's heart sank. "Very nice, though, Harriet." He looked around: everyone had finished their tea and all the cupcakes had gone.

Please go! thought Charley. Harriet was moaning softly, next to her. Walmsley leaned forward, touched her arm.

"Are you okay, Harriet?"

She peered up at him. "I just need one of my tablets."

Charley stood up and went to the sideboard where her mother's prescription drugs were kept. She passed them to Harriet.

Walmsley stood up. "Well, we'd better be going. Thanks for your co-operation, Harriet – and, uh?"

"Charley," Charley supplied.

"Charley." He beamed, and the police team trouped out of the flat.

Charley shut the door behind them and turned to face Harriet.

"What was it with the chocolate cupcakes?" she asked.

"I didn't like cannabis tea," said Harriet, "and Eddy said I could chop it up small and bake it into cakes." She looked gloomy. "I suppose the orange zest disguised the flavour."

"Sod the flavour, mother, how long before the effects kick in?"

Harriet shrugged. "I don't know. What's worse," she added, "is that I didn't get to try any of the chocolate ones myself."

"Mother! That stuff's bad for you," she said.

"Okay, sure," said Harriet, grinning. "Why don't you sit down and tell me all about you and Detective Sergeant English, or Mike as he is known and loved."

"Loved?" echoed Charley.

"Well, I think you love him, don't you, pet."

"I'm thinking about it."

Harriet punched her playfully. "Aw, you can't fool your old Mum!"

"I take it you're one of his fans?"

"If I was a few years younger and near enough to get my hands on him..." Harriet said dreamily, a faraway look in her eyes.

Charley shook her head, amused. "You'd what? You've never competed for a bloke in your life."

Harriet laid her head back against the cushion. "Don't be too sure. Just because I'm your mother doesn't mean I haven't... uh... had my moments."

"I really don't want to know."

"Some of them, you wouldn't believe," Harriet continued reminiscently.

"Mother! Shut up!"

Harriet smiled and tapped her nose. "I know how many beans make five, my girl," she said.

Charley looked at her with wry exasperation before she got to her feet and took the mugs and plates through into the kitchen.

CHAPTER TWELVE

When Seymour stepped out of his house on Saturday morning, he was surprised to see Charley squeezed into the space behind the seats of her mother's car.

"Hello, Seymour. Hop in and I'll take you for your flying lesson," said Harriet.

"Morning Harriet, Charley," he said as he lowered his length into the seat beside Harriet. "How are you, my dear?" he asked her.

"Doped up to the eyeballs," she replied as she steered away from the kerb. Shooting a quick glance at him, she elucidated, "On the dope the hospital prescribed, in case you were wondering."

"Ah," he said, nodding his head. "Think you'll last until whenever?"

She glanced at him again, then at Charley through the rear-view mirror. "I should think so. It doesn't seem to be getting much worse."

"I wish you two would stop that!" Charley cried from behind them. "Stop talking about dying so casually!"

Seymour turned until he could see her. "Sorry, Charley, but we won't – we refuse! – to get maudlin about it."

"But don't you care?" she demanded, feeling the tears springing to her eyes.

"Charley!" said Harriet sternly, "Stop crying. You can cry later, when I'm not around to watch, but just now, it's very depressing."

Charley fumbled in her handbag for a paper handkerchief. Mike's linen one was still in there, still unwashed, but she wanted the comfort of his scent, so she dabbed her eyes and cleared her nose with it again.

"Sorry," she sniffed. She swallowed hard then tried a smile. "How are your flying lessons going, Seymour?" she asked. "I'm kind-of puzzled why you want them, in view of... of next week."

He shrugged. "Just something I've always wanted to do, Charley," he replied, "like your mum wanted this car, and to try cannabis. There are one or two more things to do before we go."

"Such as?" she asked, but he would only reply by tapping the side of his nose and winking at her.

"That's for us to know, and you to wonder about," he said, mischievously.

The arrived at the heliport, and Harriet drove in a circle round the car park.

"What's today's lesson, dear?" she asked.

"The object of today's lesson," he said as if reciting from a book, "is to take off successfully, without help from the CFI."

"An important one! Good luck," said Harriet, leaning over to brush his cheek with her lips.

"See you later," said Charley as he climbed out of the car and she hiked up her short skirt to climb over the seats into the space vacated by him, giving the Air Traffic Controller in his tower, who had been admiring the sports car through his binoculars, an unexpected bonus.

*

Kay was still trying to sort out her relationship with Mark after their argument. She'd left the house early and walked down to the river which flowed round the northern perimeter of Breydon. Traffic noise was attenuated there, and a modicum of peaceful tranquillity could be found. In a small arbour planted on the river bank, a thoughtful council had placed a bench many years ago. The paintwork on its S-shaped wrought-iron end formers and the wooden laths which ran between them were cracked, but years of use had polished the wood smooth. A swan, followed by her early brood in line astern, floated serenely across the quiet waters towards her, familiar with the idea that many people used the bench from which they provided food.

Kay had brought a bag of stale bread with her. She broke it into pieces in the bag and threw the crumbs towards the mother and her young. It brought her mind back to the idea of whether she should have a baby with Mark. There were two matters for consideration. The first was fairly easy to answer: at some time in the last five years, she had gone off the idea of never having children, and in her concept of a normal situation, she would have been pleased if her husband had simply suggested they throw out their old agreement and make a baby.

It was the second matter which was causing her much heartache. Did she want a baby because Mark's mother seemed to think it was about time? And the answer to that was an emphatic no. Something as intimate and personal as whether and when to start a family was a matter, she thought, solely for the prospective parents.

In the end she decided that if Mark was going to pay more attention to his mother than to her, she would leave him. She felt a sense of peace, having come to this decision, although her heart was heavy. She hadn't married Mark with any idea of leaving him. She told herself she should have realised beforehand that he was still tethered umbilically to Violette. So now, she had to tell him he must choose between her or his mother. She was certain which way he would opt.

She returned home, still thoughtful, to find Violette's car parked in the turning circle in front of it. Kay's heart sank: she was not up to facing down Violette this morning, she wanted to get her husband alone. Well, what she wanted to tell him could wait, she thought, as she climbed the eight steps to the front door and let herself in.

The entrance hall was panelled in oak, with the study and library off to one side, the drawing room to the other, and at the rear, a dining room and door to the kitchen – once upon a time, to the servants' quarters. A beautiful staircase swept down the far wall over the kitchen door, to turn and reach the ground just in front of the drawing room. As it reached the floor, the bottom three steps broadened and angled into the space where she was standing.

She stood for a moment after closing the door, to listen for the sound of voices. She wanted an idea of where her mother-in-law was so she wasn't surprised by her. Suddenly, she heard Mark's raised voice.

"No! It's not up to me!" He dropped his voice and spoke too quietly for Kay to hear.

She went trepidatiously towards the study door. As she reached it, it was wrenched open by Violette who stopped when she saw Kay outside.

"Been eavesdropping, have you?" her complexion was livid.

"I've only just come in," said Kay, wondering what was the cause of her anger.

"Hmm!" said Violette, slamming the door and storming past her, out of the house.

Kay opened the door of the study gently and let herself in. Mark was sitting in his swivel chair in front of his computer work-station. His face was ashen, apart from two red spots on his cheek-bones. He looked up, seemingly furious, until he saw Kay, when the fury dissipated and he seemed to collapse in on himself.

"Oh! Hi!" he said.

Kay walked slowly towards him. "What's the matter, Mark?"

He pursed his lips, looking annoyed. "My mother is the matter!"

Kay privately agreed with him, but now wasn't the time to say so. She sat in an old leather armchair facing him.

"What's she done or said?"

He chewed on his lip a moment. "I need a drink," he said, getting up and going to a small drinks cabinet he kept next to a bookcase. "Want one?"

"It's a bit early... but, yes. Scotch and water, please."

He poured a generous measure of Bell's into each glass and followed it with a little water.

"Here," he said, bringing one to her before resuming his seat.

She sipped before she prompted, "Your mother?"

"We've just had an argument," he began.

"I heard the end of it. What was it about?"

He dropped his gaze and frowned. "I'm not sure I want to go into it."

"Why not? Can't I help?"

He stared at her, his face working, as if he was trying to make an impossible choice. He shook his head and closed his eyes.

"No. You can't!"

She sipped her drink and watched him over the rim of her glass. This was very uncharacteristic behaviour for him. She was accustomed to his being moody or selfish, not defeated, as he seemed now. If she'd been feeling more in charity with him, she might have felt more sympathy: he was apparently struggling with something he was not accustomed to dealing with, and she guessed he and his mother must have had a major difference of opinion – not something they'd had before. Violette must be feeling... odd, as well, Kay thought. She wasn't used to her son arguing with her.

She felt rising curiosity. Just *what* had they argued over? Getting Mark to tell her was going to prove difficult. She swallowed another draught of the fine Scottish spirit and put her glass down.

Leaning forward, she said, "If you're not going to tell me what's bothering you, perhaps I can tell you what's bothering me."

Mark looked up and found her green gaze on him. Not for the first time did the image of a cat come into his mind when confronted by those almond-shaped eyes and finely-drawn brows. She had a small nose and Cupid's Bow lips which increased the effect. He felt a twinge of fear. She often had that effect on him, and just now, after their major argument of the night before, he was particularly concerned at what she might be intending to do. Matters were made worse by the row with his mother. His normal response, to bridge the gap in his comfort until he and his mother should be reconciled, would have been to bully or cajole her, or whatever else it took for him to feel better, but now he dare not admit his neediness in case she took the opportunity to punish him even more than he felt he already had been. His mother had told him, on many occasions, that he should behave like a man; and yet, she'd skilfully kept him attached to her apron-strings. Now he was cast adrift and desperate for an anchor, and the taunt about his lack of manliness was a gauntlet waiting to be picked up.

"Go on, then," he said, inwardly wondering when he had opened Pandora's Box.

"I think it's time you made a choice," she began.

He swallowed. This sounded so much like what his mother had told him. He wetted his lips with the scotch and waited for her to continue.

"I've had a long think about our argument," she said, "and I've decided I can't continue to live here if you are going to take your mother's side whenever she sticks her nose into our business, and if you are going to discuss matters which concern only the two of us with her."

She kept her gaze on him unflinchingly. He averted his until he was staring blindly at the glass in his hand.

"What do you want to do?" he whispered.

"What I want to do is to have a normal married life," she replied. "I fell in love with a man, not his fortune or family, but I didn't realise just how different his idea of marriage was from my own."

Mark felt a flush of embarrassment stealing over him.

Kay looked at him for a moment. "Well? Have you nothing to say?" she demanded.

"I thought I was a man."

She stared at him. "I'm not talking about your biology."

"No, you don't understand! I thought I was *being* a man."

She sighed. "Have you any idea how much you've changed since we got married?"

"No. How have I changed?"

She got up and began to pace round the room. "When we first married," she began, wondering how best to phrase her complaint, "you didn't seem to rely on – your mother – like you do now. You seem to consult her about... anything that needs a decision. You used to make up your own mind: now you seem less willing to do so."

"I'm quite capable of making my own mind up on anything," he said, but he could hear the bluster in his own voice.

Her accusation that he was not manly rankled, not least because he knew, somewhere in his heart, that it was true. A quick review of the last year or so showed him how often – and it was nearly always – he wouldn't take a decision until after he'd discussed the matter with his mother.

"Are you sure it's *you* making up your mind, and not your mother?" asked Kay quietly.

He wouldn't look at her, merely shaking his head. "I talk to her occasionally," he said, "and quite often get her views first, but I always make my mind up then."

He caught the look of disbelief in her eyes. He responded with a flash of anger.

"Why don't you believe me?"

"Do you really have to ask?" she countered.

He gritted his teeth. This wasn't how it was supposed to be: his father had never been spoken to like this by his mother. She'd known her place, and – and... His churning thoughts ground to a halt. His father had been dead for over twenty years. He'd been a child when it had happened. Perhaps it was just possible, he grudgingly admitted to himself, that he had not, as a six- or seven-year-old, been truly aware of the relationship between his father and mother. One thing was sure: she'd had long enough since then to emerge from his shadow, if ever she'd been in it, and she was never short of an opinion today. Whereas, he often was.

This revelation shocked him, but as he thought more about it, he realised that his views on all the important things were shaped by his mother. He chewed on his lip, and couldn't face Kay. A terrible sense of shame settled about him: he knew – he was certain – suddenly, that she was right about his failure to fulfil his role as husband, the male half of the partnership.

"Oh!" he gasped involuntarily, clapping a hand over his mouth while staring wide-eyed at Kay. He almost ran from the room, leaving her astonished, staring after him.

She found him some time later, curled up on the bed in the spare room to which he'd moved after she banned him from her bed. She realised he was going through some kind of cathartic crisis, and hoped sincerely that he would soon come out of it. She couldn't guess what had gone through his mind, but clearly something he found difficult to accept had obviously had a powerful effect on him. It was a shock to her that he should break down as he had.

She sat on the quilt, one hand stroking his head gently, in the hope of bringing peace and tranquillity to his obviously tortured soul. She worried that she had gone too far, perhaps getting her point across too bluntly, yet she was sure it needed saying – and there was more she'd like to say, but to present him with the ultimatum of choosing between her or his mother at this time would be just too cruel. She would wait until a more auspicious moment.

Suddenly he sat himself upright, still avoiding her eyes.

"Kay, I'm sorry. I shouldn't have behaved like that," he said.

She shrugged. "Are you feeling all right now?"

"Yes, better, thanks." At last he lifted his gaze to her face. He tilted his head slightly and studied her features.

"Have you ever heard of the strange effect of very beautiful women on some men?" he asked.

She lifted an eyebrow and half-smiled, wondering what he was thinking. "No. I wasn't aware that men might find beautiful women a problem – unless it's simply a matter of stamina."

He smiled, a trifle nervously. "Have you never realised that beautiful women – like you – overawe men – me?"

She chuckled, feeling a blush bloom in her cheeks. "What are you talking about?"

"So, don't you see? I always have this idea at the back of my mind that I have to try really hard to impress you."

"You don't have to impress me, Mark. What are you thinking?"

He stared at her frustratedly. "But I feel I must! You could so easily find a better man somewhere else."

She still floundered over his meaning. "Why would I do that?" She suddenly recollected that she had considered leaving him an hour or so ago, but now was not the time to mention it.

He clenched his fists in the air and grunted with his inability to make her understand. She reached out to him and drew him to her, cradling him against her. As she did, she suddenly understood, and chuckled throatily.

"Oh, Mark! Are you trying to say that you think I'm one of these women who overawes men? That I overawe you?" she asked, shaking her head with the ridiculousness of the thought.

"What do you think I'm saying!" he retorted, his voice muffled because his lips were in the valley between her breasts.

"But I'm not like that," she said. "I'm not one of those 'stunning women' you talk about."

Suddenly he pulled himself away and looked up at her, grinning. It was his boyish grin, the one she'd fallen in love with once, a fact of which she was sure he had no idea.

"Have you bothered to look at yourself in a mirror?" he said. "Of course you are!"

She laughed, still shaking her head. "Oh Mark! It's lovely that you think I'm that good looking, but I don't understand why you should feel overawed. What have I done to give you that idea?"

"You didn't have to do anything," he said. He reached for her hands almost shyly. "Look, Kay, can we make a fresh start? I don't want to lose you. I can see that I've been wrong to involve my mother in things that were our business, and if I have to choose between her and you, I choose you, every time."

She felt her eyes mist up and a lump form in her throat. "Do you mean it, Mark?"

"Absolutely," he replied.

He cupped her head in his hands, and gazed into her eyes. She saw sincerity and warmth, and, as he leaned towards her, a glint of sudden lust. As his lips pressed against hers with growing urgency, she felt her body respond to his nearness, and slipped her arms round him. Somehow, by the time they broke the kiss, she was laid comfortably on the bed with her blouse open, one nipple being gently tweaked and tickled by his hands while the other was being lapped and suckled in a manner she found distinctly pleasurable. Her slim fingers found the buttons on his shirt and slowly loosened them, pausing at his trousers to unhitch his belt and the fastener which kept his waistband closed.

Almost her last coherent thought before he brought her to a crashing, thunderous climax was that it had been so long since he'd shown any inclination to make love to her she'd taken the opportunity to have a break from the Pill, and couldn't remember whether she'd bothered to mention it.

*

Seymour had enjoyed his morning's training. It demanded intense concentration, and careful co-ordination of hands and eyes. He'd not mentioned anything to Harriet, but he'd certainly experienced a significant amount of pain in his abdomen, reaching round to his lumbar region, and had had to take some of the tablets prescribed by the hospital. He knew they tended to slow up his reactions, and had been quite worried about whether he would be able to fly. As things had turned out, after a bit of practice, he could take-off smoothly. His attempts at landing were bumpier, but on the whole, the Chief Flying Instructor was pleased with his progress.

Walking back from the helicopter towards the hangar where the company offices were, Seymour took careful note of physical security measures, like locked doors. He was not concerned about CCTV cameras as the chances were that there'd be very little of himself or Harriet left to identify. Once in the office, he booked flying lessons for the following Monday and Tuesday afternoons. He wondered whether to book one or two further ahead, in case it should seem strange that he stopped then, but figured it didn't matter much.

Once outside the hangar in the road, he called Harriet on his mobile phone and asked her to collect him. Whilst he waited for her, he took the opportunity to check the exterior of the hangar and the fence which ran from its ends round the perimeter of the heliport. One entire quadrant was unfenced, where the heliport abutted the airport, to allow for the unencumbered passage of airport service vehicles such as fuel bowsers and fire engines, to any part of the heliport. At these points, the heliport fence joined the perimeter fence which surrounded the entire airport.

It wasn't that he was thinking of having to break in: he was simply going to turn up with Harriet, and walk through the hangar to the helicopter with the CFI as usual. The only departure from normal would come at the end of that walk. But it seemed a sensible idea just to check the place out as much as possible in case the knowledge would prove useful, if his plans didn't work out.

The throaty roar of the sports car's exhaust began to be heard over the noise of distant traffic on the main road, and a moment later, he saw it approach down the service road towards the hangar. Harriet drove round the turning circle and stopped beside Seymour.

"How was your lesson?" she asked, as Charley climbed over the seat again to sit in the back.

He explained what he'd been doing as he settled himself into the seat she'd vacated. "Well, at least I can take off all right," he concluded.

Charley chuckled behind him. "Just make sure you can land," she said.

Seymour caught Harriet's eye and smiled. "I think that lesson is on Wednesday," he said.

As Harriet drove away from the heliport, she spoke over her shoulder to Charley.

"Show Seymour what I bought him."

Charley chuckled again, and after rummaging around among the shopping bags beside her, passed him a green and yellow 'fright wig'. He laughed when it landed in his lap.

"Don't put it on out here," warned Harriet, pointing at CCTV cameras covering the street.

"Have you ever been to a football match, Seymour?" asked Charley.

"Uh, no," he replied.

She was suddenly serious and leaned forward until her cheek was almost next to his.

"So when do you expect to be going," she asked, "given that what we're not talking about is going to make it less and less likely?"

"Maybe I just wanted the wig. I don't have as much hair as I used to," he said.

She stared at him then turned to look at her mother.

"Why don't you just sit back and belt up, dear," said Harriet, detecting the movement and watching Charley through the mirror.

Charley suddenly felt very troubled and sat back, pulling the seat belt around her though not at all sure it was all her mother had meant. She began to wonder whether these two people in front of her might not be planning something they weren't telling her. Seymour's flippant comment about the lesson on landings being on Wednesday bothered her. Maybe he was simply being optimistic... or maybe he had the idea that they wouldn't be around at all on Wednesday. When she thought about it, he had never seemed to be suffering symptoms like her mother.

"Do you take pain-killers, Seymour?" she asked.

"I have tablets from the hospital," he replied. "I took some today before you picked me up."

"And like mum, you have no clear idea of what ails you?"

"It's a condition called ALS by some, motor neurone disease by others," he said.

She frowned at the back of his neck. "That's really serious, isn't it?"

He half turned to her. "That's why they've been to the trouble of telling me my time on Earth is severely limited."

"And is mother suffering from the same thing?"

Seymour glanced at her. "Your mother's condition is between her and her doctor. It's just coincidence that we were told on the same day about having only a short time to live."

Charley looked down briefly. "I suppose you are both just lucky, being able to get around more or less as normal for now."

"That's us," said Seymour, "no two luckier people alive. And when you think about it, I might not have met your mother if we hadn't both been ill."

"No," said Harriet, nodding.

"You see, dear," said Seymour to her, "you could have slipped away peacefully instead of in this vulgar truck."

She looked round at him. "Are you referring to my beautiful red sports car as a 'vulgar truck'?"

He grinned. "I know you only got it to impress me with," he said.

"I told you why I wanted it."

"To impress the boys, you said. But I know – you wanted it to show me that you still have a bit of the old fiery zest for life about you."

"And why did you arrange to drive a tank? Who was that to impress? Wasn't it a boy-thing just because I'd bought this, you wanted to drive something bigger? To say nothing of the helicopter lessons."

"They were just things I'd always wanted to do," he replied.

She drove for a while then grinned. "I bet you wouldn't have been able to tick off a parachute jump if you hadn't met me!"

He rolled his eyes. "It was a treat I could have lived without."

Charley watched them from the rear seat, developing a case of 'Wimbledon Neck' as their banter went back and forth.

"Do you two realise," she said, "how much you sound like an old married couple?"

Seymour looked down to hide a grin. Harriet pulled in outside his house.

"Come in, both of you," he invited.

Harriet switched off the engine and climbed out, while Charley tucked her skirt up and stepped elegantly over the side of the vehicle onto the footpath. She pulled her skirt down and looked up to see Seymour's eyes on her legs. He grinned.

"Like mother, like daughter," he said.

She pursed her lips and looked at Harriet. "Anything you want to tell me, ma?"

"Absolutely not," said Harriet sternly. They followed Seymour up the path to the front door.

CHAPTER THIRTEEN

Mike picked up the telephone on its second ring.

"CID: English."

The caller was a uniform sergeant stationed at Breydon.

"Uh, Mike, you were interested in a certain woman with a red sports car."

"Harriet Blythe. Yes, what about her."

"Well, her flat was raided yesterday."

Mike frowned. "Why?"

"It was the connection with the drug-dealer she was spotted with on the speed-camera photograph."

"What connection is that?"

"Well, he'd been seen visiting her flat nearly every day. She suddenly bought this nice car. The question had to be asked, where she got the money."

"And she said?"

"Bought it on her credit card."

Mike twisted his lips into a wry smile. "Did she tell you she might to be dead before the credit card bill comes in?"

The Breydon officer hesitated. "Yes. Actually, she did say something like that – not about the credit card bill, but that she was dying. That cracking daughter of hers was there and supported the story. You've heard it too, then?"

"I'm afraid it's true."

"And for the record, you know this... how?"

"I'm in a relationship with the cracking daughter. Harriet and another guy were in hospital a couple of weeks back and both received similar diagnoses. They're seeing their last days out together. Mack and Mabel."

"As long as it ain't Bonnie and Clyde," said the Breydon sergeant dourly.

They hung up after he'd said he would tell DS Walmsley of the corroboration.

Mike tried phoning Charley at work, eventually finding her when he rang her mobile phone.

"Hi, Mike," she said, suddenly breathless when she heard his characteristic bass tones. Even over the telephone, it's timbre still affected her pleasantly.

"How's your mum?" he asked. "I hear she had a visit from the local drugs squad."

"Just a small misunderstanding, sorted out."

He felt relief. "So she's not going to feature in the local newspaper?"

"They knew she'd been seeing Eddy from the eighth floor, and that she had a new car—"

He cut her off. "I understand their train of thought. But she convinced them she had no connection – and they didn't find anything?"

The line was quiet for a moment. "Do you remember the Roald Dahl story about a woman suspected of killing her husband by hitting him over the head with a heavy object? The woman invited the police to dinner, and roasted a leg of lamb – a leg which had once been frozen. Of course, after they'd consumed it, they never found the murder weapon. Well, in our case, we all enjoyed a mug of tea and some cupcakes after the officers finished searching the flat. Without finding anything, I might add."

Mike put a hand over his lips to stifle a crack of laughter.

"Are you all right?" asked Charley, puzzled by the noise.

"Oh, very! Look, are you in Breydon?"

"Yes, but I'm coming home this afternoon.."

"Any chance of your coming to a Vintage Car Club dinner?"

She hesitated. "I don't know."

"Please? Otherwise I'll be the only person there without a partner."

"Are you looking for sympathy?"

"No, I'm looking for a date."

"Oh. Okay, if you put it that way. What shall I wear?"

"Uh, I don't know. It's 'lounge suits' for the men. Reasonably smart gear for the girls, I guess."

"Okay. I'll see what I've got in the wardrobe. I don't spend my spare time buying clothes."

"The idea of you without clothes has considerable appeal. I'll pick you up from your home about seven."

He left work as early as he could and walked to his apartment, where he entered the block through the underground garage.

He kept both his vehicles there, renting an unwanted space from one of his neighbours. One car was a nondescript Ford Mondeo he kept for ordinary use. Next to it, under a tarpaulin, was his secret pride and joy: a 1951 Riley RMD Drophead Coupe in maroon with black mudguards and running boards. He folded the tarpaulin and took it up to his apartment, returning a few minutes later with a duster, to flick round the interior. He unclipped the pram top and folded it back behind the rear seats. When he'd done, he stood by the bonnet, running his hand lovingly over the curves of the bodywork, and thinking how good Charley would look in it.

He checked the battery condition, and started the 2.5 litre engine. All the gauges and indicators showed normal readings and after dipping a toe on the accelerator a couple of times to hear the throaty roar of the exhaust echoing around the cavernous garage, he turned off the ignition and returned to his apartment to shower and change for the evening.

*

After Charley had left to go home, early in the afternoon, Harriet suggested to Seymour they visit the coast.

"It's a lovely day, Seymour," she said, "and we're not likely to see many more."

"Aye," he agreed. "Let's visit Northwind Gap on the way."

"We can do a round trip, come back through Potter Heigham and get an evening meal at one of those pubs which do good food."

"Sounds like a lovely way to spend an afternoon," he concurred.

*

In another part of town, Kay was putting her shopping away. After an hour and a half in the supermarket, she was looking forward to a cup of tea. Mark had been with her for once, pushing the trolley without complaint, and taking an interest in what she was buying. They'd had one or two discussions about the relative merits of similar products, but none amounted to an argument, and all had been resolved amicably – mostly, she had to acknowledge, because she had been too surprised by his change of behaviour to insist on her point of view especially when, considering the similarity of product, there wasn't much to be gained.

Now, as she reached to put some tins away in a high wall cupboard, she became aware of his eyes on her from where he was standing, beside the breakfast bar, swishing a teabag around in the pot. As she closed the cupboard, she turned round suddenly and caught the glint of lust in his eyes again. He looked up into her face and blushed slightly, before moving towards her and slipping both hands round her waist.

"Mark! What are you—"

His response was to seek out her lips and cover them with his. Her eyes, at first wide with surprise, closed as she enjoyed his eagerness.

"Mark – the frozen food needs putting away," she protested whilst adjusting her position to ease the pressure of the worktop against which she was leaning.

"What if it does?" he said.

"We'd have to go back and get some more if it thaws."

"So?" He shrugged.

He'd never behaved so impulsively towards her before; all their love-making had been in the comfortable confines of the bedroom, and this change of venue and the unexpected nature of his move was exciting and left her breathless. She simply wanted to collapse gently against him and be held there while he brought her to the climax she realised she desperately wanted.

They remained close for several minutes, during which Kay brushed sweat from his forehead. He gently kissed her once more before moving away and pulling up his trousers.

"Perhaps you should let me put the stuff away in the high cupboards," he said.

"Perhaps you should put all the shopping away – if my reaching into the high cupboards has this effect on you, I dread to think what would happen if you saw me bending down to the low ones. Pass me that tin of baked beans, would you, please."

He chuckled. "You could easily find out," he said, passing her the tin.

"I'll save that particular journey of discovery until another time – when you've got your breath back!"

"That might be sooner than you think," he said, a dangerous edge to his voice.

She tapped him lightly on the chest. "Down boy!" she said, grinning.

*

Northwind Gap was just what it said it was: a gap through the coastal flood defences through which the north wind was funnelled. Harriet had parked in the car park used by summer visitors and local fishermen, and she and Seymour walked down the long ramp through the gap.

At a point near the bottom of the ramp, it cut through a concrete sea wall onto which they stepped to find that they were sheltered from the breeze and could enjoy the warmth of the spring sunshine. Their footsteps crunched on the thin layer of sand blown up from the beach to cover the concrete, and gulls circled out at sea in the wake of a small inshore fishing boat.

"Let's sit for a few minutes," suggested Seymour.

They sat with their backs resting against the concrete behind them, and gazed out to sea.

"I love this bit of coastline," he said, "It's wild, it's raw, there are never many people about."

"I didn't know you had a poetic streak in you, Seymour," said Harriet.

"I used to come here late at night, after Sally died. It was somewhere I felt close to her, and I didn't have to keep pretending that everything was all right."

They were silent for a while.

"I suppose I'll never know what it's like to have a real lover – I mean, someone who loves me," she said.

"Charley loves you."

"Charley is not a man."

"Her father?"

"Ten minutes of lust in the back of a dance-hall doesn't constitute love."

They fell silent again.

"Maybe if we had longer," he said.

"Longer? To do what?"

He didn't reply. He studied her for a moment, then reached out and took her hand, holding it in the warmth of his. She looked at their joined hands, then lifted her gaze until their eyes were locked on each-other.

She moved so they were almost face to face, and smiled shyly.

"Oh, Seymour," she said softly, "how long do you think you'd need?"

He ran his fingers lightly down her cheek.

"Sometimes, my dear, I feel as if it would be the easiest thing in the world to set our conditions aside, and so much harder to keep them in place. The reason why we agreed not to fall in love hasn't changed."

She dropped her gaze back to their hands.

"Seymour."

"Yes?"

"Have you not realised that I broke that particular condition when we were in Paris?"

He looked up at her, his head tilted.

"No. What do you mean?"

She returned his gesture, running her fingertips lightly down his cheek and smiling tenderly.

"I fell in love with you in Paris, and probably before, though I didn't admit it even to myself until we were half-way up the Eiffel Tower."

"I don't know what to say," he said.

She pulled away from him and frowned. "Do I need to write a script for you?"

He grinned. "Well, this is so unexpected."

"I hadn't got you down as a particularly insensitive person," she said severely.

He nodded as if in realisation of what she expected from him. "You mean you want me to say I love you, too?"

"Only if you mean it, you exasperating man!"

"Harriet," he said, grinning, "if only we had longer, I'd not only tell you 'how do I love thee' and count the ways, but I'd think it only right and proper for us to get married."

She smiled at him and glanced obviously at her watch. "Well, we've got a few hours. You could make a start."

He shook his head. "Oh, no. After this conversation, you'd just think I was trying to sweet-talk you so we could have sex."

"That's true: I might. But you could get lucky anyway. Let's go back home and you can find out."

She climbed to her feet and took his hand as he rose beside her. They made their way back to the car, hand-in-hand. Further words weren't necessary.

The gulls had moved further along the shoreline, their calls lost in the sound of the sea and the wind.

*

Charley made a careful selection of clothing from her wardrobe. She chose a smart evening gown in green silk with a Pashmina shawl, and new, silk underwear, which made her feel very slinky and sexy. Thigh-high stockings and five-inch heels completed the ensemble, along with a clutch bag. She wore the new earrings Mike had given her, with a choker that sparkled in almost any light. Old-fashioned chokers might be, but she loved the look of this one.

Most of the members of the local Vintage Car Club were considerably older than Mike. It was the first thing Charley noticed about them, dismissing them in her mind as a load of old codgers. But not *too* old, she amended when she realised how much interest they were taking in her. Rheumy eyes developed a sparkle as they appreciated her looks, and she began to feel like the prize exhibit at the Royal Norfolk Show. She decided not to let their interest bother her: they probably didn't get to see many young women. Judging by the matron-esque appearance of some of their wives, who barely concealed their disapproval of her skirt, its hemline just above her knees, any hint of flir-tatiousness by these harmless old men would promptly be suppressed.

She had been amazed and delighted earlier when Mike had arrived at the house in his Riley. She'd met him on the pavement and he'd held the door for her to swing her legs elegantly into the foot-well, then they'd gone for a spin before Mike had taken the road to Branksome Hall where the club was having its annual knees-up. It had been quite quaint really, she'd thought, when she set eyes on the four-piece band on a dais at one end of the room, and she'd been quite incredulous when Mike had taken her hand and led her onto the dance-floor to take part in a cha-cha-cha.

She'd not known the steps but he quickly taught her some basic moves to keep with him, and she found that as long as she kept to the rhythm, there was little she could do wrong. He impressed her with the fluidity of his dancing, but the unaccustomed exercise left her panting as the number came to an end.

"Wow!" she said as they left the dance-floor.

"Have you not danced like that before?" Mike asked.

"No. I was just one of those people who stood and wriggled suggestively in time to the music – and I haven't done that for years," she added.

"Want a drink?" he asked.

"Please. A vodka and tonic."

Mike went over to the bar and placed the order, getting himself a pint of bitter. Charley followed in his wake.

"I thought you said this was a dinner."

He grinned. "I do like a girl with healthy appetites," he said, his expression leaving her in no doubt he was referring to more than just food. "The restaurant is up the stairs." He pointed to an elaborate twin staircase, each wing of which curled down the wall opposite the band's dais, from a central doorway above. "Do you want to take this up, or shall we drink it down here?"

"Well, you're driving, so I guess you take your drink up," she said, "I, on the other hand, am going to have a good time tonight." Saying which, she drained her glass. Mike watched her, faintly amused.

"You have hollow legs?" he asked.

"They're just like everyone else's," she replied, taking his hand and leading him towards the staircase.

At the top, the doorway opened into a large dining room, its walls lined with Jacobean panelling in a dark, polished wood. They were shown to a table where Mike seated Charley, and took his place opposite her. A waiter presented them with menus and a wine list, and while Mike was studying the latter, several other people greeted him on the way to their tables.

They placed their order for food and wine.

"Tell me about your car," Charley asked.

It was the crack in the dam. She listened patiently while he told her various things he thought she'd find fascinating about the ageing Riley. Their wine and starters arrived, and while Charley ate, he spoke and she contrived to nod in most of the right places. She was more interested in the enthusiastic gleam in his eyes and amused by the signs of passionate involvement with the car which from time to time crept into his voice. Her plate empty, she placed her knife and fork together on it. He glanced down at his own untouched appetiser, and realised he'd been talking uninterrupted for nearly ten minutes. He glanced up at her.

"Uh, sorry. I tend to get carried away."

She smiled. "I didn't imagine you were so keen on old cars," she said, "I had you pegged for a rugby player when I first met you.".

He stared at her, astonished.

"Whatever would give you that idea?"

"Could be something to do with the way you're built."

He pursed his lips to hide a grin. "Vintage car fans have to be broad-shouldered too," he said, "as we often have to push our beloveds when they're too tired to get home under their own steam."

She gazed at him with deliberately wide-eyes. "Do you actually refer to your car as your beloved?"

He raised an eyebrow. "I don't want you to get the wrong idea: we're not engaged or anything. She doesn't mind my having a girlfriend."

"We are still talking about your car, aren't we?"

"And you, of course."

"As in, do I mind if you lavish love and affection on an old car?"

"Hmm. Of course, I see you in a quite different light from the old girl."

She stared at him, lips twitching. "Does she drink a lot?"

He nodded sadly. "Roughly a gallon every twenty miles. Speaking of which, would you like your glass topped up?"

"Thanks."

He added wine to both glasses.

They were silent for a while until he cleared his plate. The waiter, who had been hovering, swooped and cleared away their first course. The level of conversation in the room had risen, and Charley had used her opportunity, while Mike was eating, to look round at the other diners. There were one or two she recognised as former clients, and someone who featured regularly in the society pages of the local newspaper, but whose name she couldn't remember. She leaned forward.

"Anyone here you recognise from your day job?" she wondered.

He chewed silently, looking at her, then nodded.

She was all big-eyed curiosity. "Who?" She looked round the room to see if there was anyone she'd not noticed with BURGLAR or MUGGER written on their foreheads. Mike washed his food down with wine, then leaned forward.

"I can't tell you that."

Charley looked round. She pointed at the people standing at the bar behind the diners. "Is it someone over there?"

"No – and please keep your voice down," said Mike, putting a restraining hand on her arm. With her other hand, she drank the remains of the wine in her glass before pulling away from him.

The waiter chose that moment to serve their main course.

When they were alone again, she tapped him on the arm and indicated a grey-haired man with a young girl sitting together at a nearby table.

"How about him?" she asked.

Mike did not look round. "I can't tell you anything," he whispered.

"Ooh!" said Charley, "so it's him, then? The man with the child."

"She's seventeen," he said, then seeing the expression on Charley's face, rapped himself on the forehead with a hand. "Damn!"

Charley leaned towards him. "What's he done?" she asked in a loud whisper, "is he a paedophile? A rapist?"

"Will you please leave it! Oh, God! What have I done!"

"Don't worry, Mike, I can be the soul of discretion." She grinned. He was not reassured. She refilled her glass from the bottle of wine and sipped before stabbing a mouthful of food.

"Did you know he was going to be here?" she asked, halfway through her main course.

"Yes," he said, "and please keep your voice down."

She glanced past him at the man. "He's putting his hand on the girl's arm. Oh, he's so creepy."

Mike stared at her inscrutably. "Charley, please just concentrate on your dinner. Don't you like it?"

She glanced back at him. "Oh, yes, thanks. It's fine. But the idea of being on a stake-out is really quite exciting. Is that why we're here?"

"No. We're here on a date with a load of people who are interested in old cars. And their dinner guests."

"Uh-huh."

"And we're not on a stake-out."

She looked at him. "Oh, I'm sorry. I realise you probably can't tell me, officially." She swallowed another mouthful. "Are you going to arrest him and rescue the girl?"

"No."

"Is there someone else in the room who's going to arrest him and rescue the girl?"

"No."

"You're not going to let him walk out of here with her, are you?" she asked indignantly.

"Yes."

Her face fell. "Oh! Mike! I didn't think you were like that. It's condoning a crime or something, isn't it?"

"I really wish you'd keep your voice down, Charley. People are looking."

"I don't care," she replied, not lowering her voice at all, "you should go and arrest him."

"I can't."

She glared at him a moment. "Why not? Oh, you're so disappointing, Mike. I wish there was another policeman in the room."

"There is."

She looked around. The grey-haired man was studying her. She quickly scanned the other diners while a blush found its way into her cheeks.

"He's looking this way," she whispered hoarsely.

"I'm not surprised," said Mike.

He raised his fork towards his lips, but she grabbed his arm. "Mike! He's getting up. He – he's coming over. Mike! Now's your chance."

Mike sat away from the table and glanced round. The grey-haired man arrived beside it.

"Hello, Mike," he said, turning to Charley who was trying to encourage Mike with hand signals. "This your new girlfriend?"

"I'm afraid so, sir. Charley, this is Detective Chief Inspector Salmon."

The grey-haired man held out his hand. "James Salmon. Most of my colleagues call me The Trout behind my back." He glanced at Mike and winked as if to say, you didn't know I knew that, did you!

Charley stared at him, her cheeks glowing red, and took his hand nervously.

"Charley Blythe."

He studied her face for a moment. "So, your mother is Harriet, living over in Breydon, and you're a partner in Milner Blythe Associates?"

She stared at him. "How did you know that?"

"I can't possibly tell you how I know about your mother," he said, smiling and tapping his nose with his index finger. "Mike might, of course, but I might have to do something about it if I *knew* there'd been misuse of official resources. As for you, your firm did some work for my daughter. They had an extension built."

Charley's mouth had fallen open. She swallowed and her eyes dropped to the girl still sitting at the table behind Mike and looking their way. The Trout followed her glance.

"That's my granddaughter, Helen. Did you meet her when you were doing the extension? I thought you might have known her when you were so interested in us."

"Uh, uh, no," stammered Charley feeling thoroughly wretched and embarrassed. "Excuse me, I need to find the loo." She stood up and walked quickly away.

The Trout watched her go, a small smile on his lips, before turning to Mike.

"Nice girl that," he said.

"Normally," agreed Mike.

The DCI put his hand on Mike's shoulder. "Come on, Mike, you let her go off on her tangent much longer than you needed to. I could hear her quite well." He tapped a hearing aid. "These things don't filter out much."

Mike's expression gradually cracked into a grin. "Sorry about that, sir."

"No problem. Hope you didn't mind my coming over, but I could see no signs of your being about to put her straight, so I thought I'd better do it myself. Besides, I always enjoy meeting pretty, *young,* girls. We paedophiles are known for it."

"I'll be sure to point out the error of judgement to her, sir."

The Trout laughed. "Don't be too hard on her. I think she's been through the wringer enough. Car running well?"

"Yes thank you, sir. And yours?"

"Bit of pinking needs sorting out, but otherwise okay. Ah, she's coming back. I'll be off."

He returned to his table, reaching it as Charley sat down opposite Mike.

She seemed to have recovered her composure, staring at him. "You let me go on, didn't you?"

Mike forced his face to remain expressionless. "I couldn't stop you."

"You could have said he was a policeman."

"I said there was another policeman in the room, but you didn't take the hint."

"Hint? You call that a *hint?*" She glared at him.

"Best I could do in the face of your kamikaze notion about them."

She fulminated for a moment before she saw the funnier aspect of the situation.

"I do not take kindly to being made fun of," she said severely.

He noticed the twitch in her lips. "Charley, I tried to stop you. And much as I enjoy your company, do you really think I would have brought you along if I'd been here on surveillance? I wouldn't have risked your safety."

"You might," she said with a pout. "I wouldn't have minded."

"I would – especially if there was a chance you might be hurt."

"You're just trying to sweeten me up," she exclaimed.

"I'm sure it's unnecessary. What do you want for dessert?"

She eyed him for a moment before peering at the dessert menu, chalked on a blackboard on the wall. As she did so, she brushed her fingertips through her hair. A moment later, a look of horror passed across her face, and she felt once more her earlobe with the tip of her fingers. She looked down, brushing her clothes lightly, staring at the floor.

While Mike watched her in amazement, she pushed her chair away and scrabbled about on the floor, running her hands this way and that.

"What's the matter, Charley?" Mike asked, concerned.

She stared up at him, opened her mouth and couldn't find the words. Suddenly, she got to her feet, and ran back to the toilet. Mike stared after her, got up and followed her across the floor. He stopped outside, clenching and un-clenching his fists. Looking round, he spied a waitress and called her over.

"Sorry, but do you think you could go in there and find out what's bothering my girlfriend, Charley?"

The waitress pursed her lips and ran her eyes down his body.

"Okay, but can I call on you to do something for me if she ever goes out of your life?"

He smiled grimly. "I think I can make that promise, but don't hold your breath: she's going to be around a very long time, I hope."

She smiled at him in a you-don't-know-what-you're-missing kind of way and went inside the toilet.

Mike paced up and down impatiently outside the door. One or two other women stared at him as they went in-side. He began to worry that people would be getting a strange idea about him if he hung around any longer. He was about to ask yet another female who was obviously on track for the toilet if she could find out what his girlfriend *and* the waitress were doing together in there, when the possible inferences which could be drawn from such a question caused him to hesitate, and the emergence of Charley and the waitress rendered it unnecessary.

He fairly pounced on Charley. "What've you been do-ing? What's going on?"

The waitress grinned at her. "I'll leave you to answer that."

"Thanks for your help," said Charley.

"Well?" asked Mike impatiently, leading the way back to their table.

She took a deep breath and looked up at him unhappily as she sat down.

" I think I've lost one of the earrings you bought me."

He took her hand. A feeling of relief swept over him. "Is that all?" he snapped. He moderated his tone. "Sorry. I was worried it was something serious. Good job I didn't buy you the *really* expensive pair, isn't it? Don't worry, I'll replace it."

"Oh! I'm so sorry!"

"Really, don't let it spoil your evening."

"But they are beautiful."

"Fortunately, they're not unique. There're more in the shop."

But Charley was not to be placated so easily. Tears welled from her eyes.

"Oh, what will you think of me! I've embarrassed you in front of your Trout, and now I've lost your earring."

"*Your* earring. Don't wear them myself," he joked.

A sob was her response.

"Look, Charley, shall we go?"

She nodded miserably, opening her clutch bag for a tissue, but he beat her to it with another clean white linen handkerchief. She looked up at him gratefully, chuckling through her tears.

"Oh, Mike, you're always there with a handkerchief. I don't know what's the matter with me: I never used to be such a watering-pot."

"No," he agreed, "I'll tell you when the novelty's warn off and it's starting to get tedious."

She frowned at him, forgetting her tears, and blew her nose. "Are you saying I cry too much."

He shrugged. "I'm not saying anything." He went round to her chair, holding it as she stood up.

She smiled at him, tucked his handkerchief in her bag and they headed for the door.

CHAPTER FOURTEEN

Seymour was feeling distinctly edgy. One day to go before he and Harriet made their final gesture and shuffled off this mortal coil together. He'd have been happier about it, perversely, if he'd not felt quite unlike someone a few hours away from their death.

There had been this period of a quarter of an hour when their conversation had been surreal, or at least, quite unreal.

"Are we going to wait until our conditions get us, or take our destinies in our own hands and put a period to our existences before we degenerate beyond the point at which we can choose?" Harriet had asked.

They'd listed the pros and cons of doing it, or not doing it, eventually deciding to go with their original impulse and terminate their lives while they could still make and execute such decisions. Tuesday had seemed as good a time as any.

Privately, he would have liked longer, perhaps six months if they had that long – perhaps, if Harriet was willing, to marry her. There would have been a few months really together before... But that was the problem: just how long might they retain the use of their faculties? As things were, an agreement was an agreement, and he was damned if he was going to let Harriet down no matter how well he subjectively considered himself. There was no doubt she was in a lot of pain, and they needed to time their last act for when she was still able to drive them to the heliport. They'd decided that sooner was better than risking a longer wait, when the end would be the same.

Which is why he found himself taking his time over a cup of coffee in a coffee-shop overlooking the bank branch they planned to rob tomorrow. And why? How had they decided to do this? It had seemed like fun when Harriet had lightly suggested it, but he was by no means certain they'd succeed. And what if anyone got hurt? It was the last thing he wanted, and he hoped and prayed that there were no have-a-go heroes among the bank staff or customers.

He'd been taking notice of when the place seemed at its quietest. He pulled his mobile phone from his pocket and called the flying school to alter the time of his lesson. He did a few sums on the back of the menu, working out that they'd be able to fly one way to the coast comfortably on the amount of fuel that would be taken on for a half-hour flight.

He was about to leave the place and go to Harriet's when an unusual sight met his gaze. Walking towards him on the bank side of the street was David. By his side was a girl. Seymour screwed up his eyes to improve their focus.

She wore a black leather jacket covered in steel studs, and a skirt probably made of the same material. Black leather boots and tights completed her turn-out. There were several pieces of ironmongery attached to her face and ears, which were dead white, apart from purple lipstick and heavy eye makeup, which might also be tinged with purple. Her bobbed hair was black and shining. It looked the most washed thing about her, Seymour thought, and he wondered what David was doing with her.

The couple were deep in animated conversation. The girl frequently touched David's arm, and his hands were gesticulating as if he was explaining something complicated to her. They both laughed a lot and stole glances at each other. Seymour was fascinated: he was accustomed to David being somewhat taciturn, still seeming to be locked into behavioural patterns learned at the age of fifteen. The man on the other side of the street was looking remarkably normal, enjoying the company of a woman who looked anything but.

Her body language showed she was comfortable in his company. The touching, feeling, eye contact and smiling were all signs – even the way she was walking so close to him their bodies occasionally bumped against each-other. David's body language was more restrained, but there was still the smile, the eye contact, the occasional touch and the body-bumping. It was all visible if you looked for it.

His attention was diverted by the appearance of Harriet's sports car in the street. She was driving slowly, looking towards the coffee shop. He waved and got up off his stool, moving quickly outside so she could simply pause for a moment to pick him up, without having to find a proper parking space.

"Well?" she asked when he was safely installed beside her, "how'd everything go?"

"The lesson was okay," he said, "taking off is manageable. I think we'll be all right in that respect."

"Good."

He was studying her surreptitiously, and noticing how she was clamping her jaw and sucking in air from time to time.

"How are you feeling, Harriet?" he asked quietly.

"Just the odd twinge. I guess Eddy's stuff is wearing off. Did you hear about our visit from the police yesterday?"

He raised his eyebrows. "No. What happened?"

"Luckily, Charley was with me when they all arrived in their body-armour, waving search warrants."

She told him the story of the abortive police raid, and they both laughed at the idea of the police consuming the prosecution evidence baked into chocolate-coated cupcakes.

"I hope they were all right."

"Hmm. Well, I went up to the eighth floor to see Eddy, but his flat was crawling with more police and I saw him being led away in handcuffs." She sniffed. "He smiled and shrugged as he went by."

"If he's only fifteen, he won't be put in a prison," said Seymour comfortingly, "probably just somewhere he'll be better looked after than at home."

"The trouble is," she said as she pulled into the kerb outside Seymour's home, "the police ate my supplies of Eddy's medicinal compound, and I've none left. I'm beginning to feel the effects."

"Come in, Harriet, we need to talk."

He led the way up the garden path to the front door and let them in. In the living room they sat in adjacent seats.

"Now, what is it you want to talk about?" she asked.

"Tomorrow."

"Ah, yes. 'Harriet and Seymour's Last Day'. That'll be the title of my diary entry."

He stood up. "I'm having a drink – and I don't mean coffee: I've had enough of that today. Join me in a glass of something?"

"Not for me, thanks, Seymour. I have to drive."

He went to her side and squatted. "You could always stay here the night. Plenty of spare beds."

Her expression softened. "I hoped you'd say that. In that case, I'll have a drink."

"You'll stay?" he asked.

"Plenty of spare beds, you said? Well, then, how could I refuse!" Her grin broadened. "Mine's a large rum and coke, please."

He made similar drinks for each of them at the side-board. When they were both seated again, he turned to her, eyeing her over the rim of his glass.

"Tomorrow. We have to make a few final decisions."

"Well, the first thing is, you don't have to do it," she said. "You don't seem anywhere as ill as I sometimes feel, and I don't want you to end your life just because of some daft agreement we made in the aftermath of being told we had only three weeks to live."

He put his glass down and reached out so he could cover her hand with his.

"It's not as simple as that, Harriet," he said softly. "Even if I had another couple of months, I wouldn't want them without you beside me." He looked down to hide a blush he felt creeping into his cheeks. "I've already had to live beyond the death of one woman I loved, I don't want to go through it again." He picked up her hand and held it between both of his. "The fact is, I fell in love with you, too, before Paris. I think it was the night of the Masonic Ball – you looked so beautiful. Then I trod on your foot, and decided it wasn't the best moment to mention it. I didn't dare tell you later."

She covered his hand with hers. "Why ever not, Seymour?"

"I remembered our agreement. And I thought you might decide to end our comfortable little relationship."

"That's a bit how I felt yesterday at Northwind Gap. I thought *you* might decide to call it off between us."

He grinned wryly. "Can I tell you something – permission to speak freely, ma'am?"

She laughed. "Always. What?"

"I always regarded that bit of our pact about not falling in love was unenforceable, and nowhere near as serious as the decision that we would go together, and in a bang, not a whimper."

She sighed. "It was a bit of a forlorn hope," she agreed. "You're quite a catch for a woman of my age and condition. How could I hope to keep to the deal? Rather hoped *you* would, as it'd cause you a lot less anguish... as I expect you're now finding out."

"Wanted to keep all the anguish to yourself, eh?"

"Yes."

"Well, I demand my share. Harriet, we're in this together."

They touched their glasses together lightly and drank.

"Now, let's talk about tomorrow," she said.

*

It has been said, Kay reflected, that behind every great man there is a surprised woman. There was an element of truth in it, she figured, and just now, she was wondering if Mark was destined for greatness, for, by reverse logic, she had been surprised by him a couple of times in the last twenty-four hours. She needed to talk to him, to tell him that they must be careful, to use a condom.

It had been quite exciting, however: twice he'd made love to her with more vigour and enthusiasm than for a long time. The added risk she'd known she ran had made the experiences even more thrilling for her.

She poured a couple of scotch and sodas and carried the glasses through to Mark's study. He was on the phone when she went in, and waved her to a chair, nodding his thanks for the drink. He cupped his hand over the phone.

"Won't be a minute," he mouthed. Moments later he finished his call and swivelled his chair towards her, picking up his glass.

"Cheers."

"Can we talk, Mark?" Kay asked.

"Sure," he said.

"I need to tell you something." She stared up at him from her position in a lower armchair. There was a gleam in his eye which she was beginning to recognise. Her mouth was suddenly dry. "Mark – !"

He leaned forward and covered her mouth with his, pushing her skirt up and pressing himself between her legs.

Some time later, he sat back in his chair while they both put their clothing in order. She lay there panting, staring at him and wanting to laugh. She figured it was a hysterical reaction.

"Sorry about that," said Mark, "now where were we?"

"I was trying to tell you that I'm not on the Pill at the moment. I – I took a break from it. If we're not careful, I could get pregnant."

Mark shook his head. "Oh, dear," he said.

There was a hint of smugness in his voice. Somehow, she didn't think he was terribly upset. What was his game?

"Mark: are you doing this because your mother told you, or because *you* want to?"

"Doing what?" he asked.

"You know… what we did just now, what we did in the kitchen, and what we did before that in the bedroom."

"Oh that," he said, a smile twitching the corners of his mouth. "Well, there were only two of us in the room each time: my mother wasn't here. Neither was her influence." He slipped out of his chair to crouch beside her, taking one of her hands in his. "I know I've got a bit of an uphill struggle, but I really need you to believe me when I say that my mother is not running my life. I've made it plain to her that you're my girl, and the most important person in the world to me. And incidentally," he added, patting her abdomen, "if you are harbouring the next generation of Edwardses, I shall be delighted. I hope you will, too."

"Right," she said weakly. "You want us to have a child? Really?"

He leaned forward and kissed her tenderly. "You bet."

*

Harriet watched Seymour over the rim of her second glass of rum. She felt pleasantly hazed, but not enough that she didn't notice a slight frown on his face.

"Seymour? What's the matter?"

He shook his head, looked up at her. "Saw David in town with a new girl today," he said.

"What was she like?"

"One of those who dresses in black and white."

"A Goth?"

He frowned. "What?"

"They're called Goths. A little bit passé now, I believe, but under the liberal dress code of the young, anything goes anyway. How interesting," she added.

She took another mouthful of the burning liquor and felt it warm her stomach. She scratched an itch on her knee with the tip of a finger nail.

"I was thinking, Seymour..."

"Always a dangerous sign."

"I know – and it never stops! This could be our last night together."

"I know."

"Shouldn't we get the family round?"

"I wondered how you'd feel about that."

She tilted her head. "You'd already thought about it?"

He nodded. "But they don't know it's our last night. We've kept our plans to ourselves. If we suddenly change the pattern, they'll smell a rat. Besides, I would rather like there to be just the two of us together tonight. I have plans for you."

She gave him an old-fashioned look from under her lashes.

"I wouldn't want you hurting yourself, Seymour," she said primly.

"You let me worry about that," he replied with something of a smirk.

When Harriet emerged from the bathroom some time later, after readjusting her clothing and makeup, she found Seymour in the kitchen, poring over cookbooks.

"What are you doing?" she asked.

"Wondering what to cook for this evening."

She put her hand on his. "Seymour, it's your last night on Earth. Don't you think we could get a takeaway?"

He stared into her eyes for a moment, then choked on a laugh. "I suppose so."

"I feel I want to buy Charley something to remember me by," said Harriet.

Seymour put his arm round her and held her close. "Don't you think she'll never forget you?"

"I know!" she said, "but I still feel I should do something."

"It isn't natural, knowing when you're going to die. Apart from probably a handful a year, nobody knows when they're about to go. I've been trying to work out whether knowing is a blessing or a curse."

Harriet had laid her head comfortably against Seymour's chest, under his chin, hearing and feeling his heart beat. It was a solid, reliable sort of beat, the sort that could go on for ages yet, she thought. Except that tomorrow it would somehow stop.

"It's a curse, Seymour," she said, feeling tears begin to fill her eyes and leak down her cheeks onto his shirt. "If you don't know, you never really worry about how they'll manage without you, on Wednesday. In your case, where will they go for dinner on Thursday?"

He stroked her back comfortingly.

"Kay will look after David, if his Goth doesn't take on the job first."

Harriet chuckled. "I wonder what she's like and where they met."

"I've written Kay a letter," he said. "Nothing very long, just a few points about my funeral and the immediate aftermath – stuff like my passwords, for the computer and various websites."

Harriet drew her head back and looked up at him mischievously. "You're not a subscriber to *unsavoury* websites are you, Seymour? A lurker in Chat-rooms?"

"Not since I met you," he said. "No! Never!" he added, in case she hadn't got the message.

She rested her head on him again, smiling. "Methinks he doth protest too much."

"Harriet, you're not too old to have your bottom smacked."

She looked up at him again. "No, but you're too old to be making those sort of promises, especially if you can't carry them through."

He swooped down and picked her up bodily, depositing her on the settee. She giggled and struggled ineffectually while Seymour wrestled with her. She reached up and put an arm round his neck, pulling him down to her.

*

"Mostly they're for the website of shareholding registrars," he told her later, as he was fastening the buttons on his shirt. "One of these has come off, Harriet," he added, "I wish you wouldn't be so rough – with the shirt. Me, I don't mind."

"Sorry," she said, sitting up to turn the collar of her blouse the right way out. "There were too many to undo. It was taking ages."

He was searching the floor. "Well, I can't see it," he said.

"Maybe it's slipped down next to the cushion," she suggested.

"Yes. I'll have a look later." He stopped and stared at her. "I suppose I'll have to be quick, or it'll have to stay where it is."

"You can always wear another shirt."

"I was planning to."

Harriet stood up. "Seymour, I want to pop back to my flat to sort a few things out. I'll be back in plenty of time for dinner. Will you be okay without me?"

"Of course." He tapped a book on his side-table. "I've been trying to get through *Beowulf* for years. It's my last chance, so you don't have to rush."

*

Harriet was surprised five minutes after getting back to her flat when Eddy knocked at her door.

"Come in, Eddy," she cried, "I'm glad to see you."

He eyed her uncertainly. "Yo' glad t' see me, even after I been nicked?"

"Come and sit down, love. Let me make you a cup of tea."

Eddy sat down heavily on the settee while Harriet went into the kitchen and boiled the kettle. She emerged a few minutes later with two steaming mugs.

"I put two sugars in yours – that's how you like it, isn't it?"

"Yes, thanks, 'Arriet."

She sat in the chair beside him. He looked up at her.

"You seem to t'ink a cup o' tea is de – de *universal panacea!*" he said, winking at her as he used his new words.

Harriet was suitably impressed. "You haven't been wasting your time, I see, Eddy," she said.

"Yeah, well, I've had a bit o' time to t'ink – think – while the scuzzers were making up their minds what to do wid – with – me."

"And what are the, uh, scuzzers, going to do with you?"

"I guess I'll be makin' anuvver visit to de Yoof Court."

Harriet felt sorry for him. "Oh, Eddy. How dreadful."

He shook his head. "I been in detention centre before. I can handle it."

Harriet stood up and put her arm round him. Eddy was too shocked to move.

"Oh, Eddy, you poor thing!" she said, "it's terrible to hear you admit such a thing. You're so young, with your whole life in front of you. Oh, why do you not go back to school, or get a proper job?"

He wriggled free from her arms. "Are you okay, missus? I mean, Harriet."

Tears had trickled down her cheeks. He stared at them in amazement.

"Why are you cryin'?"

She shook her head, wondering how to explain. "Because I shall miss you if you go away."

"Why? You ain't my mum or nuffin'."

Harriet couldn't answer him. Eddy looked round, desperate for some clue what to do with Harriet. He wasn't used to the idea that anyone might care for him: even when his mum had been alive, she'd never put her arms round him.

A recollection came into his mind, an image of his mother and he shuddered.

"What's the matter, Eddy?" Harriet asked.

He shook his head. "I wuz jus' rememberin' findin' my muvver."

"Where was she?"

"On de table."

"Was she ill?"

"Only from de needle still hangin' outta her arm."

Harriet put a hand over her mouth. "Oh, how dreadful, you poor boy. When did this happen?"

"Las' year. Managed to keep it quiet so de Council di'n't find out. 'S when I started dealin'. Paid de rent, and bought food an 'at."

"Did the Council find out eventually?"

"Oh, yes, but I wasn' no problem to 'em. They had more worse kids to worry about than me. I reckon my file just kept being put back on the bottom of the pile. Anyway, dey ain't been back in a while."

Harriet was so moved by his story that she couldn't resist putting her arms round him again. This time, he didn't struggle, but after a moment he turned his head towards her tear-lined face.

"You gotta stop doin' this, Harriet, people will talk."

She giggled through her tears, holding him all the tighter.

Conscious of her own imminent departure from his life, she sought to prepare him as best she could.

"Eddy, life isn't fair," she said. "Sometimes, people make mistakes, and do things they wish afterwards they hadn't. I'll bet your mum at some point wished she'd never taken drugs. I bet at some point, she looked at you and wished she'd given you a better life."

"Ho! You di'n't know my muvver. Once she got the gear in her veins, she di'n't care 'bout nuttin'."

"Not then, maybe, but you don't stay high all the time, and there would have been moments, even when she was craving another fix, that she would have thought about you and wished she'd perhaps been a better mother."

He didn't respond. Harriet pressed on.

"The hard thing for me, Eddy, is that I'm dying."

He pulled away from her and looked into her eyes. "What you mean, you dyin'?"

"I'm very ill, they tell me. I might not have many more days to live."

He took a step back. "You goin' away as well?"

"Believe me, Eddy, it's not because I want to. You have no idea how much I want to stay and for us to be friends."

"'S'easy to say."

"I know. But it's true. The only thing I can do for you now is to give you everything. I have hundreds of books, some are quite valuable, if you sell them at auction. There are two paintings which might yield a few thousand pounds if they're sold. And I'm going to sign over the lease on this flat to you."

"Wassat mean?"

"The flat is on a long lease – longer than even you're likely to live. It would mean you owned the place, and you wouldn't have to pay rent. If you're careful, and can save some money, you might be able to use your savings and sell the flat to buy yourself a house."

He stared at her, still suspicious.

"An' what do I have to do for all this?"

"You have to promise to put a bunch of flowers on my grave every year, and tell me how you're doing."

"Come on!" he said. "You ain't gonna give me yo' flat and everything jus' for that!"

"I am. And when you give me your annual report, I shall expect improvement."

Tears had begun to flow freely down her cheeks. She fought to ignore them.

"Now, do I have your solemn promise?"

For a long time, he watched her. He glanced round her flat, before staring back at her. The suspicion had gone from his eyes, and they were beginning to brim with tears.

"A solemn promise is one you never have to break, ain't it?" he asked.

Harriet nodded, a huge lump in her throat.

He took a deep breath. "Then I promise, Harriet."

He moved forward and put his arms round her.

Harriet felt a sob wrack her, and she held him close. "Now when I tell you that I've grown to love you like my own son, you'll believe me."

"If I was yo' son," he asked, "would you expect me to say thank you, or just accept what you done?"

She chuckled through her tears. "Smart question, Eddy! I would have taught you to say thank you for everything good you receive. Of course, I'd *expect* you to forget, like all children seem to, from time to time."

I wish we had longer: there is so much potential in the boy, she thought. Who, she wondered, would be there to hug him this time next week?

*

Seymour's house was quiet. He went upstairs to his bedroom and opened the wardrobe, pulling out the plastic carrier bag which contained his mutilated shotgun. For an instrument of death, it was elaborately pretty. The plate around the breech was etched scrollwork, and had maybe taken a man several hours to achieve. Or a machine a couple of passes. Skill and handicraft had no place in today's drive for increased productivity, he reflected, running his finger over the marks. The stock was polished and smooth, and fitted neatly against one's shoulder. Before he'd cut off the barrels, the whole thing had had a kind of elegance: now, however, the stubby, shortened barrels made the thing look ugly, more like a killing machine than the noble instrument of execution intended by its designer.

He wondered if people would be convinced by it the next day – enough to do the things he wanted. That would amount to handing over a bag of cash in the bank, and the company pilot abandoning the helicopter when told. He didn't care how much cash was involved, neither he nor Harriet were planning the escapade to hurt people or because they needed the money: it was the doing that was important, and the measure of their success would be getting away in the helicopter and staying airborne long enough to carry out the final act of the plan, to crash into the cliffs on the north Norfolk coast.

He carefully dusted the tiny nooks and niches in the gun before wrapping it back up in the plastic bag, put it back in the wardrobe and went back downstairs.

He picked up *Beowulf* and read, 'Scyld was still thriving when his time came and he crossed over into the Lord's keeping.' Seymour had a presentiment about the next day. If he was honest, he feared that his courage would fail him when he was tested; he would at the last minute pull the helicopter out of its death-dive, and as one who still thrived, would not cross over into the Lord's keeping. He knew that maintaining the helicopter's course, lined up on the cliffs, would take every ounce of his courage.

On the other hand, Harriet was plainly very much sicker than he was. He loved her, and there were things you did for those you loved which perhaps you'd hesitate to do for yourself. He knew he could not let her down.

The doorbell rang. He let her in. As he closed the door, she turned into his arms and they kissed. He looked into her eyes, saw the signs of distress.

"Are you all right, Harriet?" he asked, "you look as if you've been crying."

She smiled. "Just saying goodbye to Eddy," she replied. "It was harder to do than I expected. I need you to witness a codicil to my Will."

"Sure. Let's use the table in the dining room."

She nodded and followed him.

"You can write here."

Harriet pulled up a dining chair and began to write, putting into effect her promise to Eddy.

∗

"You're confident you haven't been misdiagnosed?" she asked him later.

"The radiologist seemed sure of himself. Knows much more about the subject than I ever did."

She digested that for a moment. "You don't think tomorrow is too soon? I mean you don't seem that bad. I wondered—"

"If we leave it too long, we won't be able to do the things we want to. We have to commit ourselves before we're knocking on the Pearly Gates. Too late then!" He played with a forkful of stir-fried pork.

"Right." She hesitated. "I've been trying to take the measure of my life – you know, what difference have I made? Stuff like that."

"Take the measure of one's life," Seymour echoed, looking up, "I like that. I'll do it too." He dropped his voice and leaned closer to her. "I was thinking: tomorrow, we could have lunch together. The helicopter's booked for three. Give us plenty of time."

"Okay," she said, "Sounds good to me."

Later, when the dishes had been cleared away, the washing-up done, and all had been said, Seymour had led Harriet up to his bedroom, and they made long, slow, love, for much of the night.

CHAPTER FIFTEEN

A smoky, greyish-pink sun climbed out of the sea – over Ness Point, Harriet supposed, watching it from Seymour's east-facing bedroom. She remembered visiting Ness Point at Lowestoft, years ago, and being told it was the eastern-most part of the British mainland. It was funny how, when you live in a part of the country visited annually by millions of tourists, you very rarely bothered to visit the local attractions yourself. How many people living in London bothered to go to the Tower or Buckingham Palace? Here she was, living – well, she *had* been living, she corrected herself – in the heart of East Anglia, a place of pilgrimage for artists for centuries, and one which still held its pockets of old-fashioned charm for the traveller – and she hadn't visited a fraction of the places the tourists came to see.

And today it all was too late. Today it came to an end. She rubbed her side where the pain was particularly bad. Since Eddy had been arrested, he'd not dared obtain any more 'special medicine' for her, and she was having to rely on the drugs prescribed for her by the hospital. Well, after this afternoon, she wouldn't need any more. She searched her handbag for her tablets. *Take one every four hours for pain*, it said. It was possible to read that two ways, she reflected wryly, because she nearly always felt worse after taking them than before. Mostly, they made her feel sick.

Her side twinged again. Oh, sod it! she thought, and popped two of the large oval pills from their foil enclosures. In the bathroom, she filled a glass with tap water and swallowed both of them.

She found herself staring at her image in the mirror. Some of the care-lines seemed to have faded. Probably

Seymour's influence, she thought, with a smile. She wished she'd met him years ago.

She put the pack of tablets back in her handbag. Today she was going to rob a bank: no Hollywood portrayal of bank robbers in her recollection ever carried a handbag, even the female ones. Well, she decided, she would be different. In any case, her job was simply to wait outside the bank for Seymour to emerge then drive them quickly to the heliport, pausing at the charity shop on the way.

The cup of tea Seymour had made for her earlier was almost cold. She finished it. She perched on the bed beside where he'd slipped back under the covers after his visit to the kitchen.

"I'd better go home," she said. "I need some clean clothes. I hadn't expected to stay over. Need a toothbrush, too," she added, rubbing her teeth with the side of a finger.

He looked at her. "Okay. Breakfast first?"

She smiled. "That would be nice. Are you making? I haven't had breakfast made for me since Charley was at home."

He swung out of the bed and pulled a dressing-gown on.

*

In his bedroom, Seymour stared at the contents of his wardrobe. He put on a clean blue shirt and tailored trousers, and a sports jacket. No tie. He'd worn a tie every day for work until he'd given up, and now abhorred them. Besides, it was quite a stylish thing to do, going out with an open neck. Made him look quite rakish, he thought. Even the Prime Minister appeared in public like that, Seymour reflected.

His choice of shoes remained conservative, eventually picking a pair of black Oxford brogues.

In the bathroom, he gave his teeth another scrub, ran the razor over his stubble until his cheeks and chin were smooth again, and tried his best to make his hair lie down. It was light and wispy, and prone to static electricity which made it stand on end. He held one hand on his head and the other on the washbasin tap in the hope the static charge would drain away to earth, but its effect was doubtful so he gave up and hoped it would dissipate in the fresh air.

*

David had started the day earlier than he liked when he was awakened by Moon, on the pillow next to him, as she began a series of earth-shattering snorts. She didn't know it, and he wasn't going to tell her, but she currently held the record for sticking around in David's flat at one go longer than any other of his earlier girlfriends. So far she'd shown no inclination to get the vac out or clean up the stuff overflowing from the sink, but on the plus side, she was bloody good at sex. Twice now they'd both gone to sleep sticky but exhausted, and the bedclothes had begun to smell of strawberry and chocolate instead of bodies. He wondered where she got her ideas, but was too shy to ask, in case she stopped having them.

Close-up, you could see past the trowelled-on make-up to appreciate her beautiful blue eyes, which really needed no make-up at all. Her lashes curled naturally, and her lips, without the disfiguring piercings, were full and generous. She had an hour-glass figure that she liked to emphasise with her customary leather tunic and trousers, Her waist was so tiny, he could almost get his fingers to meet round it.

His father had once told him – he couldn't work out whether it was true or just a wind-up – that the gene which nipped in a girl's waist was also responsible for her fertility, and the more nipped in she was, the more fertile. Which reminded him, he needed to get out of the apartment today at least as far as the chemist's to restock on condoms: in the last three days, they'd exhausted his supply.

He swung his legs out of bed and headed for the bathroom. As he stood in front of the toilet pan, his gaze wandered around the room. There were cobwebs hanging from the ceiling, dust on the floor, and a tide-mark round the bath. When he'd finished and flushed the loo, he tried experimentally wetting a hand and running it through the stain round the tub. It left tracks, suggesting that with a bit more effort, the entire tide-mark could be removed.

Without thinking much about it, he found an old cloth in the cupboard under the washbasin, and used it to wipe the bath. There was some staining around the plug-hole he couldn't shift, even with extra soap on the cloth, but it looked a lot better than it had.

He did the washbasin while he was about it, making the steel taps gleam as they hadn't since Dorothea had done them some weeks ago. The cobwebs were a trifle more challenging, but only because he had to stand on the toilet lid, then in the bath, in order to reach them. While he was doing this, the door opened and Moon, naked, walked in yawning.

"Hi, Dave, just need the loo."

He was standing in the bath and when she sat down on the toilet, between him and the door, she effectively prevented him from leaving until she'd finished. She patted herself dry and flushed, glancing at the bath and washbasin.

"Looks better," she commented. "Just need to give the toilet a bit more elbow grease."

He climbed out of the bath and peered into the stained fitting. He shuddered.

"Uh, I don't suppose you know how to do it, do you?" he asked, "'cos I'm not very good at it."

Moon looked into his face levelly. "Dunno if you've noticed, Dave, but I'm not into the Earth-mother thing. I don't do toilets. In fact, I don't do housework. Don't mind cooking, but cleaning's the reason I tend to live with other people."

He stared at her with his best hopeless expression.

"I'd get some bleach with limescale remover, if I were you," she added, unmoved. She looked past him. "It'll probably sort out the little stain problem round the plug-hole in the bath, as well."

She smiled brightly.

"In fact, if you don't mind, I'll use the bath, now you've cleaned it. I've got about two days'-worth of chocolate sauce to wash out of my belly-button... and other places." She grinned. "So if you've finished in here, I'll have my bath while you're down the shops getting your cleaning materials."

She ushered him, speechless, out of the door.

This wasn't right, he told himself. Girls kept toilets clean: it wasn't a man's job. On the other hand, Moon did do bloody good sex. If he could get to enjoy that a bit longer, it might be worth swallowing his pride and getting his hand down the bog. His expression brightened. He could always buy himself some rubber gloves. God! but she did bloody good sex. Yup, definitely worth it.

For the first time in many months, he ventured into those relatively unexplored aisles of the supermarket which sold washing powder, drain unblocker, toilet and bathroom cleanser, kitchen antibacterial sprays, oven cleaner... and rubber gloves.

When he returned, Moon was in his tiny kitchen wearing one of his shirts and nothing else, humming while she fried some bacon. She glanced at his shopping as he unpacked it.

"Glad to see you got some more washing-up liquid," she said, nodding at the pile in the sink. "If you want to make a start on that lot now, I'll keep your bacon sarnies warm."

David's mouth fell open. He stared at her for a moment, then picked up the detergent and started sorting out the filthy plates and pans into a sensible order for washing. He began to scrub, using the hottest water he could stand. He told himself that sex with Moon was pretty good, and probably worth all this effort. He repeated this mantra to himself a time or two whilst scrubbing the pots and pans.

He'd just like to know where it was all going to end. The smell of cooking bacon and the gentle sizzle in his last clean-ish frying pan encouraged him.

About half-way through the pile, she took pity on him. She'd known perfectly well that David expected her to be so disgusted with the state of his flat that she'd clean it up. She also knew that that was no basis for a relationship – and she liked him enough to want to give a longer-term one a chance. But no way was she cleaning. On the other hand, she cooked quite well.

He didn't know it yet, but, as a girl, she'd helped her mother out at private catering functions, and picked up quite a few tips about what made a good and interesting meal. She just needed to define the relationship so he did most of the shitty jobs while she was creative in the kitchen. She figured a few more nights like the last two and he'd do anything she asked. Underneath that geeky exterior, he was a nice bloke, and she hadn't come across too many of them.

She wondered if he'd noticed yet that she hadn't replaced her facial adornments. She'd guessed he didn't like them, and maybe she might be due a change of appearance. Perhaps, she thought, this afternoon, she might buy some new clothes, maybe even a dress... and not in black.

*

Kay had brushed Mark's hand away when he'd fitted himself behind her, spoon-fashion, and reached round to caress her breast. She pulled the quilt up higher and hunched her shoulders. She'd been having a dream in which she and David were children and her mother was doing the things mothers do. In the circumstances, she was reluctant to wake and anyway didn't feel like another bout of sex with Mark. In any case, she reckoned she might be about to come on: her breasts were feeling tender and full, and she didn't fancy having them rubbed or kissed, however gently.

He walked his fingers up her spine. She lay still for a moment in the hope he'd lose interest, but having reached her neck, he'd simply reversed direction and headed south. She rolled on her back, almost trapping his hand, and turned to face him.

"Please stop it, Mark," she asked.

He shrugged. "Okay."

"I'm sorry. I was dreaming about my mum and dad. It makes me think about his not being here any more."

"Of course," said Mark, "I wasn't thinking. But the doctors don't always get it right. Some people, told they have just so long to live, carry on months and years beyond." He put his arms round her and hugged her before swinging his legs out of the bed and pulling a bathrobe on. "Fancy a cup of tea?"

"That would be great," Kay replied, "a big one, please."

"Sha'n't be long," he called as he headed for the stairs.

She rolled on her side again and pulled the quilt over her shoulders. She lay quiet for a few minutes before casting it off and swinging her legs round to sit on the edge of the bed. She heard Mark whistling something downstairs in the kitchen, got up and grabbed her bathrobe from the peg it hung on, disappearing into the bathroom before he came upstairs with her tea.

She slipped off her pyjamas and stepped into the shower cubicle. Powered from a pump, she set it to immerse her in jets of hot, cleansing water, while she poured scented gel over her skin and lightly massaged it. After five minutes, she felt better, dried herself off, and slipped on the bathrobe. On her return to her bedroom, she found a mug of tea waiting for her, and Mark tucked back into his side of the bed with the morning paper. He smiled up at her.

"You look dead sexy," he said.

She smiled. "No makeup, in a bathrobe, and my hair wet? You have a strange idea of what constitutes sexy."

"I know what I like," he said, patting the bed beside him.

She remained standing, picked her tea up and sipped it, then shook her head.

"Not this morning, if you don't mind. I think I'm getting my period."

He looked down for a moment, then grinned wryly at her. He shrugged.

"Oh, bugger," he said.

She stared at him. "You want me to be pregnant?"

"I said yesterday – if you are, I shall be delighted."

"Well, sorry to tell you this, but we were probably too late in my cycle this month."

"There's always next month. Lots of opportunities for practice runs."

She lifted an eyebrow. "It's not a military operation, you know. You're not the SAS on a midnight op."

He locked his fingers behind his head and leaned back against the headboard, staring at the ceiling.

He smiled crookedly. "Sorry. I'm just a bit disappointed. I expected you to be pregnant by now."

"Maybe I am. We'll know in the next day or two." She drained the mug: the tea had made her feel much better. "I want to go over my dad's."

"Of course, " said Mark, "we'll go over straight after breakfast."

*

Charley woke up at what she considered to be an unearthly hour: six o'clock.

She had the weirdest presentiment that this was Mother's last day. So real was the idea that she came wide awake and scrambled out of bed. She showered, dressed and grabbed some orange juice and cereal, washed it down with fresh coffee, and phoned the office. After leaving a message on Colin's voice mail to remind him she'd not be in, she let herself out of the house towards the garage where she kept her car.

The early-morning traffic was light, and she made good time to Breydon. She'd have been there earlier, but one of her tyres picked up a nail and she suddenly found the car bouncing on the rim of the wheel. Changing a wheel was not something she'd had experience of, and she contemplated phoning her roadside assistance company, but figured by the time they could reach her, she could have done the job herself.

She found the spare wheel, realising guiltily that she'd never checked the pressure in the tyre when she did the others, but it looked all right, and bounced healthily on the ground when she got it out. Next came the car's toolkit, with the jack, its handle, and the wheel-nut spanner, still in a polythene bag which had never been unsealed.

It took her half an hour, and her hands were filthy when she'd finished. Two nails, one on each hand, were broken and chipped, and there was a black streak on her skirt, where a tyre had rubbed against her. She looked at the damage to her appearance and felt tears of frustration gather. Clenching her jaw, she told herself sternly that these were not important compared with what was in store for her mother. She wiped her hands on some dock leaves on the verge, the carpet in the car, then on a duster she kept for cleaning the inside of the windscreen, and finally, when she looked in her handbag, there was a small but growing collection of Mike's hankies. She checked her face in the mirror, and found, thankfully, that it had escaped untouched.

She found herself thinking, Mike wouldn't have taken so long to change the wheel. Why is it, she wanted to know, that you never have a man handy when you need one, and at other times, you can't shake them off? It was one of life's mysteries.

She managed to get most of the dirt off her fingers and resumed her journey. The delay meant it was nearly eleven when she arrived at Harriet's tower block. She parked in the square and headed for the lift. A small man in a pair of faded dungarees and a baseball hat and heavy boots had jammed open the door of the lift car with a broom and was using a bucket of chemicals and a cloth to remove the paint on its walls.

Charley went up to him. "Any chance of a ride up to the third floor?" she asked him with a smile.

The man stopped scrubbing and looked at her. He grinned, revealing that every other tooth in his lower jaw was missing. "Not if you want more than a tenner," he said.

Charley frowned while she worked out why he'd said that. "I just need to get up to the third floor," she said sternly.

"Oh," he said, grinning, "I thought you was lookin' for a good time with ole Ben." He cackled toothily. "I mean, that was the best offer I've 'ad, ooh, since..." he glanced at his watch then back to her face "...nineteen fifty-six. Or do I mean sixty-six? Can't remember whether it was Betty or Marjory."

She lifted an eyebrow. Maybe she should use the stairs.

He pulled his broom inboard, releasing the door, and stood back so she could get inside. Charley cleared her throat and took a deep breath and walked into the car. Old Ben pressed the third floor button and turned to look at her again. When she'd thought of him as a small man, she hadn't realised he only came up to her waist.

"'Course, that was all back before these tower blocks were built," he said conversationally. "Betty used to hang out at the end of Muspole Street, and Marjory over by the Bell and Grapes." He pointed in various directions, meaningless to Charley without a view of the outside, but she had a clear picture of a couple of street girls: presumably, Ben's money was a s good as anyone else's, and forty – or fifty – years ago, he might have had something to recommend him. Whatever it was, Charley was content for his secret to die with him. The door opened and he waited while she had to brush past him. Her last view of him as she turned away was of him standing there with his eyes closed and a beatific smile on his lips. Maybe, she thought, he hadn't had a whiff of Guerlain for forty years either, even then it was doubtful.

She tapped on her mother's door, tried it, and found it locked. She rummaged through her bag for her copy of the key and let herself in, but the flat was empty.

CHAPTER SIXTEEN

After breakfast, Harriet and Seymour had driven out to Northwind Gap again. It was a token 'farewell tour' of Norfolk.

They'd enjoyed an ice cream, but afterwards, Harriet had been almost doubled-up with pain from her side. Seymour worried about her, but after a few moments, she seemed to get over it, smiled, and thanked him for his concern. A few minutes later, Harriet's mobile phone rang. She passed it to Seymour to answer while she looked for somewhere safe to stop. It was Charley.

"Your mum's just parking the car," Seymour explained to her.

"Where are you?"

He looked round. "Somewhere in north Norfolk," he replied. "Just been visiting Northwind Gap. We're following the coast road round from there. Hang on." Harriet turned off the engine and took the phone.

"Hello, dear," she said, "are you busy?"

"Mother!" Charley exclaimed, "What do you think? I I'm here at your flat."

"Oh," said Harriet, "but I'm not there."

"Do you know – I'd noticed? Are you coming home?"

"Not just yet, dear. Seymour and I are going to have lunch." She glanced at Seymour then back to the view in front of them. "Then we've got things to do this afternoon."

"But mum, your three weeks are up!"

"I know that. But these estimates are notoriously unreliable."

"Aren't you going to take it easy?"

"You mean, lay down somewhere and wait for the Grim Reaper to come by and bag me?"

"Oh," said Charley, and was quiet for a moment. "I suppose that's what I expected, but I know it isn't your way."

"Might see you later," she said. "How's Mike?" she asked as something of an afterthought.

"He took me out to a Vintage Car Club dinner and I managed to lose one of the earrings he'd bought me."

While Harriet listened to the story she smiled to herself. There was hope for her daughter. Mike was a very pleasant, dependable man, and with any luck, Charley would realise this, too. Time she found someone to settle down with, thought Harriet, and Mike might be just the person.

"Well, love to both of you," said Harriet. "Got to go now." She cut off the call and brushed tears away from her eyes. "Come on," she said to Seymour, starting the engine.

They continued along the coast road, Harriet keeping her foot light on the throttle, and spent a pleasant morning reminiscing over the memories different places held for them. Later, they turned for home, and stopped off at a roadside tavern offering a good selection of food.

Harriet looked at the menu, then glanced up at Seymour.

"I don't feel very hungry," she said.

"How's the pain?" he asked.

"Still there. I'll take another tablet."

"Would you like a glass of wine or a soft drink?"

"I'll have water, please." She looked over the menu again. "I'll just have a cheese sandwich, I think," she said, and sat back while Seymour went and ordered at the bar.

The pain was not good at all. From time to time, she felt as if someone was stabbing the red-hot point of a spear into her side, and it was all she could do not to react to it because she knew Seymour would worry, and she didn't want that. There'd be no more pain later this afternoon, she told herself.

Seymour returned to the table with a small tray containing water for Harriet, a half-pint of real ale for him, and two plates of sandwiches.

"I found I wasn't as hungry as I thought I'd be," he said, sitting opposite her, "and whilst I'd have liked a pint or two of this," – he held up the beer – "I don't think it's a good idea for what we've got in mind."

She grinned at him and pulled a lump off her sandwich. "No," she agreed.

She was beginning to feel a little charge of adrenaline coursing through her veins, and it was putting her off her food. She chewed the morsel of sandwich with determination.

Seymour consumed his sandwich with large, manly bites.

On the whole, lunch was a quiet affair.

By one o'clock, they were back in the car, on the last leg of their journey into Breydon. Harriet was trying to drive calmly, but kept noticing the speed creeping up and rebuking herself for not concentrating. The last thing she wanted was to attract anyone's attention, especially that of the police.

They arrived outside Seymour's home and went inside. Mark and a tearful Kay were in the living room. She brightened up at once as Seymour walked in.

"Oh! Dad!" she cried, wrapping her arms round him and hugging him tightly. He gave her a quick hug then moved to disengage her. "I thought you were gone... already dead, or at the hospital."

"We rang there, and they'd no knowledge of you," said Mark.

"We've been out for a drive," Seymour explained.

Kay sat down heavily. "I wish I'd known," she said, "I wouldn't have been so upset."

Seymour was conscious that time was pressing now. He glanced at the clock on the wall.

"I'm sorry to rush, but there are things to do," he said, "I have a flying lesson booked, and I need to be on my way. Our way: Harriet's taking me."

Kay stared. "You're going flying? Today?"

"Uh, yes, if that's all right with you? Got to make the most of what we have left to us."

She uttered a little sound. "Oh. I hadn't thought you would – today."

Seymour squatted next to her and cupped her cheek in his hand. "Kay, sweetheart, you've been everything a father could ask for in a daughter," he said softly. He hadn't intended to say goodbye to either of his children, deeming it too demanding on his emotions, but he couldn't ignore her need. "You'll be just fine without me. You can stand on your own feet. You have Mark, you don't need anyone else."

She uttered another little mewing sound. He realised she was trying to hold back tears, but they spilled down her cheeks anyway. He looked round at Harriet and Mark with a sort of helplessness, his own cheeks stained with tears as well. Harriet was mopping her eyes, and Mark was trying hard to control his own emotions.

Seymour turned back to Kay. "Sorry, sweetheart, but I have to go."

He stood up, conscious that his knees were aching, and glanced at Harriet.

"I'll get my things, then we can be off."

He turned to Mark and shook his hand. "Take care of my daughter."

Mark nodded sombrely. Seymour left the room and went upstairs to pick up the plastic bag containing his shotgun and the horrible green and yellow wigs Harriet had found for them. He considered changing out of the clothes he had put on that morning, but decided not to bother. Returning downstairs, he caught Harriet's attention through the doorway from the hall, and she came and joined him.

"Bye," he called as he led the way out of the house, Harriet on his heels. He wondered how long Kay and Mark would stay there. He should have mentioned the letter to her in the bureau. He shrugged and figured she'd find it soon enough.

*

They decided to hit the bank around two, when Seymour had noted there seemed to be fewer customers about. She found a place to park outside.

"Are you going to put the wig on?" she asked.

"I can't be bothered," he replied. "So what if I'm recognised?"

"Quite," she agreed. "Have you worked out what you're going to do in there?"

He shrugged. "Well, I suppose when I get as far as a till, I just point the gun at the cashier and ask them to hand over the money."

"And not set off the alarm?"

"And not set off the alarm," he amended.

"And then?"

"Come out here and get in the car and we drive down to the charity shop, then on to the heliport."

She pursed her lips while she went over the plan.

"I suppose that's how you do it."

"I never thought to check the internet," said Seymour. "They reckon you can find the instructions to make an atomic bomb on the internet; you'd think someone might have posted 'A Beginner's Guide to Robbing a Bank'."

"You'll be able to write it yourself – " She bit her lip.

He smiled. "I'm afraid it would have to be ghost-written."

She looked at him from the corner of her eye. "That is a really terrible joke, Seymour," she said, before allowing herself a chuckle.

For a moment, they stared at each other in silence. Seymour glanced at his watch.

"Well, here goes," he said, opening the car door and disappearing inside the bank clutching his shotgun in its plastic bag.

Harriet's foot kept tapping the accelerator, and she kept telling herself to stop it, because the throaty roars of the exhaust could be heard all over the street. She waited, her heart in her mouth. A twinge of pain hit her side.

"Oh, God! Not now!" she muttered, scrabbling in her handbag until she found the rest of her tablets. She popped them all out of the foil and crammed them in her mouth, forcing herself to swallow them. As the last one disappeared down her throat, the bank doors opened and Seymour came out, walking quickly. At almost the same time, the bank's alarm bell and blue beacon, thirty feet up the wall, burst into life, deafening everyone in earshot. Seymour climbed over the door, losing a few twenty pound notes as he did so, and Harriet let in the clutch.

Driving swiftly but smoothly, she drove to the far end of the street, round the roundabout, and down the side street where the charity shop was situated. The car squealed to a halt outside. Seymour grabbed the bag, remembered to remove the shotgun and put it in the footwell of the car, then rushed into the shop, threw the bag onto the counter in front of a startled elderly lady, and returned to the car.

They could hear the sound of sirens behind them, but once away from the environs of the bank, Harriet slowed down to her normal speed, and headed for the heliport. She parked outside the flying school office. As they got out of the car, she stood beside it for the last time and ran her hand lightly over its bright paintwork.

Seymour tucked the shotgun inside his jacket and waited a moment before taking her arm and led her inside. The Chief Flying Instructor greeted them.

"This is just a half-hour pleasure flight, I understand."

"That was what I booked," said Seymour.

"Okay. Let's go. The chopper's all set." He turned to Harriet. "We'll all wear headsets on board. They cut out the engine noise a lot, and enable us to talk to each other."

Harriet nodded.

The CFI turned to Seymour. "You might as well sit in the right-hand seat, if your friend doesn't mind having the rear one all to herself."

Seymour and Harriet nodded. They walked through the hanger and out onto the helicopter pad, up to the door of the Jet Ranger. With Harriet in the back, the CFI, with a little help from Seymour, carried out the pre-flight checks, and at last fired up the twin jet engines.

Seymour had noticed the fuel gauges, and realised that the machine was carrying a minimal load of fuel – more than adequate for the projected half-hour flight, and enough to get them as far as the coast.

In the headset, he heard the CFI request clearance to take off from the control tower, and glanced at Harriet. She nodded. Seymour pulled the shotgun out from under his coat, and tapped the CFI on his shoulder.

"Goodbye," he said, "and thanks for all your help. You can leave now."

The CFI stared. He'd once flown a helicopter on a James Bond movie, but even that hadn't prepared him for being evicted from his own machine. At the same time, Seymour unplugged his headset and released his seat belt, nudging the man in the side with the empty barrels of the gun. The CFI figured that trying to be a hero wasn't worth it today, and opened the door. At the same time, Seymour heard the tower grant clearance. As the door closed, he took the controls and forced the machine into the sky.

Switching to the tower frequency for inbound and out-bound aircraft, he would be able to hear any other chatter between the tower and aircraft in the area. The Jet Ranger wobbled a bit as he gained altitude, then checking the compass, he headed for the north coast. Probably the CFI had got back to the office and on the phone, because suddenly pandemonium broke out in his headphones.

Using the intercom, he suggested that Harriet squeeze between the seats and sit beside him. He settled in and began to enjoy the flight. He showed her the intercom switch.

She grinned at him. "Well, I expect the cat is well and truly among the pigeons, now."

He smiled. There was not much further to go.

*

Mark and Kay had returned home in time for lunch. She was feeling listless. Her breasts were unusually tender, and she wished her period would come so they would stop aching. She began to think of more practical things as she and Mark shared a salad in front of the television. When Seymour eventually died, who would she have to ask to the funeral? She flipped open her organiser. On the way to the listings of her contacts, it fell open at a calendar page of about three weeks before. There was a tick in the margin of 'Monday'. That was odd, she thought, because that was when her last period had started. Perhaps coming off the Pill had upset her cycle. Or...

She glanced at Mark, watching the weather forecast at the end of the news. Maybe he was going to get his wish. She wasn't going to say anything, but she made a point of remembering to buy one of the early pregnancy tests the next time she was anywhere near a pharmacy. She took a deep breath and wondered about becoming a mother. It certainly didn't feel any different, she thought. Maybe she wasn't pregnant. Maybe she was, and it was simply too soon to have any bearing on her emotions. She felt a little surge of excitement. Perhaps she could go to the pharmacy now, she thought, while Mark's watching the television?

She cleared her plate into the kitchen, and put some shoes and a coat on.

"Just going to the shop, dear," she said, "something I didn't think to get earlier."

"Want me to come with you?"

"No, I'll be fine. See you in a few minutes." Well, half an hour, but he wouldn't be timing her. She left the house and walked the half-mile to her nearest shops, returning in due course with the important little box in her coat pocket.

"That you, Kay?" called Mark from his study.

"Yes," she replied, removing her shoes and coat and heading for the bathroom with the little box in her hand.

Fifteen minutes later, she was still in there, staring at the crossed blue lines on the indicator, and trying to come to terms with the knowledge she was now a mother – albeit of only a few cells. She heard Mark calling her.

"Kay! Are you all right?"

She put the tester carefully in the pedal bin, flushed the toilet, rinsed her hands, and went to find him.

*

When her mother had cut off the telephone call, Charley had felt very alone. It was not at all how she'd wanted to say goodbye to her mother. She'd sat in Harriet's kitchen and worked her way through half a box of tissues, thinking at one point that she was undoubtedly the watering-pot she had denied being to Mike.

The thought prompted her to phone him.

"Charley – I'd been wondering where you were," he said.

"You could have rung me."

"Yes. Well, I tried your office, but they said you were on leave. I was just about to try your mobile, but you beat me to it."

She took the phone from her ear and gazed at it with a sceptical lift of her eyebrow before replacing it.

Mike was still talking. "How are you? Have you seen your mother? Is she all right?"

"I'm feeling lonely. I drove over here to Breydon to see her – her three weeks are up today and I wanted to be with her. I expected... Oh, I don't know! I suppose I expected her to be in bed waiting for the end."

"And?"

"She was out with Seymour, gallivanting round the north coast, on a sort of farewell tour."

"That sounds like just the sort of thing she would do," he said. "I like your mum."

"I wouldn't have thought she was your type at all."

"Why? You are – why not your mum?"

"Because she can be a bit – what do you mean, I am?" Charley asked, diverted.

"Just that. I hope we can last a bit longer than a month this time."

She took the phone away from her ear again and stared at it for a moment. She felt her heart skip a beat.

"How – how much longer?" she asked.

She heard him suck air in between his teeth. "Well, that sort-of depends."

"On what?"

"Well, for instance," he began, teasingly, "if I buy you any more jewellery, will you look after it, and keep it on a bit longer than the earring lasted?"

"As long as it goes with what I'm wearing – oh!" she exclaimed. She'd just figured out that 'keep it on' didn't sound like he was planning to buy her something to dangle from her ears, or hang round her neck, it sounded... as if he had something else in mind. Or was she reading too much into what could have been just a careless use of language?

"Are you all right?" he asked.

"Yes," she said, and sounded breathless to her own ears.

"Good, because I wondered if you'd like to come to my place and let me cook you a meal this evening."

"Oh! I haven't anything to wear," she said, the first thing that came into her head.

"Shouldn't worry about that," he said, "I wasn't planning for us to go out anywhere."

He wanted a quiet night in, with her, she thought. That would be different! She didn't want to go back home, feeling the need to stay in Breydon in case her mother should need her.

On the other hand, she owed him over the missing earring.

"Mike, why don't you come to Harriet's place, and let me do the cooking?" she suggested.

"That's okay with me," he said. "What time?"

"Seven-ish?"

"See you then. But if you hear anything about your mother, phone me. I won't mind if we have to change plans."

"Right, Mike. Thanks," she said softly, "see you later."

She cut the call gently, reluctantly. Now, apart from having to worry about Harriet, she had to decide on a menu for the evening meal.

She left Harriet's flat and headed back towards the lift, but choosing the stairs rather than risk another meeting with Old Ben. When she reached the ground, he'd gone anyway. She got in her car and decided to buy some fresh vegetables in Breydon's excellent permanent market. She drove into the centre of town and parked up not far from the gaily-coloured market stalls.

She bought herself some lunch before spending almost an hour looking at the different stalls, gradually collecting a selection of vegetables which would give her a wide choice of what to cook for Mike. As she was finishing, there was a slight kerfuffle when somewhere an alarm bell started ringing. She glanced round, but couldn't see the source of the noise, but for a moment, thought she saw her mother and Seymour drive past the other side of the market place in something of a hurry. It was only a glimpse, and she couldn't be sure. Harriet's wasn't the only red sports car in Breydon.

She was still frowning over the incident when she got back to her car, loaded the boot with her shopping, and set off back to the flat.

In Harriet's kitchen, she scoured some of her mother's recipe books for dishes she could make using her purchases. While she prepared some vegetables, she had the local radio station on in the background,. Suddenly, it interrupted its afternoon magazine programme to issue a news bulletin.

"We have just received news that a branch of Robinson's Bank in Breydon has been robbed at gunpoint. The thief, a man in his fifties, pointed a sawn-off shotgun at Mary-Ann Nugent, 22, and demanded the contents of her till. The man then left the bank. No-one was hurt in the raid, and the thief got away with less than five hundred pounds. Miss Nugent, who raised the alarm, was praised for her courage in a frightening situation by Ernest Cliffe, branch manager."

Maybe that had been the alarm she heard, thought Charley.

"The robber got away in a bright red sports car, driven by a woman, also, according to eyewitnesses, in her fifties," the bulletin concluded. The police were appealing for witnesses of both the raid and any sightings of the distinctive sports car. CCTV footage in the vicinity of the bank was being studied.

By the time the programme reverted to music, Charley realised her mouth was hanging open. Surely – surely! Not! Not her mother and Seymour?

*

Seymour was trying to remember how to go faster. Lift the collective, left pedal and forward cyclic. He carefully moved the two levers controlling collective and cyclic pitch of the rotors and pressed the left pedal. The Jet Ranger dipped its nose and picked up speed towards the coast.

His headset crackled as the Tower suddenly opened the frequency and began to give directions to another aircraft with the call-sign 'golf-papa-alpha'. He realised he had seen a helicopter with that lettering, parked on the pad near the Jet Ranger: the one belonging to the Police Authority. He guessed they were coming looking for him and Harriet. Well, he thought, as the coast flashed by beneath the helicopter, they'd be too late.

Beside him, Harriet was being very quiet. He glanced across at her, and when she looked round, he saw her pupils were dilated, and she was almost asleep.

"You all right, Harriet?" he asked. "Have you taken something?"

She smiled peacefully at him. "Thought I'd take the rest of my tablets," she said.

His first inclination was to turn back, but he realised why she'd done it, and almost wished he'd thought of it, too, so they could both slip quietly away when the time came. But then he wouldn't have been able to fly. He would just have to deal with it fully conscious. It would be mercifully quick. He patted her arm.

"Not long, now, Harriet," he said, feeling a huge lump grow in his throat. "I wanted to say – I love you. I wish we'd had longer together." He shut up, unable to say any more, and concentrated on turning the machine round until it was facing the cliffs. Harriet gazed at him, smiling.

"I love you too, Seymour," she whispered. He saw her eyes close, blinked away tears which had gathered in his own and tipped the nose of the aircraft down towards the tops of the waves.

The Tower began broadcasting again, this time using their call-sign, and demanding they return at once to the heliport. Seymour didn't reply. An alarm started ringing in his headset, possibly two. He didn't care. He pulled the headset off. His mobile phone vibrated in his pocket. He decided to ignore it. Another few minutes and it would be mangled in the wreckage. It continued. He lifted it out and glanced at the screen. To his surprise, it was neither of his children, nor was it the police, nor the air traffic people: it was the hospital. He glanced at it a second time then accepted the call and put the phone to his ear.

The cliffs were less than a quarter of a mile away when he aborted the plan. Drop the collective, right pedal and aft cyclic. The machine began to slow down. The nose tilted upward and he had to cram on power now to lift it over the cliffs. The jet turbine roared. Alarms started ringing in the cabin. Seconds after the cliffs passed a few yards below the helicopter's skids, the engine ran out of fuel. There was scarcely any height above the turf, and the aircraft fell like a stone. He saw the police helicopter heading rapidly towards them from a mile away, then everything went black and silent.

CHAPTER SEVENTEEN

When Seymour opened his eyes it was to find his vision restricted to a thin slit. Into his field of view loomed the image of the nurse he'd last seen three weeks ago. She smiled, but not broadly.

"And how are we feeling, Dr Whittle? Few aches and pains, eh?"

"Just tell me: is this heaven or hell?"

She grinned. "Somewhere in between, Dr Whittle."

"You mean I'm still alive? On Earth?"

"Oh, indeed you are! Back in Breydon General. And Mrs Blythe, too."

Seymour tried to move and discovered it hurt. His left arm was in plaster and there was a strapping round his neck.

"Is she around?"

"I'm right next to you, Seymour." Harriet's voice drifted in from over to his left.

He couldn't turn towards her, and the bandage round his skull prevented him from seeing her out of his eye corners.

"Indeed, she is, Dr Whittle."

Seymour looked at the nurse sourly, though his expression was hidden beneath his bandage.

"Glad to be able to tell you that my hearing's fine, thank you," he said.

"Good," said the nurse, "you'll be able hear the doctor when she comes to talk to you. How do you feel?"

"My neck's sore, my arm's sore, my ribs hurt like hell."

The nurse nodded. "That's about what I thought. See you later."

She moved out of his view.

"Nurse!," he called.

She re-appeared.

"Yes?"

"Why is my head bandaged?"

She smiled. "Because the doctor said so, and you know how doctors are: their word is law."

"I'm a doctor. Will you take the bandage off, or at least fix it for me to move my head. My nose itches."

She moved out of view to his right and he heard the papery rasp as a tissue was pulled out of a box. She loomed close, suddenly, and rubbed his nose gently with the tissue. It was tender.

"Ouch!"

"Sorry. It's bound to be a bit tender for a few days."

"You mean, it's broken?"

She nodded. "A real boxer's nightmare. They did their best to restore your good looks."

"They shouldn't have bothered on my account," Harriet said.

The nurse glanced up at her. "Don't you want him restored, Mrs Blythe?"

"Serves him right for a really terrible landing. He told me he could do it, you know: didn't want any help. And when I took him at his word and had a nap, leaving him to cope by himself, what does he do? Uh, actually, I'd like to know: what did he do?"

"I'm told he landed a helicopter rather too quickly," replied the nurse. "On the subject of your nap, you'll be pleased to know we pumped your stomach and have done our best to purge your system of all the drugs swimming around in it. You should feel a lot better now."

Harriet groaned.

Seymour was privately glad to hear her voice.

"How are you, Harriet? Anything broken?" he asked.

"I've got a plaster on my left wrist, otherwise, it seems to be cuts and bruises."

"It's a Colles Fracture, Dr Whittle," said the nurse. "She certainly escaped with fewer serious injuries than you did, probably because she was unconscious at the time of the crash. She was relaxed. It often helps if you are."

"I'll try to remember that," Seymour replied drily.

The nurse grinned. "Well, I'll leave you two to pursue 'auld acquaintance' and discuss driving standards while I give the doctor the good news that you're both alive and eternally grateful to us. That reminds me," she added, peering at Seymour, "you owe me two teabags."

He lifted an eyebrow, which was lost on the nurse as she couldn't see it beneath the bandage.

"I'm touched that you remember me so well, nurse," he said. "But I have a nasty feeling I might become something of a minor celebrity in the near future, and you'll be dining out for several minutes at a time on the story that you once helped out Doctor Whittle and Mrs Blythe with a teabag each."

She frowned at him, shaking her head. "I've had promises like that before from men. I think I'd rather have my teabags back than rely on the chance of reflected glory in the future. It might never happen."

"Oh, woman of little faith," muttered Seymour.

"I've had a lot of boyfriends, Doctor Whittle."

He was aware of a snort from the next bed.

"I'm sure she didn't mean that, nurse," he said.

"We all like to have a man in our lives – well, most of us," said Harriet, "but that doesn't mean you can trust him with your teabags."

"Absolutely!" agreed the nurse.

"I'll let you into a secret, dear."

"What?"

"I've never allowed him free access to my packet of Tetley's."

"Well, I've learned my lesson – again – Mrs Blythe," said the nurse. "I shall bear that in mind. The next man who wants one of my teabags can die of thirst, and see if I care."

"That's the spirit, girl," said Harriet encouragingly.

"Better go and make the doctor's day."

"I expect you have to do that quite a lot," said Harriet sympathetically.

"You've no idea: it takes it out of you," said the nurse tragically, as she left them.

"I suppose you had to put up with being surrounded by attractive nurses in their crisply starched pinafores and caps when you were training, Seymour?" asked Harriet.

"You must be thinking of Hattie Jacques and Shirley Eaton in *Carry On, Doctor*."

"Actually, I was thinking about Florence Nightingale and Edith Cavell."

He choked back a laugh. "I'm only three years older than you, Harriet, and I didn't go to school with Methuselah."

The door to the room opened and footsteps approached the bed.

Whoever it was stood between the beds. Seymour could just see a few iron-grey curls and the shoulder of someone wearing a white coat with a stethoscope round their neck. He tried turning his head, but stopped when something felt as if it was stabbing him in the chest.

The nurse bobbed in and out of view, picking up his notes and handing them to the doctor. Seymour heard pages being turned.

"Well?" he asked. "Why aren't we dead?"

The iron-grey curls turned towards him and he heard the pages of his notes fall closed as they were returned to the nurse.

"Doctor Whittle!" said the doctor: he still couldn't see her face.

"Yes?" Seymour replied.

"You are very lucky. When you managed to crash your helicopter, it didn't fall very far, so although you got shaken about, and have broken your nose, arm and collar bone, you escaped serious injury."

"Thank you. Now why aren't we dead?"

He saw the shoulder elevate in a shrug. "It wasn't your time, I suppose."

"It was three weeks to the day," said Seymour, "Harriet and I were both due to die today."

"What are you talking about?"

There was a hasty, whispered conversation between doctor and nurse before the doctor resumed.

"Ah! Well, it appears that there might have been a problem with your prognosis, three weeks ago. I'm advised I mustn't talk about it in case you sue the hospital. It was a different doctor then, who no longer works here. But so far, let me assure you, I've found no reason for either of you to think your life-expectancy is any different from anybody else's."

"What about all the pain I've been in?" asked Harriet.

"It's possibly nothing more than gall-stones. It wasn't helped by your use of, uh, cannabis along with your prescription meds. They tended to increase the irritation as well as react with each other."

Seymour heard Harriet mutter an unladylike imprecation.

"I wish I'd known," she said.

"Can we get out of here?" asked Seymour. The curls turned towards him.

"You can be released into police custody as soon as we're satisfied you're on the mend."

"Police custody?" squeaked Harriet.

The curls turned back towards her. "Yes. It's nothing to do with me, but I gather they think you robbed a bank and stole the helicopter. They want to talk to you."

"Do you think you could hold them off?" she asked.

"Don't see why not, but why should I?"

Seymour shifted uncomfortably. "Is there any chance I could get out of these bandages?"

The doctor sighed. "I'll check the x-rays, then consider it."

"It's rather like being in the next bed to the Invisible Man," said Harriet.

The doctor had moved out of Seymour's field of view, and he heard the sound of x-ray film being removed from its envelope and jammed against a viewing panel. Fluorescent tubes flickered into life.

There was a moment of silence, then the lights were switched off and the films unclipped and returned to their envelopes. The doctor returned to Seymour's bedside, and this time he could see her face. It looked very familiar.

"Mrs Edwards? Violette?" croaked Seymour, somewhat aghast.

She looked up sharply into his eyes.

"No! Why? Do you know my sister?"

"She must be your twin. We've met."

"She's the elder by thirteen minutes. How well do you know her?"

Having recovered from her shock, the doctor began gently unravelling the bandage around Seymour's head.

"She's my daughter's mother-in-law."

As the bandage came off, Seymour looked round at Harriet in the next bed, the nurse at the foot of it, and the doctor, who was sitting on the edge of his so she could reach the bandage round his head. As she finished removing it, she studied his face.

"I heard she'd married her son off."

"Your nephew made a very good move in marrying my daughter," Seymour said, feeling the need to defend Kay.

The doctor, whose name, now Seymour could read her badge, was Edith Reagan, raised an eyebrow.

"I wonder if she did as well for herself? What I know of him, he was a real mother's boy."

"I take it you've not had much to do with your sister's family? You weren't at the wedding, I know."

"Violette and haven't spoken since we were in our teens. I think we fell out because she poached a boyfriend of mine, a young man I particularly liked. The fact that he went off with her rather put me off the idea of men. I was always more bookish than Violette, so I concentrated on becoming a doctor while she continued her search for the right kind of husband material."

She stood up.

"How soon before we're fit to leave here?" Seymour asked.

"You were unconscious for quite a while," she said, "and I think we need to keep you in till Friday. Just in case. Then, of course, it'll take some time for your arm and collar-bone to mend, to say nothing of your nose. Apart from the bang on the head, I'd think of you as walking wounded – no need to stay here."

"What about me?" asked Harriet.

Doctor Reagan looked across Seymour's bed at her other patient, stood up and walked round to her.

"You're walking wounded, too, Mrs Blythe. Apart from the Colles' Fracture, which, like Mr Whittle's broken bones, is likely to take six to ten weeks to repair, your main problem has been, uh, chemical. When we tested your blood, after you were brought in, we found a high level of opiates, and a low level of cannabis."

"Opiates?" asked Harriet. "I never took opiates."

"If you took your prescription pain-killers – and it looks as though you took the lot! – you took opiates. Heroin got its name for being the world's best painkiller, though we prefer to call it diamorphine or a couple of fancier names these days."

"Oh, dear!" Harriet looked chastened.

"But it would seem you were also taking cannabis. Your body reacted badly to the presence of both drugs in your system at the same time. Then there was the matter that brought you in here in the first place: we think now that it was gall-stones."

"The doctor we saw before thought it was a cancer."

"Yes. Well, I can't discuss that with you. He no longer works here, or anywhere else in the health service, and has an appointment with the General Medical Council " She turned to include Seymour in her comments. "You two weren't the only ones misdiagnosed."

Harriet smiled weakly. "I suppose that's good news," she said.

"You don't sound convinced," said the doctor.

"We – we've been doing a few things we wouldn't normally have done, on the basis that we wouldn't be around to answer for them. I bought a horribly expensive car – on a credit card. Seymour took us to Paris. And – and we robbed a bank."

Doctor Reagan gazed at Harriet with something like awe.

"You just went out and... robbed a bank?"

"It was a last act of, uh, daring, I suppose."

"Good God!" said the doctor. She gazed at Harriet and then at Seymour. "So, it's true, what the police say? You robbed a bank, then stole a helicopter?"

"Yes."

"What did you do with the money?"

"Dropped it off at the hospice charity shop in Station Street," said Seymour.

"Really?" She thought for a moment. "So it was all done just the for hell of it?"

"That's all," said Harriet.

The doctor looked round at Seymour. "You're the one who went into the bank with a shotgun?"

Seymour looked sad. "Yes. I bought it years ago. I've never used it."

"Was it loaded?"

"No. I never got round to buying any cartridges. Besides, there's no way I was going to shoot anybody."

"How romantic," said Doctor Reagan. She turned back to Harriet. "Was it his idea or yours?"

"Mine. I feel terrible now. He'd never have thought of doing it otherwise, and now I'm responsible for his being wanted by the police, stealing a helicopter, and being back in here with some dreadful injuries."

The doctor lifted a sceptical eyebrow. "Are you telling me he didn't have a choice?" She lowered her voice to a stage whisper. "And let me tell you, his injuries aren't so bad, so if he comes the 'Old Soldier', don't have too much sympathy."

Harriet turned to smile at Seymour. "We're in it together," she said simply.

The doctor stood up. "Well, I'd better go. I'll be back later."

Seymour and Harriet stared at each other after the door closed behind both doctor and nurse.

Harriet looked at her injured wrist and at Seymour's more extensive strappings.

"So… we're still alive, and… and not going to die," she said.

"Not this week, apparently," replied Seymour.

He watched as Harriet's eyes suddenly filled with tears, which cascaded down her cheeks. She wept silently. He struggled to sit up, gritting his teeth against the pain from his broken bones.

"Harriet!" he said softly, "Harriet, it's all right. We're not going to shuffle off this mortal coil just yet. That's good news isn't it?"

She allowed a sob to escape. "But Seymour! What have we done? We're in a mess now, and it's all my fault."

He swung his legs cautiously out of the bed and hobbled across to her side, sitting next to her and putting his good arm round her.

"Nothing was your fault alone," he said, "neither of us forced the other."

She shook her head sadly. "But Seymour: you were a respectable man, a doctor, and now you're a bank robber. And a helicopter hijacker. We both are. And if I hadn't suggested it, you wouldn't have agreed to it, and we wouldn't be – fugitives from justice." Another sob racked her.

He pulled her towards him and kissed her on the cheek, tasting the salt of her tears.

"We'll sort it out, my love. Don't worry about it now. We've both had a bit of a stressful day, and it probably makes things seem worse than they are."

She turned to look at him, and chuckled damply.

"A stressful day? Is that what it's been? Stressful!" She giggled. "Not dreadful, or catastrophic: just stressful?" She ran her fingers down his cheek, feeling his stubble, and giggled again. There was a touch of hysteria in the sound. "I thought moving house was stressful, or marrying or getting a divorce. Somehow, I didn't include robbing a bank in the same category."

He kept his voice light. "Come on, you've got to see the funny side. We rob a bank because we think it's the last thing we'll ever do, and now... well, all that psyching ourselves up has proved pointless and unnecessary. But wasn't it different? As experiences go, we'll never have one like it again. It was frightening, but it was a bit of a thrill, too, wasn't it?"

She considered the question for a moment. "Yes. I suppose it was."

"There, you see! Got the adrenaline rushing around. It's a while since anything did that for me. Probably never happen again."

"I suppose it was exciting." She looked up at him, with a gleam in her eye. "Perhaps it's too soon to say it'll never happen again."

"What do you mean? What's going through your mind?" asked Seymour with a hint of alarm.

"I have a cunning plan," she said.

*

Charley received a phone call from the hospital around five o'clock.

She'd been beside herself after hearing the news bulletin on the local radio station, and phoned Mike as much as anything simply to share her feelings. He'd been unable to leave work, but had promised to travel to Breydon as soon as he could. She had to settle for that. For some time, she'd fretted about where her mother might be, and thought she'd probably call her as soon as she could. She took her mobile phone from her bag and stared at it. When she'd tried to call her mother's, she'd simply been diverted to the messaging service.

In the event, the first call she received was from the hospital. Charley's name had been listed on their records as Harriet's previous visit as next-of-kin.

"I'll come over at once," Charley had said, but the nurse advised against it, on the grounds that the police wanted to interview Harriet and Seymour before they spoke to anyone else.

"But she's definitely not in any serious danger from her injuries," added the nurse.

Charley frowned. "But she and Seymour Whittle were supposed to be on the verge of death," she said, "and now you tell me they aren't?"

"Uh, no," said the nurse. "The original diagnosis was not quite right. Your mother and Dr Whittle are fine."

In the end, Charley could do little but wait and hope that Mike wouldn't be long. He eventually arrived at Harriet's flat just after eight.

Charley opened the door at his knock, and allowed herself to be enfolded in his arms as he stepped inside.

"Sorry I'm late," he said, but she brushed his apology aside. She told him quickly all she knew and he held her close so she could feel the comforting heat of his body.

After disengaging themselves, she led him into the kitchen so they could talk while she made some coffee.

"The main thing is, she isn't going to die," he said.

She sighed. "It seems to me the main thing is, she and Seymour appear to have robbed a bank and hijacked a helicopter."

Mike sucked in his cheeks, as if trying to repress a smile. He gave up, smiling wryly. "I probably shouldn't say this, but I think your mother and Dr Whittle are just great! Lovely, colourful people."

She echoed his smile. "So do I, but what can we do about what they've done?"

They sat side by side on Harriet's settee. Mike tried to think of a way to calm some of Charley's fears.

"All I can tell you is that, if this is their first offence, that alone will count in their favour. I don't know anything about the details of the allegations so I don't know what else is involved."

"The radio news said it was only a small amount of money taken, but one of the cashiers was frightened."

Mike sighed. "I don't know what to say, Charley. Maybe if it was only a small amount taken and they gave it back, it would help their case. I'm sorry, I'm not very comforting."

She leaned towards him and kissed him. "It's comforting that you're here," she said. She nestled against him and he held her tight, so she could listen through his chest to the steady beat of his heart.

Suddenly, she sat bolt upright. "Dinner! I forgot to cook! Oh, damn!"

Mike gazed at her, but the hunger in his eyes was not for food, she realised as she stared at him. A shiver ran through her, and settled into a pool of heat deep inside her belly. The feeling was so strong it almost took her breath away. Blood rushed to her cheeks. Mike cupped her face in his hands and smothered her lips with his own. She felt her strength and will-power ebb away and was content to let him do with her as he wished.

This time there were no interruptions.

CHAPTER EIGHTEEN

Harriet slept fitfully, woken every few hours by powerful and frightening recollections of the moments before the crash. The ward began to come to life between six and seven. A new nurse, whom she didn't recognise, came in and checked Seymour's dressings, then Harriet's bound wrist and arm.

The usual business of feeding the patients and handing out their medication went on. Harriet got up and dressed herself. The nurse returned and saw her.

"You're not supposed to leave, Mrs Blythe."

"Why not? Doctor Reagan said I could yesterday."

The girl, who looked younger than Nurse Buxton, was confused. "There's nothing on your notes," she said.

"Maybe she hasn't written them up yet?"

"But Sister said–." She bit her lip.

"What did Sister say?" asked Harriet.

The nurse looked at her wide-eyed. "That you hadn't to leave until the police had talked to you."

"Oh, that," said Harriet, nodding. "Don't worry, I know all about that."

"So you'll see the police?"

"Undoubtedly," replied Harriet. "I think my daughter's going to marry one." If only this little escapade doesn't put him right off any association with Charley and me, she added silently.

"Oh," said the nurse.

"But I'm not leaving without Dr Whittle, here," Harriet said, nodding at Seymour.

"He's not supposed to be fit to leave before Friday," said the nurse.

271

"So you see, dear, you needn't worry about me. I'm not leaving until *he* does."

"Oh, that's all right then." She flitted about, checking bed notes, taking temperature, pulse and blood pressure, before leaving.

Harriet went to Seymour's bedside and studied his face. His features were relaxed but both eyes looked to be bruised, as if he'd been given a matching pair of black ones. A large dressing covered his nose. He opened one eye and studied her for a moment before opening the other.

"What are you staring at, woman?" he asked.

She turned away. "Just seeing if you were awake." She walked back to her own bed. "I see your injuries have done nothing to increase the amount of honey on your tongue."

"Huh! Think I should be sweet-talking you, do you?"

She sat on her mattress and looked at him. "We're a right old pair of wrecks, don't you think?"

"Is *that* what you think I am?"

She grinned. "You know what I think you are."

He smiled. "So, how are you this morning?"

"I'm good," she said. "What about you?"

"My face hurts. They assured me it would, but that it would all be worth-while once it healed."

She hesitated. "You know the police are waiting to pounce?"

"Yes. I hope they don't decide to do it today. I haven't thought up a really convincing alibi."

"There's a good reason for that," she said, "but I don't know how we're going to cope with going to prison."

"At our age," he added, ironically. "Well, we'll just have to grit our teeth and bear it. Stoic to the end, et cetera."

"I was thinking," she said.

"Yes?"

"We'd never have done the bank job or the helicopter heist if we hadn't believed we were about to die."

"No. And you wouldn't have bought that car, or decided we should jump out of helicopters."

"And we wouldn't have gone to Paris," she said. "Do you regret Paris, Seymour?" she asked softly.

He gazed at her through his puffy eyelids and shook his head. "I don't regret anything we did."

"I'm glad," she said, "because I think the main thing of all was that we did these things together."

They were interrupted by a tap on the door. Charley and Mike entered. Charley crossed the room to her mother and hugged and kissed her.

"Hi, mum."

"Hello, Charley," Harriet replied, her eyes on Mike.

He smiled at her. "Hello, Harriet." He turned to the other bed. "Seymour." He looked back at Harriet. "Good to see you both alive and kicking. You gave everyone a fright."

"I'm sorry about the girl at the bank and the CFI," said Seymour. "They were collateral damage."

Mike regarded him, raising his eyebrow.

"Mike promised me he's off duty, and here as a friend," explained Charley, "and in any case, this isn't his patch."

Mike nodded. "It's true. I'm here as your daughter's boyfriend, just sucking up to her mum in order to create a good impression."

Harriet laughed. "I don't think you'd know how to suck up to anyone," she said, "and you certainly don't have to suck up to me. I thought I'd already cast fate to the wind and given you both my approval – not that you need it."

Charley pulled two chairs over between the beds so she and Mike could sit down.

"We have an announcement," she said. "Oh, but first, something I was asked to bring with me."

She felt in her handbag and produced a sealed envelope, which she passed to Harriet. Harriet casually placed it on her bedside cabinet then turned back to her daughter, who she saw was bursting with news. She glanced at Mike, who was smiling fondly at Charley.

"Mike asked me marry him," said Charley. She looked round at her new fiancé. "Actually he offered me a partnership and my own hammer and chisel in his do-it-yourself sideline business, but it wasn't enough of an incentive. He came up with the right one eventually."

Harriet didn't quite understand, but it was clear from the way they looked at each other that her daughter and Mike shared a private joke.

"Congratulations, love. I'm so pleased for you," she said.

"Yes, indeed. Congratulations," Seymour echoed.

Charley looked across at him, smiling. "Thank you, Seymour." She looked at him and her mother. "Uh, now you two have a future to look forward to, don't you think you should be considering making my mother an honest woman?"

"Charley!" exclaimed Harriet.

"Somebody should," agreed Seymour.

"I guess she'll never try to rob a bank again," said Charley.

"I don't need you to defend me, Charley," said Harriet.

"No, but she has a point, Harriet," said Seymour. "I think you were an honest woman up until that point, weren't you?"

"Yes, of course. That's why I don't need anyone to 'make an honest woman' of me."

"Quite. That's why I think it's a rather old-fashioned phrase."

Charley frowned. "Well, are you going to propose to her?"

Seymour struggled to sit up, wincing with pain and using his one good arm. Mike helped him.

"As my children used to say to me, MYOB. It's a matter for me to decide. I'm waiting until the moment seems propitious and your mother's defences are down."

Charley smiled at Harriet. "And what will you answer?"

"None of your business, my girl!" said Harriet sharply. "You'll find out soon enough."

Charley shrugged. "Okay. I just thought, if we had a double wedding, we could probably negotiate big discounts for a joint reception."

"The situation hasn't arisen," said Harriet. "Now change the subject."

"We've been told we only have five minutes," said Charley, "but we just had to tell you." She turned towards Mike. He smiled down at her and planted a kiss on the tip of her nose.

"It's great news, love," said Harriet.

"But what's going to happen now?" asked Charley.

"The police are waiting to interview us. I thought they weren't going to allow visits from family members until they had," said Seymour.

"Having a policeman on my arm probably helped," said Charley.

"Probably," said Mike, "but I think we should be going." He looked back at Seymour and Harriet. "See you later."

Seymour smiled as they left the room. "Have a good life," he said.

Harriet and Seymour stood together for a moment in the empty room.

"Time for your cunning plan, I think," he said.

"Your telephone calls seem to have worked," she said, nodding at the envelope containing Harriet's passport.

"Have you had all you want of your old life?" he asked.

She nodded.

"Then let's go and see if we can find another."

She reached up and kissed him.

When the nurse came back into the room, it was empty.

EPILOGUE

The Caribbean sun sank slowly towards the west. Seymour Whittle, former General Practitioner of Medicine, one-time bank-robber and failed helicopter pilot, adjusted the brim of his sun-hat to keep the dying rays out of his eyes. Harriet brought a blue-coloured cocktail out of the cabin which they'd rented, and set it down on the table beside his chair. A gentle breeze disturbed the leaves on the banana trees growing round the edges of the little bay, and every now and then, one of the coconut palms would give up one of its fruit, which would fall to the white crystalline sand with a thud. The blue water of the Caribbean Sea made half-hearted attempts to climb up the beach towards Seymour. In a while, he knew, he would have to retreat up the beach as the tide grew stronger, but first, there was a drink to be sipped, and the letter from Kay to be read. He'd waited until the evening before opening it, but now, with Harriet beside him, it seemed like the time was right.

He grinned as he read the first few lines. "Seems I'm going to be a granddad, my daughter tells me."

"Oh, that's wonderful news," said Harriet, smiling.

He read further. "She says the police have put our case on the back-burner, after we arranged to pay the money back to the bank. They have bigger fish to fry. The helicopter loss was covered by my insurance. Your car has been repossessed."

"Ah, well, it was great while it lasted," she said.

"Kay got a severe slap on the wrist for helping us get away."

"Hope she's all right."

"It seems so."

They sipped their drinks in companionable silence for a few minutes.

"It's been nice here," said Harriet.

"Great place for a honeymoon," he agreed.

"Wonder if Charley and Mike would join us for theirs?" She gazed at the gentle waves breaking on the sand.

"It's like working in a chocolate factory," she said after a longer pause.

"What is?"

"All this." She waved at the beach and the trees. "Sun, sea, sand –"

"–Sex!" Seymour added.

She looked sideways at him. "We can have that any-where!"

He nodded, grinning. "And you're thinking: you can have too much of a good thing?"

"Not really," she replied, "I'm thinking that we're let-ting time slip by, and there are other things we could do."

"Getting restless!"

She smiled at him. "Yes. I want to take another heli-copter flight – with someone else driving, if you don't mind, Seymour – and fly over the Grand Canyon. I want to go swimming with dolphins. I want to cross the Rocky Mountains and the Sahara desert." she explained.

"You have such a long list, Harriet," Seymour said. "I guess we'd better get started."

He stood up and slipped his mended arm round her waist, picking up his drink and newspaper with the other hand, and led her slowly back up the beach.

THE END